PETER DAMES

REGINALD Evelyn Peter Southouse Cheyney (1896-1951) was born in Whitechapel in the East End of London. After serving as a lieutenant during the First World War, he worked as a police reporter and freelance investigator until he found success with his first Lemmy Caution novel. In his lifetime Cheyney was a prolific and wildly successful author, selling, in 1946 alone, over 1.5 million copies of his books. His work was also enormously popular in France, and inspired Jean-Luc Godard's character of the same name in his dystopian sci-fi film *Alphaville*. The master of British noir, in Lemmy Caution Peter Cheyney created the blueprint for the tough-talking, hard-drinking pulp fiction detective.

PETER CHEYNEY

DAMES DON'T CARE

DEAN STREET PRESS

Published by Dean Street Press 2022

All Rights Reserved

First published in 1937

Cover by DSP

ISBN 978 1 914150 89 0

www.deanstreetpress.co.uk

Chapter One
SOFT PEDAL FOR SAGERS

Is it hot!

I ain't never been in Hell, but I'm tellin' you that I reckon it ain't any hotter than this Californian desert in July.

I am drivin' along past Indio an' I reckon that soon I am going' to see the Palm Springs lights. An' I am goin' some—the speedometer says eighty. If it wasn't so hot it would be a swell night; but there ain't any air, an' there was a baby sand storm this afternoon that caught me asleep an' I gotta lump of the Mojave desert or whatever they call it stuck right at the back of my throat.

Say, did you ever hear of Cactus Lizzie? Well, there is a song about this dame an' I am singing it. Not that I gotta voice, because I ain't, but I am one of them guys who always feels that if Ma Caution hadda fixed it so's I was born with some honest-to-goodness vocal chords an' a face that wasn't like the Santa Domingo coast line, I reckon all the lovelies woulda queued up to hear Lemmy tear off a couple of swing numbers that woulda made croonin' history.

Revertin' to this Cactus Lizzie. I oughta tell you that this dame was in a song; an' for some reason that I don't know this song is sorta buzzin' in my head, keepin' time with the hum of the car. I got this jingle off some cowboy on Sonora two years ago, the time I brought in Yelltz for murder an' kidnappin'. All this cowboy had was a guitar, smokers' throat an' a hey-hey Mexican jane who took a run-out powder on him. He usta keep singin' it all the time until the noise of somebody readin' your death warrant woulda sounded like a comedy number—it woulda been such a relief. Well . . . here we go . . .

Livin' on the desert . . . swing Cowboy,
Ridin' on the desert . . . Love is sad an' strange. . .
Hit up that banjo . . . sing Cowboy,
Your girl's got the jitters an' the cattle's got the mange.
Cactus Lizzie . . . grieve Cowboy,
I loved her plenty an' she give me the air,
That Cactus Lizzie—she got me dizzy,

Oh hear me grievin'—'cause the dames don't care.

This is the jingle I am singin', an' it's one of them rhythms that sorta keep with you—you know, one of them things. . . .

I am on the straight run now an' I can see down the road the Palm Springs lights. They tell me that this Palm Springs is one swell desert town. You can get anythin' there—a diamond necklace from a ritzy jeweller's shop, perfume at fifty dollars a bottle, an' a smack in the puss with a whisky bottle at some of the road houses they got out on the desert highways—the sorta places where you can save time by losin' your reputation an' your suspenders at the same time.

I am just runnin' into the town now, an' I'm good an' tired. I was tellin' you about Cactus Lizzie, wasn't I? Well, I reckon that there's a lotta dames playin' around like Cactus Lizzie. They're afraid of spiders but they'd just as soon stick a stiletto into their boy friend as call for a chocolate sundae. Janes are like that, but maybe you've had your own troubles.

Me, I like women. There's something fascinatin' about 'em. They got rhythm. They got technique—and how!

I am nearly through Palm Springs now. A bit further ahead on the right I can see a light an' a neon sign. The sign says 'Hot Dogs,' an' I reckon that this is the place I am lookin' for. I slow down. When I get outa the car I feel as stiff as a corpse, an' why not? I have been drivin' ten hours.

I ease over to this joint an' look through the window. It is one of them fancy eats houses. Everything is just sweet an' clean an' there are a pair of janes servin' behind the counter. They are swell babies. One of 'em is a redhead with eyes that indicate trouble for somebody, some time, an' the other has gotta figure that makes me wish I was on vacation. There are one or two little tables stuck around all about the place an' there ain't anybody there except the girls an' a guy sittin' at a table eatin' frankfurters an' tryin' to look wicked at the blonde with the figure.

I look at my watch. It is half-after midnight; then I give the brim of my fedora a snappy tweak an' I go in.

"H'yah, Gorgeous," I say to the redhead. "Meetin' up with you calls for a Hamburger an' a cup of coffee with a lotta cream, because my mother says I need buildin' up."

She grins at the other dame.

"Say, Alice," she cracks. "Here's Clark Gable."

She gets busy at the coffee urn.

"Not for me," says the blonde. "For me he's Spencer Tracy. He's got that certain something they talk about, ain't he? Where's he been all our lives?"

"No fightin' now," I tell 'em. "If either of you honeys wasn't here I could go for the other in a big way, but you're a sweet pair an' you sorta cancel each other out—an' don't forget the mustard an' *no* onion."

"Seein' somebody?" says redhead.

"Not a hope," I say. "I just never eat onion. It's dangerous. You never know what's goin' to happen. I once knew a guy who ate Hamburgers *with* onion an' one hour afterwards some jane he was tryin' to make called up the War Department for a gas mask."

She pushes over the eats.

"You're new around here, ain't you?" she says.

She looks sorta friendly.

"Yeah," I tell her. "I come from Magdalena, Mexico. I'm lookin' for a friend of mine, a guy named Sagers—Jeremy Sagers. Some guy in Arispe has left him some dough an' I thought he'd like to know about it. Ever seen him?"

"Ain't that a scream," says redhead. "I reckon we know this Sagers. I see him talkin' to Hot-Dog Annie, an' I reckon the old girl pushed him into one of them dumps she gets around to—one of them select desert road houses around here."

"You got them, too?" I crack. "Say, this town is the berries."

"You betcha," she says. "We got everything around here. Now we got you, we're all set for a big ride!"

"Nuts to you, sweetheart," I crack, "Say, who is this Hot-Dog Annie?"

"She's an old peach," says blondie. "She starts drinkin' double Martinis about six an' by midnight she's good an' high. Then she comes in here an' takes in a cargo of hot-dogs. She says it sorta absorbs the poison an' stops her from seein' handsome cowboys where there ain't any. That's how she got the monniker." She pipes down. "Hold everything, here she is," she mutters.

I screw around.

Some dame has just blown in an' is certainly an eyeful. She is wearin' a sorta jumper an' a pair of blue hikin' shorts. She has gotta pair of sand shoes on, an' a jag that woulda lasted any ordinary guy for about three years. But in some funny way she has got class . . . if you know what I mean.

She goes over to a table an' flops down. Behind the counter the girls are busy. They have gotta plate of hot-dogs an' a large cup of coffee all ready, an' I pick it up an' take it over an' put it on the table in front of this dame.

She takes a look at me.

"An' who might you be?" she says.

"Me . . . I'm a guy who believes in fairies," I say. "Listen, lady," I go on before she can pull anythin'. "Maybe you can help me. The girls here tell me that you gotta job for some guy I'm lookin' for—a guy called Jeremy Sagers. I got some good news for this guy—some palooka's left him some dough."

She goes into a huddle with a hot-dog.

"I got him hired at the Miranda House Hotel," she says, "but he was so lousy they gave him the air. Then he fixed himself up. He's workin' at a dump way out on the desert—The Hacienda Altmira—an' as far as I'm concerned he can have it."

She starts cryin'. This dame is plumb full of stagger-juice.

"Take it easy," I say, "an' tell me where this Altmira is."

She comes back to earth.

"Go through the town an' keep goin', cowboy," she says, "an' when you're out the other side turn right at the gas station an' take the desert road. Keep goin' some more an' when you've done about thirty miles an' there ain't much more road, you'll see it away on the right. Only if I was you I'd leave your bank-roll behind. They're funny guys out there."

I say Thanks a lot; I pay Redhead an' I scram.

I drive fast an' plenty. Bit by bit I get out into the desert. I pass plenty places, road houses, an' hang-outs an' a dude ranch or two.

Pretty soon they start stringin' out, an' a bit after that there ain't nothing, nothin' but foothills an' joshua trees, cactus an' highway. The speedometer says I have done twenty, an' so I start singin' Cactus Lizzie again, because I have found that whenever I sing this song I seemta go faster.

I am wonderin'. I am wonderin' just how this guy Sagers has been gettin' along an' if he has found life interestin' around here. I get to thinkin' about him. He is a young sorta guy. . . .

Then I see the dump. The road has sorta tailed off an' is good an' bumpy. It curves around to the right an' inside the curve, stuck right in the middle of a swell spot of desolation, is this Hacienda Altmira. It is the usual sorta *adobe* building, with a plaster veranda all the way round, an' a laid out front with some ornamental cactus stuck around. There is a bunch of neon lights over the front, an' as I get near I can hear hot music. Some guys are playin' guitars an' playin' 'em good.

I find a place for the car an' leave it. When I say I find a place for it I mean I leave it on one side of this dump in the shadow of a mud wall just so's I can put my hand on it quick if I wanta get outa this place in a hurry. There have been times before when I have wanted to vacate some spot very quickly an' I have always found it is not good to have your car stuck right in the front of the place where some guy can stick a knife in the tyres.

I go in the front door. The place is built Mexican fashion, an' there is a sorta passage with a curtain at the end. The guitar playin' is comin' from the other side of the curtain. I string along the passage an' pull the curtain an' lamp in.

I am surprised. The place is sweller than I thought. It is a big *adobe* walled room with a wooden floor. Dead opposite me is a bar and by the side of the bar is a flight of stone steps leadin' up the wall, turning left to some room half-way up an' then turning right an' leadin' on to a wooden balcony that goes all around the room, except on the side to my left which has got big wire windows from floor to ceilin'. There are tables set all around the place and there are a bunch of people stickin' around.

In the middle of the tables there is a floor that has been planed down an' polished, an' dancin' on this floor, doin' a heavy tango with a dame that is old enough to be his mother, is what looks to me like the desert's swellest gigolo.

He is tall an' slim an' supple an' he is wearin' a pair of Mexican breeches, a silk shirt, an' a silly smile, an' he is pushin' this dame around as if he would rather have been flirtin' with a rattlesnake. The band, four guys in chaps on a little platform on the left of the bar, is hittin' up some swell Spanish stuff, an' there are four or five other guys stickin' around the bar. Most of these guys is wearin' cowboy chaps, or breeches, an' I reckon that maybe they come from some of the dude ranches that I passed on my way.

From above my head, in some room leadin' off the balcony I reckon, I can hear a lotta laughin' an' conversation. At a table away on the left near the windows three guys who look like Mexicans are havin' a few words over some *tequila*. On the right, there is a party of pretty high guys in tuxedos with some women wearin' some swell jewellery, an' as I have not seen any cars around this place I reckon that there must be a garage on the other side of the house where I couldn't see it.

When I go in the guys at the bar take a look at me, an' then go back to their wisecrackin' with the fly-lookin' jane who is workin' the bar.

I pick myself a table on the edge of the dance floor, an' I sit down. After a bit some guy, who looks like he would die any minute, he is so thin, comes over and says what do I want. I give him an order for some ham an' eggs an' a lotta whisky an' he goes off. I then amuse myself watchin' the guy on the dance floor doin' his stuff.

He goes on pushin' this dame around an' by the way the guys who are playin' the guitars are lookin' I can see that there is a big laugh somewhere. Maybe they think that the big boy is playin' her for a sucker, and I gotta admit that he is certainly goin' on like a hired dance partner. When they come around opposite me he turns her around so that he is lookin' at me an' he gives me a sorta apologetic grin an' a double wink.

After a bit the boys stop playin' an' the couple go off to a table where I can see there is a bottle of champagne, and then after a minute some guy in a swell cut tuxedo an' a silk shirt comes outa the room halfway up the stairs. He sees me an' sorta smiles an' runs down the stairs an' comes across to me.

"Good-night to you, señor," he says. "I am mos' pleased to welcome you to Altmira. I 'ope you get everything you want."

I grin.

"Me too," I tell him.

Then I shut up.

"You are in thees neighbourhood a long time?" he asks me. "I deed not theenk I 'ave seen you before. You see, señor, you are ver' lucky to find us open at these time—eet is nearly three o'clock—but to-night we 'ave a little party 'ere as you see. I 'ope we shall see you some more."

The waiter guy comes back with the whisky. I pour myself a stiff shot an' pass the bottle to this guy.

"Have a drink," I tell him, "an' who might you be?"

He smiles an' waves his hand that he don't want a drink.

"I am Periera," he says. "I manage thees place. Eet is a ver' good place, when you get to know eet."

"Swell," I tell him. "I'm sticking around the neighbourhood for a bit," I go on, "so you'll see some more of me."

He grins an' he goes off.

After a bit the waiter comes in with my ham an' eggs an' I start eatin'. After a bit the guitar guys start playin' again, an' sure as a gun the gigolo guy gets up an' starts cavortin' around with the dame. This old lady is so keen on doin' a hot rumba that it looks as if she is goin' to bust outa her gown at any minute.

As they come swayin' around my way, I swallow some whisky quick an' make out that I am a little bit high. When they get opposite me I look up at the guy an' I grin. He grins back.

"H'yah, sissy?" I say, good an' loud.

You coulda heard a pin drop. The party on the right stop drinkin' an' the guys at the bar spin around. The big boy stops dancin' an' takes the dame back to the table an' then he walks sorta casually over to me.

"An' what did you say?" he asks me.

"I asked you how you was, sissy," I tell him.

This guy is quick. He takes one step forward, an' as I am about to get up he kicks my feet sideways an' busts me in the nose at the same time. I go down with a wallop, but I am pretty quick an' I shoot after him an' mix it. I put up a quick uppercut, which he sidesteps an' when I try a straight one he blocks it. I get hold of his shirt an' yank over to me an' he trips me, Japanese scissor fashion, an' we go down again. The band has stopped playin' an' as I flop I can see Periera comin' across.

As I go to get up sissy smacks me down again, an' when I do get on my feet I am lookin' not quite so hot.

I stand there swayin' a bit as if I was high, an' I let out a hiccup so's they'll be certain.

Periera stands smilin' at me.

"Señor," he says. "I am sorry that you should make some troubles with people in my service. Pleese don't do eet some more. Eef you are hurt I am sorry."

He starts brushin' off my coat where it is dusty.

The sissy has gone off back to his table to the dame. I look across at him.

"Pleese not to start sometheen else, Señor," says Periera. "We do not like some troubles here."

I flop down in my chair.

"I reckon you're right at that," I tell him. "I reckon I had too much before I come here an' anyhow he was right to smack me in the puss. It looks like he ain't as big a sissy as he looks," I go on.

He smiles.

"Listen, Periera," I say. "You go across to that guy an' tell him I'm durn sorry, an' that I'd like him to come an' have a drink with me so's there ain't any feelin's over this. I'm goin' over there for some air."

I get up an' I stagger across the room to the side where the windows are, an' I pick a table in the corner. Periera goes across to the sissy an' speaks to this guy, an' after a bit he gets up, says something to the fat dame an' comes over. As he stands facin' me he hands me the double wink again.

"Listen, pal," I say, nice an' loud, "I reckon that was a not very hot thing to say to you. I reckon that if you are a sissy then I'm in Iceland. Sit down an' have a drink on it."

We shake hands an' he sticks something in my hand. I yell for the waiter guy an' get the whisky an' glasses brought over. Nobody much is payin' any attention to me now, the fun bein' over, an' after I have poured the drinks I light a cigarette an' start waggin' my head an' smilin' like I was makin' a lot of light talk.

Under the table I look at what he put in my hand. It is his Federal badge. I slip it back to him.

"O.K., Sagers," I tell him smilin' nice an' polite, with a swell hiccup, for the benefit of all concerned. "What do you know?"

He gives himself a cigarette an' under cover of lightin' this he starts talkin' quick, smilin' an' gesticulatin' like we was havin' some airy conversation.

"Plenty," he says, "but nothing that seems to look like anything. I come out to Palm Springs an' started to muscle around for a job. Told 'em I'd been tryin' for extra work at the coast studios. I contact some old lady who gets me a job at the Miranda, but pretty soon I see this is the job I want, so I get myself fired. The only way I can get in here is by doin' this pansy dancin' partner act.

"This place is the berries. They got everything. They'll take you for a toothpick. There's some play goes on upstairs that would make the Federal reserve Bank look like a five an' ten, an' the roulette wheel's so crooked that one night when some guy won something the croupier went into a decline. The guy over in the corner with fancy moustache is runnin' nose candy. This is the feller who beat the New York Narcotic Squad to it three years back—what he don't know about sellin' drugs could be typed on the back of a stamp. The guys who come here ain't so hot, neither. Some of 'em are the usual Palm Springs daddies lookin' for somethin' swell with curves an' some of 'em look like they could do with ten to fifty years. The women are a mixed bunch. Some of 'em work here an' some I don't know. There's all sorts of janes bust around here."

He pushes the bottle over.

"What's your front?" he asks.

"I'm fakin' to come from Magdalena, Mexico," I tell him. "I'm supposed to be bringin' you some news that a guy's left you some money an' that I've got a roll on account for you. That gets you outa here. Then I'm aimin' to stick around for a week or so before goin' back—that is unless something breaks. Now . . . where's the dame?"

"She's around," he says. "She gets me guessin' an' she'll get you guessin'. Caution. If she owns this place then I'm a greaser. The manager guy Periera treats her like she was nothin'. She does a hostess act around here an' looks like she could bite a snake's head off. She's permanently burned up. She's got class an' she dresses like a million dollars. The real boss is Periera."

"Does she live here?" I ask him.

"Nope. There's a little rancho, way back over the intersection off towards the Dry Lake. She lives there. It ain't far—about ten miles from here. I've cased it. Usually there ain't anybody around there except some woman who cleans up. Pretty often there ain't anybody there at all."

"O.K." I tell him. "Now listen. In a coupla minutes I'm goin' to blow outa here an' take a look at this ranch. If there ain't anybody around maybe I'll have a look inside. When I scram you spill the beans about how this guy in Arispe has left you this dough an' that you're firin' yourself an' goin' to Mexico to collect. To-morrow mornin' pack up an' get out. Go into Palm Springs an' make a big play that you are goin' to Mexico. See the Chief of Police an' tell him to lay right off this dump while I'm stickin' around. Tell him to tell the Bank Manager here to keep his trap shut about that counterfeit bond. Then fade out for the border by car. When you're well away switch; ditch the car at Yuma, grab a plane an' get back to Washington. Tell 'em I'm here an' all set. Got me?"

"I got you," he says. "But I don't like it, Lemmy. I sorta got an idea in my head that somebody around here's leery to the fact that I ain't an honest-to-god film extra bein' a dancin' partner. I reckon they're suspicious."

"So what?" I tell him. "Suspicion don't hurt nobody. O.K., Sagers."

We start drinkin' an' talkin' again, an' after a bit I put up a big act of shakin' hands with him, an' call for the bill. I pay it an' give a big *buenos noches* to Periera who is stickin' around the entrance, smilin' like he was in Heaven, an' then I get the car an' scram.

I drive along till I come to the intersection an' I take the main desert road. It's still plenty hot. I step on it an' pretty soon I see this ranch. It is the usual sorta place. I pull up behind a joshua tree an' get out an' take a look around. There ain't no lights an' there ain't a sign of life. I go around the back an' it's just the same. There is a stake fence around this place an' after a bit I find a gate an' I go through. I amble up to the back veranda an' knock on the door, but nobody don't take any notice.

I think I will try a fast one, so I put in a little heavy work on the door with a steel tool I got, an' in about two minutes I've got the lock open as good as any professional buster-in coulda done it an' I step inside.

I pull out my electric flash. I am in a sorta little hallway that is furnished not too bad. In front of me is a passage leadin' through to the front hall an' doors each side. At the end of this passage on the right is some stairs leadin' to the floor above. I reckon that maybe what I am lookin' for is likely to be in a bedroom, so I ease along the passage an' up the stairs an' start gumshoein' around tryin' to find the dame's bedroom.

There is four bedrooms up there. One looks like a hired girl's room an' the other is a sorta boxroom—there is all sorts of junk lying around. On the other side of the hall there are the other two rooms. One of 'em might belong to anybody, an' it don't have any special features that attract my attention. When I try the last door I find it is locked an' so I think that maybe this is the room I am lookin' for.

I take a look at the lock an' I think that it might fall for the spider key I got in my pocket, an' I try it out an' it works. I have the door open pronto an' go in. Directly I get into the room I can smell that this is what I am lookin' for—the perfume comes up an' hits me. It's swell—I always did like Carnation.

I go over an' pull the shades over the windows before I switch on the flash, an' then I take a look around.

It is a dame's room all right. There is a wrap lyin' over the back of a rest chair, an' there is a long line of the swellest shoes you ever saw. Oh boy, was they good? There is little shiny patents with French heels an' there is dress shoes in satin an' crêpe-de-chine. There is polished brown walkin' shoes, ridin' boots an' a pair of pink quilted satin mules that woulda knocked a bachelor for the home run. I tell you these shoes was swell. They sorta told you that the dame who owned 'em knew her way about, an' I reckon that if the rest of her kit was on the same level, well, she was an eyeful any time.

I nose around. I am tryin' to figure out where a dame—a clever dame—would hide some papers so that nobody would guess where to find 'em supposin' they figured to look. I reckon that either she'd have 'em stuck on her body an' carry 'em around, or she'd put 'em in an innocent sorta place where no smart guy would think of lookin' for 'em.

Over in the corner is a pile of books standin' on a little table. I go over an' look at 'em. I run the pages of the top books through my fingers an' they are O.K. but when I grab the fourth book—a leather bound book of poetry, do I get a kick or do I? Somebody has cut a big square out of about fifty pages in the book, an' stuck inside is a packet of letters. I look at the address on the envelope of the top one, an' I do a big grin because it is addressed to Granworth C. Aymes at the Claribel Apartments, New York City.

It looks as if I have pulled a fast one on Henrietta. I stick the packet of letters in my pocket, put the books back, close an' lock the door behind me an' scram downstairs. I stick around for a bit just to see if anybody has been tailin' me, but everything is O.K.

I go out the same way as I come in, an' fix the back door so's it looks all right. I go over to the car an' I head back, intendin' to take the main desert road back to Palm Springs, but before I have gone far I come to the conclusion that I will go back to the Hacienda Altmira an' just have a look around an' see how the party is goin'.

I am there in about fifteen minutes.

The electric sign is turned off an' the place is all dark. There ain't a sign of anything. Way up on the top floor facin' me I can see a little light comin' between the window shades.

I go up to the entrance an' it is all fastened up. Then I think of the wire windows around on the left, an' I get around there. They are locked too, but they are pretty easy, an' I have one open pronto.

The moon has come up an' there is a lot of it tricklin' through a high window above the bar.

I shut the window behind me an' start easin' across the floor. I am keepin' quiet an' if you asked me why I couldn't tell you. It just seems sorta strange that this place shoulda closed down so quick—especially when everybody looked like they was having such a swell time.

When I get past the band platform, where the bar starts, I stop and take a look, because from here I can see the bottom of the adobe stairs that lead up the side of the wall. There is a piece of moonlight shinin' on the stairs an' as I look I can see somethin' shinin'. I go over an' pick it up. It is the silver cord that Sagers was wearin' in his silk shirt, an' there is a bit of silk stickin' to it, so it looks like somebody dragged it off him.

I turn off the flash an' stick around. I can't hear nothin'. I lay off the upstairs an' start workin' around the walls, nice an' quiet, feelin' for door knobs. I miss the entrance wall because I know that the passage leads straight out front.

I get over the bar because I reckon that there will be a door behind, probably leadin' upstairs an' connectin' with the balcony some place. There is a door all right an' I have to spider it open because it is locked. On the other side is a storeroom. I go in an' use my flash. The room is about fifteen feet square an' filled with wine an' whisky cases an' a coupla big iceboxes. There is empty bottles an' stuff lyin' all over the place.

I ease over an' look in the first icebox. It is filled with sacks. In the second icebox I find Sagers. He is doubled up in a sack an' he has been shot plenty. I reckon he was on the run when they got him because he is shot twice in the legs an' three times through the guts at close range afterwards. I can see the powder burns on his shirt. Somebody has yanked his neck cord off him an' torn his shirt open.

I put him back in the icebox an' close it like it was. Then I get outa the storeroom, lock the door with the spider an' mix myself a hard one in the bar. I get over the bar an' scram out the way I come in.

I go back to the car an' drive towards Palm Springs.

It's a hot night; but it wasn't so hot for Sagers.

CHAPTER TWO
THE LOW DOWN

ANYHOW I have got the letters.

When I am about ten miles from Palm Springs I slow down. I light a cigarette an' I do a little thinkin'. It looks to me as if it is no good makin' any schmozzle about Sagers bein' humped off, because if I do it is a cinch that I am goin' to spoil the chance of my gettin' next to this counterfeit bezusus.

I suppose whoever it was ironed Sagers out will take him out some place an' bury him some time before dawn. As a bump off it was a nice piece of work, because if Sagers had told 'em what I said he was to tell 'em, that he was blowin' outa here an' goin' back to Arispe to get the dough that this guy was supposed to have left him, then that is goin' to account for his disappearance, an' who the hell is goin' to worry about one dancin' partner more or less. Anyway it looks like I had better have a few words with the Chief of Police around here an' tell him about the Sagers bump off, an' get him to lay off things while I am flirtin' around with this proposition.

When I get into the main street I pull the car up under a light an' I take the letters outa my pocket an' I read 'em. There are three letters altogether. The handwritin' is good. Nice regular sorta letters with nice even spaces between the words, the sorta handwritin' that is swell to look at.

The first letter is addressed from a hotel in Hartford, Connecticut, and it is dated the 3rd January. It says:

"Dear Gransworth,

"I know that you always have thought that I am a fool, and I haven't minded this particularly, but I do insist that you credit me with a certain amount of intelligence.

"Your evasions and excuses during the last two months confirm my suspicions. Why don't you make up your mind about what you are going to do, or are you so selfish that you are prepared to take what advantage you can from the fact that the community regards you as a happily married man who has no need to sow any further wild oats, whilst at the same time you continue to carry on an affair with this woman.

"When you denied this previously I believed you, but having regard to the events of the last day or two, and a letter which I have received from a person who is in a position to know, it is quite obvious that you have been making a fool of me and other people for some time past.

"I'm fairly good-tempered, but quite candidly I've had enough of this business. Make up your mind what you're going to do, and be prepared to let me know very shortly. I shall arrange to come back and hear your decision.

Henrietta."

The second letter is from the same hotel, five days afterwards, the 8th January, an' it says:

Gransworth,

"I have received your letter and I don't believe a word of it. You're a very bad liar. I am going to have satisfaction one way or the other. Unless I do get satisfaction I am going to be rather unpleasant, so make up your mind.

Henrietta."

an' the third is just a few lines dated four days after, on the 12th January. It says at the top "New York" and goes on:

Gransworth,

"I shall arrange to see you this evening. So I've GOT to be tough!

Henrietta."

I put the letters back in my pocket an' I light another cigarette. It just shows you, don't it, that things are not always what they're cracked up to be. Up to now everybody believed that when Granworth Aymes died Henrietta Aymes was outa town in Hartford, an' here is a note which definitely shows that she was fixin' to see him on the day he died, an' that she was feelin' tough.

It's pretty easy to see why Henrietta was so keen on gettin' those letters back, but what a mug she was to keep 'em. Why didn't she burn 'em? Anyhow it looks to me that if I have any trouble with her, maybe I can use these letters as a means of makin' her talk, because I am beginning to think that this Henrietta is not such a nice dame as she tries to make out. In fact I am beginnin' to develop a whole lot of ideas about her.

I get out my notebook an' I look up the address of the Chief of Police here. He is a guy named Metts, an' he has got a house just off the street I am parked in. I reckon he is not goin' to be so pleased about being dug up at this time of the night, but then I have always discovered that policemen ain't pleased with anythin' at any time.

I drive round an' park the car on the opposite side of the street. Then I go over an' ring a night bell that I find. About five minutes later he opens the door himself.

"Are you Metts?" I ask him.

He says yes an' what do I want. I show him my badge.

"My name's Caution," I say.

He grins.

"Come in," he says. "I heard about you. I had a line through the Governor's Office that probably you'd be handlin' this thing. I suppose you're down here about that phoney Registered Dollar Bond business."

"You said it," I tell him.

I go in after this guy an' we go to a nice room on the ground floor where he gives me a big chair an' a shot of very good bourbon. Then he sits down an' waits. He is an intelligent lookin' cuss, with a long thin face an' a big nose. I reckon I ain't goin' to have any trouble with him.

"Well, Chief," I tell him. "I don't want to be a nuisance to you around here. I just want to get this job I'm doin' finished as soon as I can an' scram out of it. The co-operation I want from you ain't much. It is just this. When this counterfeit Dollar Bond business broke an' I was elected to handle it, I got through an' got a guy in the "G" Office at Los Angeles put over here workin' under cover, name of Sagers. He's been working out at the Hacienda Altmira as a dancin' partner.

"I blew in to-night with a phoney tale about his comin' into some money so as to relieve him, but somebody got wise to the job. When I went back to this dump later I found his body in a sack in the ice safe. Some guy had given him the heat in five places. He's still there. I'm reportin' that to you officially because a murder around here is your job; but I don't want you to do anythin' about it yet. I'll advise Washington that Sagers is due to have his name put on the memorial tablet at headquarters, an' we'll just leave it like that for the time being, because if you start gum-shoein' around tryin' to find out who bumped him off we're just goin' to get nowhere. O.K.?"

He nods his head.

"That looks like sense to me," he says. "That's O.K. by me. I'll get out an official report as from you on Sagers' death, an' we'll file it and sit on it till you say go."

"Swell, Chief," I tell him. "Now the other thing is this. Who was the guy who sent the information through to Washington about that Dollar Bond bein' phoney? Was it you? If it was where did you get your information from? Was it the bank manager? How did it happen?"

He pours himself out a drink.

"I'll tell you," he says. "I got it from the bank manager. When this Aymes woman came out here, she opens a checking account at the bank. The bank manager, who is an old friend of mine, told me she opened this account with 2,000 dollars. She draws on this checking account until there is only ten dollars in it, and then one day she blows down to the bank an' sticks a five thousand U.S. Registered Dollar Bond over the counter to the receivin' teller an' asks him to pay it into her account.

"Well, that bond is a nice piece of printin'. He looks at it an' it looks good to him, and it is only an hour afterwards when the manager is havin' a look at it that he twigs it is counterfeit.

"He rings up Mrs. Aymes an' tells her that the bond is as phoney as hell. She just seems a little bit surprised, that's all, an' accordin' to him she didn't seem to take very much interest. She says O.K. an' she hangs up. Next day he writes her a line an' says he'll be glad if she'll look in at the bank.

"She blows in. Then he tells her that this business is a little bit more serious than she might think. He tells her that he has got to report that a counterfeit bond has been paid into his bank, an' that the best thing that she can do will be to tell him just where she got the bond from an' all about it. She says O.K. she got the bond from her husband an' she got it with a packet of 200,000 dollars' worth of U.S. Registered Dollar Bonds that he bought in New York for good money an' gave to her.

"When the manager asks where he bought 'em, she says he bought 'em from the bank, an' when the manager says that it's not easy to believe that because banks don't sell counterfeit bonds, she says that's as maybe but that's all she knows. With that she gets up and is just about to go out when he asks her where her husband is as he reckons that somebody will be wantin' to ask him some questions.

"She turns round an' she smiles a little bit, an' she says she reckons it will be durn difficult to ask her husband questions because he committed suicide in New York on the 12th January this year. Naturally this staggers the manager for a bit, but he says to her that she ought to be good an' careful because it is a federal offence to change bonds that are screwy, an' that he reckons she had better bring the rest down to see what they look like.

"So she drives off an' she comes back with the rest of this stuff—195 thousand dollars' worth of Registered Dollar Bonds in denominations of fifty thousand, twenty thousand, ten thousand, five thousand an' one thousand dollars, with the usual interest bearing coupons that go with them.

"In the meantime Krat, the manager, has been on to me about this an' after she has left the stuff at the bank, I go over an' look at it. The whole durn lot is counterfeit, but the job has been done so well that you have to have one helluva look before you see it.

"Well, there is the story. The same day I put the report through to the State. I suppose they pass it on to Washington an' you get the job. What are you goin' to do? Do you think she was in on this game? Do you think that she an' this husband of hers got this stuff made before he killed himself?"

"I wouldn't know, Chief," I say. "Nothing matches up in this deal. I've handled some screwy jobs in my time, but I don't think I've ever got one quite like this, an' maybe it won't be so hot for her before I am through with it."

"One of them interestin' things, huh?" he says.

"Yeah," I tell him. "An' how! It's one of them funny ones—you know, nothin' matches up, but as a case it's durned interestin'. Here's how it goes:—

"This guy Granworth Aymes an' the dame Henrietta Aymes have been married about six years. He is a gambler. He plays the market an' sometimes he makes plenty dough an' sometimes he's scrabbin' around for the rent. They do themselves pretty well though; they live in the Claribel Apartments, New York, an' they are heavy spenders an' put up a good front. They are supposed to be plenty happy too, in fact this Claribel Apartments dump is just another little love nest, an' you know how they usually end up?

"O.K. Well, at the end of last year this Granworth Aymes gets a hot tip. He plays it up well an' believe it or not the deal comes off. He muscles in on a big stock-pushin' racket an' he walks out of it with a quarter of a million dollars profit. The boy is now in the money.

"Well, it looks like he has a meeting with himself an' he comes to the conclusion that he's had enough of bein' up an' down on the market an' for once he is goin' to be a sensible guy an' salt down some of the profits. So he pays fifty thousand dollars into his checkin' account at the bank and with the other two hundred thousand bucks he buys himself that much worth of U.S. Registered Dollar Bonds. He brings 'em along to his downtown office an' he makes 'em up into a parcel an' seals it down an' he calls his lawyer on the telephone an' tells him to legally transfer the Dollar

Bonds to his wife Henrietta Aymes. He says that if it's her money then they'll be all right in the future because she is a careful dame, an' will stick to the dough an' not let him go jazzin' it around.

"The lawyer guy gets a bit of a shock at hearin' Granworth talk like this, but he is pleased that he is getting some sense, an' he draws up a deed of gift to Henrietta Aymes an' the deed is registered an' the lawyer then hands the bonds over to Henrietta, an' the bonds he handed over was O.K., they wasn't phoney, they was the real stuff.

"All right. Well, Granworth is on top of the world, ain't he? He's got a swell wife—because they tell me that this Henrietta is one swell baby—he's got fifty thousand dollars in his checkin' account. He don't owe no money an' everything is hunky dory.

"An' it looks like Granworth is learnin' some sense. He plans to buy some more insurance. He is insured on an annuity policy at this time with the Second National Corporation an' he waltzes along an' he says he wants to take out additional insurance. He wants to pay a down premium of thirty thousand dollars. They examine him for health an' they find him O.K. They give him the new policy, but there is just one little snag.

"Two years before this guy Granworth Aymes has tried to bump himself off. He tries to commit suicide by jumpin' in East River. He'd been havin' a bad time an' was broke an' didn't like it. He was fished out by a patrolman.

"Havin' regard to this little thing the Insurance Corporation make a proviso in his policy. The proviso says that, havin' regard to the fact that he has tried to commit suicide on a previous occasion, in the event of future suicide on his part the policy is nullified. They will pay on anything else but not suicide.

"Got that? Well, everything goes along O.K. an' he makes a bit more dough on the market, an' on the 12th January this year he does another little deal that nets him twelve thousand. He has got forty thousand dollars in his checkin' account at the bank, no debts, a wife with two hundred thousand Dollar Bonds an' is in the best of health accordin' to the Insurance examination of a few months before. So what? So just this. He goes an' commits suicide. Can you beat that?

"On the evenin' of January 12th he is workin' late at his office with his secretary, a guy named Burdell. His wife is stayin' in Hartford, Connecticut; he has fixed to go out to a party with some guys he knows, an' this Burdell guy says he was plenty excited about something.

"He packs up at about eight o'clock an' rings through to the garage for his car. He helps himself to a big drink, says good-night to the Burdell bird an' scrams. Burdell says he was lookin' a bit strange when he went outa the office.

"He used to drive a big grey-blue Cadillac—a car you couldn't forget. At ten minutes past nine he is seen by a wharf watchman drivin' the car down to Cotton's Wharf which is around there, an' while this guy is watchin' him Granworth drives the car into a wooden pile, bounces off an' goes over the edge into East River.

"Next mornin' they yank the car out. Granworth is smashed up pretty good. They get him along to the morgue an' Burdell is telephoned for an' comes along an' identifies him. In his pocket, inside his wallet, is a note sayin' that he is feelin' funny in the head an' that he reckons he had better take this way out an' to give his love to his wife an' say he is sorry for what he is doin'.

"All this stuff comes out at the inquest, an' his wife is brought back an' is knocked out by the news, an' they bury this guy an' that is that.

"All right. They clear up his business affairs, an' after everything in fixed up Henrietta reckons that she will come out here an' give herself a holiday at the Hacienda Altmira which was a property Granworth had bought when he was out here two years before an' leased to this guy Periera who calls himself the manager out there. She goes off, an' she hands over Granworth's office business to the secretary Burdell, because Granworth had said one time that he would like him to have it.

"All right. Well the Aymes dame comes out here, an' she brings with her about five thousand dollars that was what she got after probate was fixed out of Granworth's checkin' account, an' I suppose she brings out the two hundred thousand bucks in Dollar Bonds. The next thing is that Washington is advised by the State here that a phoney Bond has been slipped over by her an' that she has got another 195,000 dollars' worth of phoney Dollar Bonds, an' they put me on the job.

"I do a little bit of delvin' around an' I get the shorthand notes of the inquest an' get the dope that I have just told you. I check up with this Burdell guy, an' he confirms everything, includin' the fact that this Henrietta was a durn good wife an' a swell dame to get along with; that she was too swell for a piker like Granworth.

"Meantime, I reckon that it will be a good thing if somebody keeps an eye on this dame out here. So I get Sagers put on the job. He gets orders to get along here an' fix himself a job out at the Altmira somehow an' just case out the situation out there. He told me all he knew to-night an' it wasn't much. So there we go, an' what do you know about that?"

Metts scratches his head.

"I reckon that's durn funny," he says. "It looks as if somebody had got the original real Bonds off her an' slipped her the phoney stuff in their place."

"Maybe," I tell him, "an' maybe not. Listen, Chief," I go on, "you tell me something. When this bank manager Krat found out that the first Bond she tried to slip over was phoney, who did he tell besides you?"

"Nobody," he says. "He told me that he hadn't said a word. He was the guy who found out that the Bond was screwy an' he told the boys in the Bank to keep their traps shut an' say nothin' to anybody. He said that it would be a federal job an' the least said the better. Naturally, I ain't told a soul. I reckoned a federal agent would be along here pretty quick an' I never talk."

He looks at me old-fashioned.

"Say," he says with a sorta snarl, "you don't think . . ."

"I don't think nothin'," I tell him, "but I'm just askin' you to get a load of this. I got my instructions to handle this job ten days ago. I was in Allentown, Pennsylvania. I ease right along to New York, an' park myself at a hotel dump I use on East 30th Street. The second day I was there somebody sent me a note with no signature on it. This note said that I would probably do a durn sight better for myself if I was to get out to Palm Springs an' take a look around the dump where Mrs. Aymes was stayin', that I might find some interestin' letters there.

"Well, I was lucky. Sagers tipped me off about this place to-night, an' I went over there. There wasn't anybody around an' I had a look around an' I found the letters. They was hidden in a book with the inside cut out—you know, Chief, the old stuff—an' these letters show that things wasn't so good between Henrietta an' Granworth as the world believed. More than that they show that she wasn't in Connecticut the night he bumped himself off. She was in New York, an' she'd gone there to have a show down with him. An' how do you like that?"

He whistles.

"That's a hot one," he says, pourin' me out some more bourbon. "Maybe there was something screwy about that suicide of his. Maybe she bumped him somehow. Women can get like that sometimes."

"You're tellin' me," I say, "an' what does she bump him for? Does she bump him because she's found that the two hundred grand in Dollar Bonds is phoney, huh? Does she find that out an' get annoyed with him? That would be a motive all right, but I reckon that if she knew the Bonds was fake she wouldn't have been such a mug as to try an' cash one in on a bank. She'd have tried a fast one on somebody who wasn't so wise as a bank guy."

I shake my head.

"I can't get it," I say. "It's not so hot."

He grins.

"Dames is funny things," he says. "They do all sorts of screwy things—even the best of 'em."

I sink the bourbon.

"You're tellin' me," I say. "I know 'em. Dames don't care. Once they got an idea they just do something tough."

"Yeah," he says. "So what are you goin' to do?"

I grin.

"Well, Chief," I tell him, "I'll tell you what I ain't goin' to do. I ain't goin' to run around here flashin' a tin badge an' shoutin' out loud that I am a Federal Agent. I am goin' to check in at the Miranda House Hotel, an' I'm goin' to keep up the front that I am from Magdalena, Mexico, that I come here to tip Sagers off about comin' into the money, an' that I am goin' to stick around here for a bit an' take a little vacation.

"To-morrow night I am going out to this Hacienda Altmira. I am goin' to get next to these guys. If they want to play faro, then I'm playin'. I'm goin' to get next to this Henrietta dame an' stick around until I find out what the hell this dame is playin' at an' whether she is on the up an' up or is just another female chiseller who has tried to pull a fast one.

"I gotta find out who bumped Sagers an' why. I gotta try an' get next to somethin' solid about these phoney Bonds, because, right now, it looks as if nothin' makes sense."

"O.K. by me," he says. "An' I reckon you don't want me or the boys interferin' around at the Hacienda?"

"You're dead right," I say. "Say, is this place as lousy as they say?"

He shrugs.

"It's just one of them places," he says. "We've had plenty complaints from guys who've lost their dough there. Gamblin's illegal an' we put up a raid now an' then just to amuse the children, but what's the use of tryin' to stop people playin' faro or shootin' crap for big dough if they're built that way? Ten months ago some guy is found out on the desert away back of the Hacienda. He'd been clubbed till he looked like a map of Europe an' he was good an' dead. Plenty people said he'd been done at the Hacienda after they took him for his dough, an' I tried all I knew to get a case goin' but I couldn't make it. I couldn't prove a thing."

"O.K. Chief," I say an' I shake hands. "Now I reckon I ain't comin' to see you any more. It's no good you an' me being seen around together. But if I want to contact you I'll call you. If you want me I'm at the Miranda House an' I'll be using the name of Frayme—Selby T. Frayme of Magdalena, Mexico."

I scram. I get the car an' drive over to the Miranda House an' check in. Then I go up to my room an' drink some coffee an' read the three letters again. But I still can't make any sense outa this thing.

One little thing is sorta stickin' around in my mind an' that is this. I would very much like to know who the guy was who sent me that anonymous letter sayin' I should find these three letters out here at Henrietta's dump. I wanta know who this guy was, an' I am goin' to guess once an' take a shade of odds that I am right. The only guy mixed up in this business who mighta known that I was stayin' on East 30th Street would be Langdon Burdell, Granworth Aymes' secretary, an' maybe I am goin' to talk cold turkey to this guy pretty soon.

But even if it was him, how did he know that the letters would be out at the rancho? An' how did he know that Henrietta had taken 'em?

Another thing is that I have always found this ferretin' out business comes hard. Nothin' in this "G" game is easy. *An' I found them letters too durn easy.* Maybe I was meant to find 'em.

I go to bed because, as I have told you before, I am a great believer in sleep. If the tough guys an' dames was to stay in bed more instead of rootin' around raisin' hell generally, "G" men could take time out for eatin' cream puffs.

I am wonderin' what this dame Henrietta is like. They say she is one swell baby. Well, I hope they are right, because if I have gotta pinch a dame I would as soon pinch one who is easy to look at.

You're tellin' me!

CHAPTER THREE
HENRIETTA

NEXT day I just stick around. In the afternoon I ease along to the telegraph office an' I send a code wire to the "G" Office in New York askin' them to let me have a list of the servants an' people employed by Granworth Aymes at the time of his suicide an' their locations right now, that is if they can find 'em out.

I have got a sorta hunch about this Aymes suicide. It looks to me like there is something screwy about it, an' if I can dig up anything that is goin' to help me along, then I reckon I am goin' to dig.

The main difference between the sorta things that you read about in detective fiction an' the things that happen in real life is that the real life things is always a durn sight more strange than the ones in the book. No writin' guy ever had the nerve to write a story that he knew was true—nobody woulda believed him; but in the books there is always a bunch of clues that the crook leaves lyin' about just like they was banana skins for the dick to slip up on.

Me—I always follow my nose an' just go right ahead. That's my system. I don't believe what anybody tells me on a case till I've checked on it, an' even then, like as not, I still don't believe 'em.

One snag is that the New York coroner who was responsible for the inquest says that Granworth Aymes committed suicide, and it ain't any business of mine to go gumshoein' around bustin' that verdict wide open unless it's got some direct bearin' on the counterfeit business. You gotta realise that I am a Federal Agent an' it is not my business to check up on police work or try an' prove that they are wrong—not unless I have got to.

At the same time I reckon that I will do some delvin' because it stands to reason that the counterfeitin' of these Dollar Bonds mighta been done in more than one way. First of all somebody might have pinched the original certificates an' substituted the counterfeit ones *after* they had been handed over to Henrietta Aymes. This coulda been done without Granworth knowin' anything about it, or else it coulda been arranged by him an' done with his knowledge, although where this woulda got him I don't know.

Then Henrietta mighta got the counterfeit stuff made after Aymes was dead, thinkin' that she had a better chance of passin' it than anybody else just because everybody knew that Aymes had given her the regular bonds. But even if this was so you woulda thought she wouldn't have been such a mug as to try an' push one over on a bank. Anybody will cash a Registered Dollar Bond if they've got the money, an' there was plenty of other places she coulda tried first.

Supposin' that she is tryin' a fast one. Well, where are the original certificates an' who's got 'em?

I can't help thinkin' back of my head that there is some connection between the counterfeitin' business an' this schmozzle that is goin' on between Henrietta an' Granworth over this woman just before he dies. It also looks very screwy that Henrietta was aimin' to go an' see him on the day that he bumped himself off; an' here is another little thing that I cannot understand:—The New York police told me that at the inquest on Aymes, Burdell, his secretary, an' the other servants workin' in the Aymes' apartment all said that Mrs. Aymes was away in Connecticut until after the suicide, when Burdell sent her a wire an' she came back pronto so's to be at the funeral.

Anyway, I reckon that I will take a look at this Henrietta as soon as I can, an' maybe she an' me can do a little talkin' an' see if we can get some of this business straightened out.

Sittin' on the veranda outside my bedroom window, drinkin' a mint julep, I get to thinkin' about Sagers. I am tryin' to find some reason why some guy shoulda bumped him off. Nobody could know that there was any connection between Sagers an' me, an' the act we put on at the Hacienda Altmira the night he got his was watertight. Nobody woulda suspected that he was reportin' to me while we was doin' that big makin' friends act.

So it looks to me like somebody out at the Hacienda thought that Sagers knew a durn sight more than he did, an' when he blew along an' said that he had come into this money an' was scrammin', they thought they'd better make a certainty of him an' give him the heat. Even so I reckon he was shot in a funny sorta way.

The way he was lyin' on those stairs looked to me that he was comin' down 'em when he was shot. There was a powder burn round one of the bullet holes where he was shot in the stomach an' that particular shot was fired at pretty close range—about four feet away I should think.

So I work it out this way:—Sagers was up in one of the rooms leading off the balcony that runs round the inside wall of the Hacienda. Somebody shot him in the guts an' Sagers, not havin' a gun on him, evidently thought he'd better blow before they ironed him some more. So he turns around, gets along the balcony an' starts runnin' down the stairs.

The guy who is doin' the shootin' leans over the balcony an' puts a coupla shots into Sagers' legs. Sagers falls down an' the guy then walks over an' standin' at the top of the stairs puts another shot into his body. This would account for the fact that there wasn't any powder marks around the other bullet holes.

The shootin' guy then walks down the stairs, steps over Sagers' body, an' standin' two or three stairs below him, gets hold of his silver shirt-neck cord so as to pull him over his shoulder. In doin' this the cord breaks an' the little tassel falls off the end on to the stair where I found it. The killer then carries Sagers along to the store behind the bar an' dumps him in the ice chest, all of which is very interestin' only it don't get me any place except that I have gotta sorta idea that one day I would like to bust this shootin' guy a coupla hard ones an' get him the hot squat afterwards.

After all this thinkin' I go inside an' lie down an' read a detective magazine because it takes my mind off my business, an' then, when the evenin' starts arrivin' I get up an' I put on a very swell "soup-an'-fish" that I have got, dinner pants an' a white serge tuxedo that makes me look like the King of Japan, after which I eat my dinner an' wisecrack with the girl in the reception.

At eleven o'clock I get the car an' I take the desert road an' make for the Hacienda Altmira. I reckon that I will just stick around an' see if something is happenin' that is interestin'.

It is a swell night, an' when I get there I can hear the guitars goin'. A half a dozen horses are tied up around the back, an' there are a coupla dozen cars parked in the garage round at the side. I leave the car an' walk around to the front entrance.

Periera is there. He is all dressed up an' I can hear from the noise comin' along the passage that there are plenty people around. Periera says will I have a drink on the house an' I say yes, an' while I am checkin' in my fedora they bring me a highball. I say good health to him an' drink it, an' he takes a quick look at me an' says that if I would like a little game of anythin' there will be one goin' some time after twelve o'clock an' that it will be in the room on the balcony right at the top of the stairs. I say thanks a lot an' that I am game for anything that is a gamble from crap shootin' upwards.

He laughs an' I walk along the passage an' pull the curtain an' stand lookin' on to the main floor.

The place is crowded. All the tables are full of guys and there are some swell dames with 'em. Two, three cowboys—real or dude I don't know—are standin' up against the bar, an' the piece of dance floor is pack full of people dancin'. There are coloured streamers hangin' from the balcony, an' on the walls are long Spanish shawls an' here an' there a Mexican blanket—the place looks swell I'm tellin' you. The band know their stuff an' they are playin' a hauntin' tune—some Mexican tango, an' one of the guys on the band platform, who has got the sorta voice that makes a temperamental dame wanta go into a convent, is singin' a song about dyin' for love that is breakin' some of them janes' hearts.

There are two or three tables around the band platform an' the women sittin' at 'em are lookin' up at this guy like he was an angel or something. When one of the men with 'em—they look like business men from Los Angeles—says anything the dames sorta shut him up in case they miss a bit of the song, which only goes to show you that some dames are screwy as hell. These dames marry some business guy an' he buys 'em swell dresses an' takes 'em places where they can sling a warm look at a cheap palooka who is singin' in a club band. Sometimes they go the whole hog an' run off with these crooners, after which they get wise an' spend the rest of their lives tryin' to find another business man that they can get next to an' marry, so that they can get some more dresses an' sling longing looks to some different band guys.

I'm tellin' you that the place was a sight, one of the prettiest pictures I have ever seen, an' then just as I was goin' to move down an' walk over to a table I see a dame walkin' my way. She's comin' from the left of the room over by the windows. This dame has got what it takes—an' then a bundle! She is tall an' slim, an' she has got all the right curves. She's as pretty as a picture an' she has got her nose stuck up in the air like she was a queen. She is a brunette an' the way she has her hair done is aces. It was swell.

An' she looks tough. Her mouth is set in a hard line an' I see that she has got a jaw. Somehow for no reason at all I know that this is Henrietta.

I look back down the passage. Periera is still standin' there wise-crackin' with the girl who is checkin' in the hats. I nod my head at him an' he comes along.

"Who's the baby, Periera," I say, "the one who has just sat down at that table over there, the one by herself? I didn't know you had dames around here like that."

He grins up at me. This guy Periera reminds me of a snake. I don't like him a bit.

"Señor," he says, "we got everything. Thees lady ees the Señora 'Enrietta Aymes."

"You don't say," I crack.

I look surprised.

"Say listen, Periera," I say. "She ain't the dame that was married to that guy—what was his name—Granworth Aymes—the guy who bumped himself off in New York? I was there at the time. I read about it in the papers."

He nods, an' he puts on an expression like he was very sorry. Then he makes himself out to be the big guy. He says how this Henrietta came out to the Hacienda Altmira thinkin' that it belonged to Granworth, her husband, an' when she gets out there he has the sweet duty of tellin' her that the place is mortgaged over to him; that Granworth didn't pay off the mortgage, an' that it is his place.

He spread his hands.

"Then, Señor," he says, "there is some more troubles for thees unfortunate lady. There ees some argument about her money. She tells me she has no money. So," he goes on, "I let her stick around. I am a good man, you understand, Señor. I feel sorry for thees poor woman. I let her stay around here an' be hostess until she makes up her mind what she would like to do."

"Yeah," I tell him. "It looks like you're a good guy, Periera. How about meetin' the lady?"

He nods, but just then I tell him it don't matter, because goin' towards the table where Henrietta is sittin' is a guy. He is a big guy an' he looks pretty regular to me. He has got a nice sorta face. I can tell by the way that this guy is lookin' at Henrietta as he goes towards the table an' the way that she looks back at him, that these two are pretty friendly. I grin at Periera.

"Looks like she's got a boy friend," I say, "nice lookin' guy. Who is he?"

"'Ees name is Maloney," says Periera. "'E comes around here a lot. He plays. Maybe he plays to-night."

I nod.

"Well, I hope I take some dough off him," I say. "By the way my name's Frayme—Selby Frayme. Do you play high stakes around here?"

He shrugs his shoulders.

"What you like, Señor Frayme," he says. "For us the roof ees always the limit."

I say O.K. Then I go an' sit down at a table and order myself a highball. I reckon it is not very much good my tryin' to muscle in an' talk to Henrietta while this guy is stickin' around.

The time goes on. Periera takes me over an' introduces me to some party sittin' at a big table. These guys are pretty warmhearted guys an' the women with them can certainly dance. If I hadn't had my mind on the job all the time I would certainly have enjoyed that dancin'.

About two o'clock people start movin', an' in half an hour's time the place is pretty empty, except for about ten or twelve people who were stickin' around. It looks to me like these people are the ones who are goin' to do the playin'.

My party scram out of it, an' as I am sayin' good-night to 'em, Periera comes over. He tells me that play will be startin' any minute now, an' that I know where the room is, the one at the top of the stairs. I tell him yes but I think I am goin' to have a walk around first. I go out the front way an' I walk around the place sniffin' the air. I am very funny about any sorta gamblin'. I like the game to get started before I bust into it.

About twenty minutes afterwards I go back. One of the waiter guys is closing down the windows on the left hand side of the club. The band have packed up and most of the lights are down. I walk across the floor, up the stairs an' go into the room at the top. It is a fair sized room, with a big table in the middle. There are some guys playin' baccarat at this table, an' at another little table in a corner another three guys an' two dames are playin' poker.

Maloney is at the baccarat table an' standin' near to him watchin' the play is Henrietta. All the guys up there are wearin' tuxedos, an' one or two of 'em at the baccarat table look plenty tough to me. It looks like everybody has been doin' some drinkin' too because there is that sort of atmosphere that comes when people get high.

After a minute Periera comes along, looks in an' then goes off some place. I just stick around and watch.

Maloney ain't doin' so well. He is losin' plenty an' he don't look so happy about it. Also he is lookin' a little bit puzzled as if he cannot quite understand somethin', an' I am wonderin' if somebody has been doin' a little fast stuff with the cards.

After about ten minutes Maloney goes banco an' flops on it. He loses a bundle. He turns round an' he looks at Henrietta with a silly sorta grin.

"It don't look anythin's comin' my way," he says "I never seem to get any luck at all around here."

She smiles, an' believe me her teeth match up with the rest of her, an' did I tell you that she had sapphire blue eyes. Me, I have always been very partial to sapphire blue eyes!

"Why not give it a rest?" she says. "Or would you like me to play a hand for you?"

On the other side of the table is a big guy. He is a broad-shouldered fellow with a thin face an' a lotta black hair. I have heard him called Fernandez. He is watchin' Maloney all the time whilst they are talkin'. Then he chips in:

"It looks like both your lucks out," he says, "But," he goes on with a snicker, "maybe you always expect to win. Maybe you don't like losin'."

Maloney goes red.

"Whether I like winnin' or losin' is my business, Fernandez," he says, "An' I don't need any wisecracks outa you. I don't mind losin'," he goes on, "but I said that I've got a funny habit of always losin' when I play around here." He grins sorta sarcastic. "But maybe it is only my imagination," he says.

"You don't say," says Fernandez.

He gets up sorta very slow an' pushes his chair back. Then he leans across the table an' be busts Maloney a hard one right on the puss. You coulda heard the smack a mile away.

Everybody stops everything. Maloney does a swell back fall over the back of his chair. He gets up an' he is lookin' groggy. By this time Fernandez has walked around to the end of the table. He gets Maloney off his balance an' chins him again. This guy Fernandez is lookin' like a burned-up tiger. He is all steamed up an' I get the idea that he is a dope. I stand over in the corner an' light a cigarette. I am just beginnin' to get interested.

Henrietta has gone back up against the wall. She is watchin' Maloney. Her eyes are glitterin' an' I know she is sorta prayin' that he can get up an' hand Fernandez something. In the corner one of the dames playin' poker, who is very high, starts cacklin'. She thinks it's funny.

Maloney gets up. He is shook all right, but wades in at Fernandez. He swings a right which Fernandez blocks, an' before Maloney can do anythin' about it Fernandez gives him another haymaker. Maloney goes down again an' he is not lookin' pretty. One eye is closed up an' his face is covered with blood.

The guys playin' poker in the corner get up. One of 'em—a little guy—comes over.

"Why don't you two mugs cut it out?" he says. "What do you think this is? Madison Square Gardens or what? An' what's the matter with you, Fernandez? Why must you always start something around here?"

Fernandez turns round an' grins at him.

"Don't you like it," he says.

He wipes this little guy across the face with the back of his hand.

"If you don't like it," he says, "get out."

There is a sorta silence—the sorta stuff that they call atmosphere. Nobody says anythin'. Then the little guy who has just been smacked down gets up an' walks outa the room. His party go with him. Maloney has got up. He is standin' against the wall an' he

don't look so good to me. I reckon that first punch of Fernandez'—
that one across the table—shook him considerable.

I go over to him.

"Listen, big boy," I say. "Why don't you go some place an' get
that mug of yours cleaned up. It ain't pretty. An' whilst you're
about it I'd have a drink if I was you. You look as if you could do
with one."

I turn to Henrietta an' I grin.

"Look, lady," I say. "Take him away an' do a big nursemaid
act." After which I say "I reckon we might play a little game of
cards around here."

While I am talkin' Periera has come in the room. He is standin'
just inside the doorway an' he is lookin' quite pleased. It looks
like this Fernandez is a friend of his, an' the big guy around here.
Henrietta don't say anythin' at all, but if she had gotta gun I reckon
she woulda shot Fernandez. She just grabs this guy Maloney and
pushes him towards the door.

Fernandez looks over at them as they are goin' out an' laughs—
he has gotta nasty sorta cackle.

"Take that sap away an' lose him," he says.

Henrietta turns around. She is as white as death. She is so
burned up she don't know what to do with herself. Fernandez
looks at her an' grins. Then he walks over to her an' before she
knows what he is goin' to do he kisses her right on the mouth.

"Run along, sister," he says "an' don't get het up because it
won't get you no place."

He comes back to the table.

"Now maybe we can get ahead," he says, pickin' up the cards.
The other guys, four of 'em at the big table, get set. They are goin'
to play poker.

"Are you comin' in?" says Fernandez to me.

I nod.

"Yeah," I tell him, "but justa minute. I gotta do something."

I turn around and go outa the room. I can see Henrietta takin'
the Maloney bird into a room way down along the balcony. I ease
along there an' look through the door. She has put Maloney on

a couch, an' she is in the corner gettin' a basin of water ready. Maloney don't look so good.

I go in.

"Say, sister," I start, "I reckon that your boy friend got a raw deal. Maybe he ain't in fightin' trim to-night. He certainly can take it."

She goes over to Maloney an' starts dabbin' his face with a towel.

"I wish I was a man," she says. "I'd kill Fernandez." She stops work an' turns round an' looks at me. Her eyes are flashin' an' she looks good. I always did like dames with tempers. "Jim here would have smashed him to bits," she goes on, "but he can't use his arm properly. He broke it two weeks ago and it's not working properly yet. It was easy for that moron to be tough."

Maloney starts comin' up for air. He struggles to get off the couch, but he can't make it. He falls back.

"Let me get at that . . ." he mutters.

I do a bit of quick thinkin'. I think that maybe I can do myself a good turn by gettin' next to this Henrietta in a big way. Maybe if I play my cards right she will talk, an' it looks as if this is the opportunity.

"Don't worry, Maloney," I say. "You never had a chance with that arm, an' he caught you off balance." I look at Henrietta. "I was feelin' pretty burned up myself when that lousy bum went over an' kissed you like that," I go on. "That was a pretty insultin' thing to do in a room full of guys."

"Oh, yes," she says. "Well, I didn't see you doing anything about it."

I smile.

"Listen, lady," I tell her. "When you got your friend here all fixed, just come along back to the card room, an' you an' me'll have a little talk with this Fernandez guy."

I scram.

I go back to the card room. They are waitin' for me. Fernandez grunts like he is impatient to begin, an' I sit down an' ante up.

We start to play poker. They are playin' ten dollar rises which is quite big enough for me, but I am not doing badly in the first coupla hands. I win. I look at Fernandez an' grin like I was sorta pleased with myself. He gives me a big scowl.

We go on. There is a round of jackpots an' finally Ferandez opens it. He opens it for fifty dollars an' everybody plays. There is about two hundred an' fifty dollars in the pot. While we are drawin' cards I hear Henrietta come into the room. She comes an' stands just by where I am sittin'.

Fernandez bets. He bets a hundred. The other guys throw their cards in. I stay in. I reckon he is bluffin' an' I am goin' all out on my two pairs.

I see him. I was right. He has got two pairs sixes high an' I am tens high.

I scoop in the pool.

"You oughta learn to play this game, sucker," I tell him.

He looks up.

"An' what did you call me?" he says.

I get up, I put my hands under the table ledge an' I throw the table over, sideways. This leaves a space between me an' Fernandez. I jump in. As he puts his arms up I drop my head an' give it to him under the chin. As he goes back I follow with a left an' right an' I connect on each side of his jaw. I stand off an' wait for him to come in. He does, but he is a bit shook an' I sidestep an' smash him one on the nose that busts the works properly. He goes down, an' while he is goin' I call him by an old-fashioned name. This sorta riles him. He gets up, an' he comes for me like a bull. I sink my head an' he gets it in the guts. He brings his knee up but I miss it an' hit him again in the stomach. This hurts him plenty, an' he goes up against the wall. I go after him an' I paste him. I get to work on this guy like I have never worked on anybody before. Once or twice he tries to make a comeback, but he is not so good. The one I gave him on the mark has finished him for a bit.

Eventually he is just leaning up against the wall an' I smack him down. He stays put on the floor. I look at Periera. He don't look so pleased now.

"Listen, Periera," I say. "You take this punk tough guy outa here before he gets me really annoyed. Because I am a guy who is liable to hurt somebody some time. But maybe I will do the job myself."

Periera don't say nothin'. I get hold of Fernandez by the collar. I yank him up an' I take him over to Henrietta.

"Tell the lady you're sorry, punk," I say, "because if you don't I'm goin' to smack it out of you. Get busy."

Just to help him along I flatten his nose—which is not so well anyhow, with my thumb.

He comes across, an' says his stuff.

I take him outside to the top of the stairs leadin' down to the dance floor an' I kick him down. He bounces considerable. When he gets to the bottom he sits up like he was tryin' to remember what his first name was.

I go back.

"Listen, Periera," I say. "Where does this guy Maloney live?"

He says he lives in some dump near Indio, so I tell him to get out a car an' drive Maloney home. He looks like he is goin' to object but he thinks better of it. I tell him that he had better take the Fernandez bird off as well, an' he says all right.

I turn around to Henrietta. There is a little smile in her eye. I give her a big wink.

"Get your wrap, sister," I tell her. "You an' me is goin' to do a little drivin'. I wanna talk to you."

She looks at me an' she laughs.

"You've got your nerve, Mr. Frayme," she says.

Chapter Four
PORTRAIT OF A "G" MAN

Sittin' in the car, drivin' easy with Henrietta smokin' a cigarette an lookin' straight ahead in front of her, I was feelin' pretty good. I was thinkin' that if there wasn't so much crime mixed up with this "G" business it would be a swell sorta job.

After a bit I ask her if she wants to go any place in particular, an' she says no, but that if we keep ahead an' take a turn right pretty soon we will come to some dump where they are open all night an' that she reckons that we might as well drink some coffee while we are talkin'.

I take a peek at her sideways, an' I'm tellin' you that this dame is certainly the goods. She has got that peculiar sort of way of talkin' an' doin' everything that gets you guessin'. Most dames woulda been hot to know what I wanted to talk to 'em about, but this Henrietta just don't ask a thing. She sits there lookin' straight ahead with them sapphire blue eyes of hers, an' a little smile playin' around her mouth. She gets me curious because she don't seem interested in anything much—not even herself—an' there ain't many dames like that.

Pretty soon we come to the intersection that she has talked about an' we turn right. Away ahead I can see the lights of this place where we are goin' to get coffee. I slow down a bit because I want to put in a spot of thinkin' myself about what spiel I am goin' to pull on this Henrietta. I reckon that I have gotta tell her some sorta stuff that is liable to make her open up an' yet I have also got to keep who I am an' what I am doin' around here under cover. However, I have always found that if you are goin' to tell a fairy story you might as well make it a good one, so I get busy thinkin' about the idea that I am goin' to pull on her, after which I step on the gas an' we travel plenty.

Suddenly she starts talkin'.

"I think that was a swell job you did on Fernandez, Mr. Frayme," she says, lookin' at me outa the corner of her eye.

"He thinks he's tough. But maybe he'll alter his opinion after that little session he had with you."

"That wasn't nothin'," I tell her. "Anyhow, I don't like this Fernandez. He looks to me like a punk, an' I didn't like to see him bustin' your boy friend about. He looks a regular guy that Maloney bird."

"He's pretty good," she says, "I like him."

I pull up an' she stops talkin'.

We go in this place. It is the usual one story adobe building with a few tables stuck around an' a guy who is half asleep takin' coffee to a coupla odd guys who are sittin' at a table. Besides these there ain't any one else there.

We sit down an' I order some coffee. I give her a cigarette, an' when I have lit it she holds it up an' looks at the smoke curlin' up.

"I'm afraid that you won't be very popular with Fernandez after this, Mr. Frayme," she says, "and what he is going to do about me I don't know. . . ."

I ask her what she means by that crack.

She laughs, an' I can see her little teeth gleamin'.

"Fernandez wants me to marry him," she says. "He thinks he's madly in love with me, but what he'll think tomorrow after he's had a little facial treatment and got rid of some of the black eyes and bruises, I don't know."

"Well, well, well," I say, "an' here was I thinkin' that you was stuck on this Maloney. You don't really mean to say that you would consider hitchin' up with a bird like that Fernandez," I tell her.

She smiles again. She certainly is a mysterious dame.

"I don't know what I think," she says. "Maybe I'll *have* to marry Fernandez." She looks at me an' she gives a little laugh. "Don't let's worry about him just now," she says. "You tell me what you want to talk to me about."

The guy brings the coffee an' it smells good to me. When she lifts her cup her wrap falls off her shoulders an' I see that she has gotta pair of shoulders that mighta been copied off this dame Venus that you probably heard about, an' who seems to have started plenty trouble in her time. Henrietta sees me lookin' an' she gives me a sorta whimsical look like you would give a kid who was bein' naughty, an' I begin thinkin' that this dame has gotta way with her that I could go nuts about if I was a guy who went nuts about the shape of dames' shoulders, which is a thing I would probably do, only just when I am getting good an' interested in things like that I get sent off to the other end of the country on some bum case or other.

Well, here we go, I think to myself, an' I start in on the spiel I have thought up in the car while I was drivin' to this dump.

"Look, lady," I tell her, "this is the way it is: I work for a firm of New York attorneys who have got a branch office in Magdalena, Mexico, that I run for 'em. Well, a month or so ago I am in New York on some business an' I get around with a guy who is workin' in the District Attorney's office there. This guy starts tellin' me about your husband Granworth Aymes bumpin' himself off last January an' he tells me that they have got some interestin' new evidence an' that they reckon they may re-open this case."

I stop talkin' an' start drinkin' my coffee. Over the top of the cup I am watchin' her. I can see that her fingers holdin' the cigarette are tremblin' an' she has gone plenty white round the mouth. It don't look to me that what I have just said has pleased her any.

She takes a pull at herself but when she begins to talk her voice ain't so low as it was before. There is a spot of excitement in it.

"That's very interesting," she says. "What new evidence could they find. I didn't know there was any question about my husband's suicide. I thought it was all over and finished with."

She stubs out the cigarette end on an ashtray. By this time she has got hold of herself. I put my cup down an' give her another cigarette an' light one for myself.

"You see it's this way," I go on. "A coroner's inquest don't matter very much if the D.A. in charge of the case thinks that he's found some new stuff that means something. Anyhow this guy in the D.A.'s office tells me that they have discovered that you wasn't in Connecticut on the night that Granworth Aymes is supposed to have bumped himself off. They have found out that you was in New York an' another thing is that they have gotta big idea that the last person to see Granworth Aymes before he died was you, see?"

"I see," she says. Her voice is sorta dull, the life has gone out of it.

"These guys get all sorts of funny ideas in their heads," I say, "but you know what coppers an' district attorneys are. They just gotta try an' hang something on somebody. They wouldn't be doin' the job they do if they didn't like pullin' people in.

"You see it looks like somebody has dropped a hint around there that Granworth Aymes didn't commit suicide. That he was bumped off."

She flicks the ask off her cigarette.

"That seems ridiculous to me, Mr. Frayme," she says. "The watchman on Cotton's Wharf testified that he saw Granworth drive the car over the wharf. That looks like suicide . . . doesn't it?"

"Yeah," I tell her, "that's O.K., but I gotta tell you what happened. This guy in the D.A.'s office tells me that they got information that you slipped a counterfeit Registered Dollar Bond over at the bank here, an' of course that was reported to the Federal Government. The Feds. evidently put a 'G' man on the job, an' this guy gets around in New York an' he grills this watchman on Cotton's Wharf an' after a bit he gets the whole truth about this business. What the watchman said he saw an' what he really saw is two different things, believe me, lady, because the watchman tells this 'G' man that he saw Granworth Aymes car drive slowly down the wharf, an' that when it was half-way down an' in the shadow the off-side door opens an' somebody gets out. He can't see who it is, but he can see it's a woman. He sees her turn around an' lean inside the can an' then shut the door. The car starts off again, gathers speed, bounces off a wooden pile an' goes right over the edge into the river."

"I see," she says. "And why doesn't this watchman tell this story at the coroner's inquest?"

I grin.

"He had a reason, lady," I tell her. "A durn good reason. He kept his mouth shut about that little incident because a certain guy by the name of Langdon Burdell—a guy who was your husband's secretary—gave him one thousand dollars to forget everything except seeing the car bounce off the pile an' go over the edge."

She looks at me as if she has been struck by lightning.

"It looks like this Burdell guy is pretty friendly towards you," I tell her, "because when this 'G' man had seen him previously he said that you wasn't in New York that night, you was in Connecticut, an' it looks as if he not only said that but that the night after the death he had scrammed down and bribed the watchman good an' plenty to keep his mouth shut about that woman.

"Well, what does that look like?" I say. "It looks like Granworth Aymes mighta been dead an' stuck in that car. It looks like the woman mighta been drivin' it, don't it?"

She don't say anything for a minute. I see her wet her lips with her tongue. She is takin' this stuff pretty well, but she is frightened, I reckon. But she soon gets a hold of herself again.

"If Granworth were killed they could have discovered it at the post mortem," she says.

"Maybe," I tell her, "an' maybe not. But the guy in the D.A.'s office tells me that Granworth was smashed up through the fall into the river. Remember when that car hit bottom he banged plenty hard against the wind shield. His head was all smashed in, but that mighta been done before he was put in the car."

"I don't understand any of this," she says. "And I don't understand why Langdon Burdell should have bribed the watchman to tell some story that was not the truth. Why should he do that?"

"Search me, lady," I tell her. "But I expect that the D.A.'s office can find that out if they wanta start gettin' funny with somebody."

I ask her if she would like some more coffee, an' she says yes, so I order it. While we are waitin' for it to come I am keepin' a quiet eye on Henrietta an' I can see she is doin' some very deep thinkin', which don't surprise me because it looks like I have given her something to think about.

When the coffee comes she drinks it as if she was glad to have something to do. Then she puts the cup down an' looks straight at me.

"I'm wondering why you took the trouble to tell me all this, Mr. Frayme," she says. "What was in your mind? What did you expect me to do?"

"It ain't what's in my mind, Henrietta," I tell her. "It's what's in the mind of these guys in the New York D.A.'s office. The thing is this. My friend who works there says that nobody gave a durn about whether Granworth Aymes committed suicide or not until this counterfeit business turned up. The inquest was all over an' everything was tied up an' put away, an' then this Registered Dollar Bond thing happens. Well, that's a Federal job, an' the 'G' people at Washington have made up their minds good an' plenty to find out who it was faked those phoney bonds. If they can find that out everything's hunky dory an' they ain't likely to worry about the inquest or anything else.

"When I went to the Hacienda Altmira last night that guy Sagers, the feller who was workin' there an' who was leavin' for Arispe to-day, told me you was Mrs. Henrietta Aymes, an' I made up my mind to tell you about this business, an' here's why:

"Supposin' for the sake of argument you know somethin' about this counterfeitin'. Supposin' you know who fixed it. Well, if I was you I'd come across. Slip me the works. Then, when I go back to New York I can hand the information quietly to my pal in the D.A.'s office an' if it's good enough for them to pass on to the 'G' people at Washington an' satisfy their curiosity, well, I don't reckon that they'll want to re-open that case about your husband.

"You see these guys reckon that you must know something about that counterfeitin'. An' if you don't come across with some information, it's a cinch that they'll re-open the business about your husband's death just so that they got something to pin on to you that will *make* you talk. See?"

"I see," she says, "but I've no information to give any one. The package of Dollar Bonds which I brought with me out here was taken from my husband's safe deposit where I kept them. I understood from Mr. Burdell that the safe deposit was opened with the key taken from my husband's dead body by his lawyer, who handed them to me. That is all I know. As for their re-opening the question of my husband's death and the suggestion that I was in New York on that night, well, they'll have to prove that, won't they?"

"Yeah. I suppose they will," I tell her. I am thinking that all the proof wanted is in the three letters from her to Granworth that I have got stored away in the safe at the Miranda House hotel.

"Anyhow it was very nice of you to give me this warning," she says. "It seems that I have a lot to thank you for, Mr. Frayme, and now, if you don't mind I think I'll be getting back."

We go out an' get into the car an' I drive back. I make out that I do not know where she is living an' she tells me the way. I drop her at the door, an' I wonder how she will feel when she finds out that somebody has pinched those three letters—three letters that may spell a bundle of trouble for this dame.

She says good-night. She gets outa the car an' she walks up to the door of the rancho. When she gets there she looks back at me an' smiles.

I reckon Henrietta has got nerve all right.

I start the car up an' I just drive along. I don't take any notice of where I am goin' because I am busy turnin' over in my mind what she has said. By an' large she seems to be takin' this business pretty calm.

There is one or two things that I cannot understand about this Henrietta. I cannot understand why she made that crack about *havin'* to marry Fernandez, an' I certainly cannot understand why she kept the three letters she wrote to Granworth—the letters that prove she saw him on the night he died—instead of gettin' rid of 'em pronto.

But I don't think that she knows anything about Sagers bein' bumped off. When I brought his name up an' said that he was the guy who was leavin' for Arispe I was watchin' her like a cat watches a mouse an' she never batted an eyelid.

An' I reckon she has got enough nerve to have bumped off Aymes. Let's do a bit of supposin'. Let's suppose she goes back to New York after writin' the letters because she has made up her mind to have a show down with Granworth about this woman who he is supposed to be runnin' around with. Maybe Granworth meets her some place in his car, because when I talked to Burdell about it when I was in New York before I come down here, he tells me that Aymes left the office to "meet some people" an' he was lookin' a bit excited. Maybe he was goin' to meet Henrietta. All right, well they meet an' they have one helluva row. It might be possible too, that in between whiles she has discovered that the Dollar Bonds he gave her was phoney. So what? Aymes is sittin' in the drivin' seat of the car in some quiet place an' she smashes him one over the head with a gun-butt or something an' knocks him out. Then she has an idea. She remembers how he tried this suicide business once before in East River, an' she thinks she can pull a fast one. She shoves him outa the drivin' seat an' pushes him over in front of the passenger seat. Then she gets in an' drives round by the back way until she gets to Cotton's Wharf which is pretty deserted. She don't see the watchman standin' at the end of the wharf. She gets out, leavin' the engine runnin', turns the wheel so that the car is pointin' to the edge of the wharf, leans over an' presses the clutch pedal down with her hand an' shoves the gear lever into gear. Then, as the car moves she stands away an' shuts the door. This would account for the car runnin' into the wooden pile before it bounced into the river.

I reckon she coulda done it that way, an' I reckon that she has got the nerve. The fact that she's pretty don't mean a thing. I have known pretty janes bump guys off before—an' get clean away with it too.

I have been drivin' back along the road nice an' easy, an' away in front of me in the moonlight I can see the white walls of the Hacienda Altmira. I wonder if Periera has delivered this guy Fernandez back where he lives, an' I wonder how the Maloney bird is feelin'. It looks like this Maloney has fallen for Henrietta. I could tell by the way he was lookin' at her earlier in the evenin'. He's got that sorta nutty look that a guy gets when he starts gettin' excited about a jane, an' I am thinkin' that he'd better watch his step with Henrietta. I reckon that one could play him for a sucker too, if she wanted to. Maybe she's playin' him off against Fernandez—you never know with dames.

I drive past the front of the Hacienda an' turn around an' run pretty slowly past the back. I start gettin' curious. I start wonderin' whether thy have took Sagers outa that sack in the ice safe yet an buried him some place in the desert. I reckon that was done pretty early yesterday mornin'.

An' for some reason that I don't know I think I would like to have a look. I sorta get a hunch about this, an' when I get a hunch I always play it.

I stop the car behind some old broken down adobe wall that runs away from the end of the garage, an' I look up at the windows an' case the place. I can't see any lights an' I can't hear anything. I keep in the shadows an' I get around by the wall until I come to the windows on the side of the dance floor an' in about two minutes I am inside.

The place is dark, but there are big patches of moonlight here an' there. I listen but I can't hear anything, an' I ease over to the bar, get over it, an' start workin' on the door of the store room behind the bar. I get this open an' go in. After I have closed the door I switch on the flash that I have brought outa the car an' go over to the ice safes. I look in 'em both an' I see that Sagers is gone. I thought he would be, because whoever bumped him would get him moved before the club opened again.

Over on a shelf in the corner is some bottles. I go over an' look a 'em, an' I see one is a bottle of *tequila* that has been opened. I sit down on a box an' take a swig at this bottle, an' although the stuff is durn strong it is better than no drink at all.

I sit there with this bottle in my hand flashin' the torch around an' wonderin' why I had this hunch about comin' back to see if they'd moved Sagers. I mighta known they woulda done this. While I am thinkin' about this the light flashes on a garbage can in the corner. Stickin' out from under the lid is what looks like the corner of a letter. I go over an' take the lid off an' start lookin' at the rubbish inside. There is all sort of junk in this can, an' I turn it over with my foot.

All of a sudden I turn over what looks like a photograph that has been torn in two. I take the two pieces out an' put them together. The picture has been cut out of a newspaper an' underneath it I can see the caption that is indistinct because it has been folded over.

I take this picture back to the box an' sit down an' have a look at it under the flash. I get a sorta idea that I have seen this guy in the picture before. Then do I get a start? I am lookin' at a picture of myself cut out of a newspaper. I straighten out the caption an' read it. It says "Portrait of a 'G' man. Exclusive picture of Lemuel H. Caution, the Federal Agent who brought in the Yelltz kidnappers."

Then I remember. This was a picture of me published in the *Chicago Times* two years ago after the Yelltz case. I remember how burned up I was at havin' my face in a newspaper so's every durn crook would know me on sight.

Round at the side of the picture on the plain edge of the newspaper is some writin'. I look at it close. It says "This is the guy."

I get it. Now I am beginnin' to understand a thing or two. It looks like somebody has sent this picture of me along here, an' has written on it "This is the guy" so's somebody would know me when I got here. I reckon that somebody back in New York, who knew I had been put on this case sends this picture along here so that the guys this end will know that something is goin' to happen.

. An' that is why they killed Sagers! It hits me like a bullet. When I blew into the Hacienda Altmira the first time they knew who I was. They was wise to my act with Sagers. So they guessed he was workin' with me, an' when he told 'em that night that he was scrammin' to Arispe like we arranged, they bumped him. They thought he might know a bit more than he did an' they aren't takin' any chances.

An' if they'll bump Sagers, well, I reckon they will bump me if they get the chance.

I take a spot more *tequila* an' start doin' a little concentratin'. Who would be the guy who would get this old newspaper an' cut the picture out an' send it out here so's they would be waitin' for me. Wouldn't it be the same guy who went to the trouble of writin' me that anonymous note in New York so as to get me out here after the letters that Henrietta had got? You bet it would.

This guy knows about the letters. He fixes to get me out here after 'em. In doin' this he knows that he must be puttin' the idea in my head that Henrietta bumped Granworth Aymes, an' he also takes the trouble to send a picture out to somebody here so's they'll know I'm me.

An' what is the big idea behind all this? Is it to get me out here because it will be easier to rub me out in this place—easier than anywhere else?

I get up off the box. This counterfeit case is beginnin' to look sweet an' interestin' to me. It is gettin' so tied up that in a minute I shall think I done it myself.

But way back in my head is an idea that I'm goin' to work on. The idea that it was this secretary bird Burdell who sent me that anonymous letter so's I should get out here an' get next to Henrietta, an' maybe start something that is goin' to end up with her bein' pinched on a first degree murder charge. An' if I am right about this what is he doin' it for? Is he doin' it because he thinks that he is helpin' justice that way or because he's got some reason for wanting to put Henrietta on the spot.

I take another swig at the *tequila* an' I put the picture of me back in the garbage can—which is where a whole lot of crooks would like to see me too—an' I scram. I get outside an' get the car goin' an' I slide back in the direction of Palm Springs, because I think that it is time that I got busy on this case. I reckon that if nobody else won't start anything then I had better start something myself.

When I get back to the Miranda House Hotel I find a telegraph waiting for me. It is coded an' is in answer to the one I sent the "G" office in New York askin' for information about the people in Granworth Aymes' employ at the time of his death. It says:

"Aymes employees as follows stop. Langdon Burdell secretary in service seven years now carrying on Aymes business under own name New York stop. Enrico Palantza butler at apartment in service four years present location unknown stop. Marie Therese Duhuinet maid to Mrs. Henrietta Aymes now in service Mrs. John Vlaford New York stop. Juan Termiglo chauffeur service three years present location unknown stop. Despatching to you photographs Palantza Dubuinet and Termiglo within two days stop."

This don't tell me very much an' between you an' me I didn't see just then that havin' pictures of these guys was goin' to do me much good neither.

I light a cigarette an' I do some thinkin'. I reckon that just for the moment I ain't goin' to do much good around here. Whether Henrietta decides that she is goin' to hitch up with Maloney or Fernandez ain't goin' to get me no place.

Another thing is that I wanta have a little conversation with this guy Burdell. I reckon he can tell me a coupla things I would like to know, an' if he can then I reckon that I am comin' back here to start something good an' proper.

Back of my head I have gotta big idea that Henrietta is holdin' out on me; that she is twicin' me good an' proper. There is something about that dame's face that is very nice, but that don't prove nothin' at all.

I remember a dame in Nogales on the Arizona-Mexico border. She was a honey. This dame had a face like a saint an' she spoke that way too. She was Mexican an' she figured to get some more culture an' teach herself English by readin' the History of the Civil War to her husband every night. He was a bit older than she was an' of a very doubtin' disposition. While she was readin' the History of the Civil War with one hand she was mixin' in arsenic in his coffee with the other.

One day this guy peters out. He gives a big howl and hands in his dinner pail. Some suspicious dick pinches the dame for murder although she says it musta been the History of the Civil War that give him the pain in his stomach.

When she goes for trial she gets a hot lawyer who knows all the answers an' he tells her to put a veil all over her face an' cry all the time she is in court. She is lucky. The jury disagree an' another trial is ordered. This time she gets another lawyer. He don't know anything about law, but believe me he knows his onions. He gets her all dressed up for the trial in a skin tight black lace dress an' flesh coloured chiffon silk stockings. He sticks her on the witness stand with a hand-picked jury of old gentlemen all over seventy an' they take one look at her an' say not guilty without goin' outa the jury box.

The judge—who is also an old cuss—gives her the once over an' says he agrees with the verdict. After the trial he gets her a job in the local dry cleaners an' the way the old boy used to rush around every week for his laundry was just nobody's business.

All of which goes to show you that you never know where you are with dames—especially when they got sex-appeal. The more S.A. a dame has got the more trouble she causes.

An' Henrietta has got sex-appeal plus. Boy, she has everything it takes an' then a lot. When I was lookin' at her when we was havin' that coffee I was thinkin' that maybe she was like the dame in Nogales.

Even then I reckon I wouldn'ta minded bein' her husband. I just wouldn'ta drunk coffee, that's all.

CHAPTER FIVE
NEAT STUFF

I AM back in New York.

Maybe you think that I am a mug for takin' so much trouble but the way I look at it is this:

It woulda been easy for me to pinch Henrietta on suspicion an' bring her back here. I coulda got the New York police to re-open the Aymes inquest an' the production of the letters she wrote Granworth woulda maybe justified it. But what good's it gonna do if she really an' truly don't know anything about the counterfeitin', an' even if she did kill Aymes still you gotta realise that I am a Federal dick investigatin' a counterfeitin' job an' not a guy rushin' around tryin' to teach New York coppers their business.

Besides which I have gotta bunch of ideas stewin' around in my head. I have gotta hunch an' I'm goin' to play it, an' that hunch certainly takes in this Langdon Burdell who, if you ask me, is tryin' to play me for a mug. You'll see why pretty soon.

I check in at the airport, fix myself up in my usual dump, have a shower an' change, an' after just one little bourbon just to keep the germs away, I jump me a yellow cab an' scram down-town to the Burdell office.

Burdell is runnin' Granworth's old business, an' is in the same office building.

I go up in the elevator an' walk in. In the outer office there is a fancy dame smackin' a typewriter about. She has got four-inch trench heels an' a pompadour that woulda made Marie Antoinette look like a big cheese.

She is wearin' long jade earrings an' an expression like somebody was burnin' cork under her nose all the time, an' when she gets up from the typewriter as I go in she has gotta wiggle when she walks that woulda won her a beauty contest anywhere where the judge's wives weren't around.

She uses a beauty parlour plenty by the look of her pan, an' she has gotta mouth made up with a lipstick that is about four shades too light.

It is a durn funny thing but I have only found about one jane in sixty-four ever uses the right shade of lipstick. An' whenever I strike this odd one she is always goin' some place or is married or somethin' else that don't help me along any.

I tell her I wanta see Mr. Burdell an' she says he's in but I'll have to wait because he is in conference. I crack back that any time I have to wait to see Mr. Burdell I will commit hari-kari with a tin-opener an' I walk straight into his room which is at the back of the office behind a fancy oak door.

Burdell is sittin' behind a big desk helpin' himself to a shot of rye out of a swell flask.

He looks up an' smiles.

"Pleased to see you, Mr. Caution," he says. "Come right in, I ain't busy."

I stick my hat on a big bronze figure of a boxer that he is usin' as a paper weight, an' I sit down in the big chair opposite him an' help myself to a cigarette out of a swell silver box.

"Listen, Burdell," I tell him. "I wanna talk to you, an' I want you to listen an' not make any slip-ups, otherwise I'm goin' to get very tough with you."

He looks surprised. This Burdell guy is a bird about five feet four with sandy hair an' a thin face like a weasel with indigestion. He has got red eyes an' a pointed chin. He is one of them guys who might be good or bad or just nothin' at all. You just wouldn't know a thing by lookin' at him.

"Listen here," he says. "You don't have to talk like that, Mr. Caution. I've always told you anything you wanted to know, ain't I?"

"Sure you have," I tell him, "but I wanta know some more that's all. Now stay quiet an' listen to this.

"Two weeks ago when I get put on this counterfeitin' job I come around here an' I ask you a lotta questions. Well, the main thing is that you say that you and the servants at the Aymes apartments have given evidence at the inquest that Henrietta Aymes wasn't in town the night that Granworth bumps himself off.

"O.K. Well next morning I get around an' I talk to this watchman down at Cotton's Wharf—the guy who saw the car go over the edge, an' I grill this guy plenty. Finally he comes across that the mornin' after Aymes killed himself you got down there an' he told you that he saw some woman get outa that car way down the wharf. He says that you gave him a thousand dollars to keep his trap shut about that little fact, an' that he kept it shut.

"O.K. Three days afterwards I get an anonymous note sayin' that I oughta go to Palm Springs an' check up on some letters that Henrietta has got. Right, well I checked up an' I have found them letters.

"Now I am very interested in who the guy was who sent me that anonymous note, an' I have come to the conclusion that the guy is you. You sent it to me, Burdell, an' you're goin' to tell me why, because you are a very contradictory sorta cuss. First of all you graft this watchman to keep quiet about the dame; then at the inquest you an' the servants say Henrietta Aymes wasn't in town on that night, an' a few months afterwards, after I have seen you an' heard one thing from you, you send me an anonymous letter that gets me out to Palm Springs where I find some letters that might hang a murder rap on Henrietta. So what? I'm listenin' an' I wanta hear plenty. Did you write that letter?"

He looks serious.

"Yeah," he says. "I wrote it, an' I'm goin' to tell you why, an' maybe when you've heard you'll understand why I played it like I did.

"You gotta get the set up," he says. "In the first place I knew Mrs. Aymes was comin' to town to see Granworth because I saw the letters she wrote. I knew she come to town on the night he died, but I kept my trap shut about it at the inquest, an' I told the servants at the flat to keep quiet too, an' I'll tell you why.

"Granworth Aymes was a lousy dog. We none of us liked him, but we liked her plenty. We knew he usta play around with a lotta janes an' that he gave her a raw deal. But when he made that dough an' told us that he was goin' to give two hundred grand in Registered Dollar Bonds to her I thought that maybe he was goin' to start over an' be a good guy. I believe this because he acts that way, an' because he takes out extra insurance an' says he's goin' to be a regular feller.

"On the night he died he went outa this office an' I knew that later he was goin' to meet up with Mrs. Aymes an' talk to her about this dame that she was so burned up about. The next thing I hear is when the police ring up the next mornin' an' say that they have fished Granworth outa the river an' want identification. I go down an' do it.

"I also knew that Mrs. Aymes had gone back to Connecticut late the night before, because Granworth told me she was goin' back after she'd seen him.

"Now I worked it out this way. I worked out that she'd seen him an' told him plenty; that she'd told him he was a lousy double-crossin' dog an' that she was goin' to leave him an' after that she'd started back for Connecticut. Well, I know Granworth. He was an excitable sorta guy an' he probably was a bit upset, so I reckon he has some liquor an' maybe makes up his mind that he will bump himself off. Knowin' him I reckon that he woulda been drinkin' with some jane somewhere an' that she was the woman that the watchman saw.

"But I think that if I say that he saw Mrs. Aymes that night that the police will think that the dame with Granworth was her; that they will bring her back here an' start givin' her the works an' makin' things tough for her. So I get around to the apartment, an' I have a talk with the servants, an' we fix to keep quiet about her bein' in town that night. I take a thousand that Granworth had in the drawer of this desk an' I graft the watchman to keep his trap shut. I thought then that Granworth had bumped himself off an' I didn't see why she should be brought into it. He'd caused her enough trouble anyway.

"All right. Everything works out swell an' the inquest finishes an' that's that. But a few months afterwards you come along an' you say that Mrs. Aymes has tried to pass a phoney bond down at the bank at Palm Springs. You ask me a lotta questions before I have time to think this thing out, so I give you the same story as I handed out to the coroner at the inquest. But after you went I got down an' I did a little thinkin'. I knew durn well that the bonds that Granworth's lawyer handed over to Henrietta Aymes was the real stuff. They was got outa Granworth's safe deposit where they had been kept. I started thinkin' that if she had tried to pass a phoney bond then she musta got it from somewhere an' knew it was phoney.

"Another thing. I looked in the drawer of this desk where Granworth had put those three letters. They was gone, an' I remembered that when she came down from Connecticut after the inquest I found her at this desk one day. I begin to get a screwy idea in my head. I get the idea that maybe I have been a mug, that maybe she did bump Granworth after all; that she was the woman the night-watchman saw, an' that's why she wanted the letters.

"Well, I may have sympathised with her in the first place, but I don't hold with murder an' I began to get a bit uncomfortable. Especially with you musclin' around because you have got a hot reputation, Mr. Caution, an' I start wonderin' what is goin' to happen to me if you find out the truth. I was right here because the first thing you do is to go an' grill the truth outa the watchman, although I didn't know that at the time.

"So I sit down at the typewriter an' I send you that letter, without any signature, because I work it out that way. If you get down to Palm Springs an' get them letters, well you can do what you like about it. If you think she bumped Granworth you can set out to pin it on her, or you can leave it alone, just as you think. I thought that you might not worry about who wrote the letter providin' you got the information, an' I also thought that if you did pin that letter on me I would come across with the whole works. Well, there it is. That's how it was, an' I'm sorry if I've caused you any trouble by bein' a mug an' not tellin' the truth first go off."

I get up an' I hold out my hand.

"Fine, Burdell," I tell him. "I reckon you're a wise guy to come clean. I'm beginning to think that this Henrietta bumped Granworth all right, an' if she did, well she'll have to fry for it."

He shakes hands with me an' I scram.

I say so-long to the dame with the french heels outside, an' I take the elevator down. I ease along pretty quick to the caretaker's office on the entrance floor an' flash my badge an' grab the tele-phone. I get chief operator at the telephone exchange.

I tell the chief operator who I am an' I also tell him that I have just left Burdell's office an' that I have got an idea that Burdell will be puttin' a long-distance call through to somebody at Palm Springs pretty quick. I say that they are to listen in to that call an' take a note of it an' who the guy is at the other end who takes it. I say that they are to keep this shorthand note for me to call for an' that they can check up on my authority in the meantime.

The chief operator says O.K.

I then go back to my hotel an' give myself a swell cigar. First of all it is quite plain to me that this second story of Burdell's is not so hot either. I'll tell you why.

Supposin' he did know that Henrietta had taken the letters outa the desk drawer because they proved she'd seen Granworth on the night he died. Well, wouldn't it have been sensible for Burdell to think that she took 'em *to destroy 'em,* not to carry 'em about with her? How did he know they was at Palm Springs? There's only one way he coulda been certain of that an' that was if some-body down at Palm Springs had told him that she still had 'em an' had 'em in the rancho where she was stayin'.

So I reckon that after I have got out of his office he is goin' to telephone through to this guy an' say that I have blown in an' tell him that I have fallen for this story an' that everything is O.K., an' that the job has been played the way this Burdell bird wants it played.

An' this brings me to another little thing. What about that picture of me cut out of the *Chicago Times* an' sent down to some-body at the Hacienda Altmira at Palm Springs? Don't it look like Burdell sent that too. An' the reason he sends it is easy. When he has sent me the anonymous letter he knows I will scram out to Palm Springs so he gets 'em good an' ready for me. He searched around until he finds a newspaper that has gotta picture of me in it an' he cuts it out, writes "This is the guy" on it, an' sends it down to the Hacienda.

An' this Burdell bird is goin' to slip up plenty in a minute. Mind you, the guy has got brains—plenty brains. He knows that

I can figure out that it was him that wrote the anonymous letter to me, an' so he has a swell story all ready for me when I blow in; but what he don't know is that I am wise to that picture business, an' that is just where he is goin' to slip up.

I reckon that you will agree that this bezusus is gettin' good an' interestin'. It is beginnin' to get me interested—almost!

I stick around till it is six o'clock, an' then I get another idea. I thing that I will ring through to the New York "G" Office an' ask 'em if they have despatched them pictures of the Aymes' servants, the butler, the chauffeur an' the maid, that they was goin' to send to me at Palm Springs. I am lucky. They tell me that they have sent off one lot but they have got a duplicate set an' they fix to send these around to me at the hotel. I also ask 'em to send somebody around to the main exchange office an' see if they have gotta transcript of the shorthand notes of any telephone conversation that Burdell has had since I went outa the office, an' they say they will do this.

After which I give myself another shower to pass the time an' change into a tuxedo just so's I can feel civilised for one night anyhow.

At seven o'clock things begin to happen. An agent comes round from the "G" Office with a note of a conversation that Burdell has had with Palm Springs. He leaves this an' he leaves the packet of duplicate pictures an' after he has had a little rye with me he goes. I read the note of the Burdell conversation, and do I get one big kick outa it. Here it is:

New York Central Exchange
Time: 5.24 *p.m.*
Report of long-distance telephone conversation from office of Langdon Burdell Central 174325 *and Hacienda Altmira, Palm Springs, Calif.*

Call from Burdell Office 5.24
Burdell Office:—Hello. Long-distance call please. This is Central 174325, *office of Langdon Burdell, calling Palm Springs* 674356.

Operator:—You are Central 174325 Langdon Burdell call-ing Palm Springs, California. Palm Springs 674356. Hang up please I will call you.

Time: 5.32

Operator:—Hello, Central 174325. Here is your Palm Springs number. Take your call please.

Burdell Office:—Hello, hello, Hacienda Altmira?

Hacienda:—Yes, who are you? What do you want?

Burdell Office:—This is Langdon Burdell. Is Ferdie there?

Hacienda:—Sure. I'll get him. How you makin' out Langdon? Hang on, I'll get Ferdie.

Hacienda:—Hello, Langdon?

Burdell Office:—Is this you, Ferdie?

Hacienda:—You betcha. What do you know?

Burdell Office:—Listen, kid. Get an earful if this an' don't make any mistakes. Are you listenin'? O.K. Well, this afternoon this goddam Caution comes bustin' around here askin' plenty ques-tions. He has fell for this business an' he is on to me for writin' the anonymous letter to him an' startin' him off after the letters at Palm Springs. I tell him the works. I tell him how I tried to cover up for the Aymes dame until this counterfeitin' business starts an' then I get a screwy idea that after all she has prob-ably bumped Granworth an' that I do not want to be a party to a murder rap so am cashin' in with the truth. The big mug listens with his ears floppin' an' then shakes me by the hand an' scrams. I have also wised him up to the fact that the original bonds that was given to Henrietta was O.K. an' that she musta got the phoney ones herself. Now listen, Ferdie, I reckon that he is comin' back to Palm Springs plenty quick an' that he is lyin' to pinch Henrietta just as soon as he can get his hooks on her. Because if he can pin the murder thing on her an' she gets the chair, the Feds are goin' to take it for granted that she pulled the counterfeitin' too because that will be the easiest way to close the case down. You got all that?

Hacienda:—Swell, Langdon. Okie doke. An' I play it the way we said.

Burdell Office:—You bet your life. What you gotta do is to get hitched up to the dame. You gotta make her marry you. You can do it easy. When that big mug Caution comes back an' starts gumshoein' around she's goin' to get good an' scared. Then pull your stuff. You tell her that the only way she can beat this murder rap is if we say that our original evidence was right—that she wasn't in New York the night Granworth did the high divin' act. After that everything's easy. You got all that, Ferdie?

Hacienda:—You said it. I got it O.K.

Burdell Office:—Give Periera a lovin' kick in the pants for me an' tell him I'll be seein' him directly this job's finished an' we get where we wanta. So long, Ferdie. Keep your nose clean baby an' no gun play if you can keep off it.

Hacienda:—'Bye, Langdon. An' don't you get your nose dirty either. I'll be seein' you.

Call ends.

Operator:—G. O. Tarnet.

Shorthand notes by V. L. O'Leary.

Is this sweet readin' or is it? It looks like I am dead right in my ideas about this Burdell guy, an' I reckon that before I am through with him I am goin' to hand him something for callin' me that big mug Caution. It is an extraordinary thing how all these guys who are up to funny business always think that any kind a policeman is a mug. It's a sorta rule with them, but now an' again they find out that the drinks are on them.

But believe me I ain't said nothin' yet. When I have read through the notes I undo the package of pictures. There are three of 'em—Dubuinet the maid, Palantza the butler an' Termiglo the chauffeur, an' when I look at this last mug do I get a kick? Because Termiglo the chauffeur is nobody else but Fernandez, the big guy at the Hacienda Altmira, the guy I smacked down, an' threw down the stairs! Boy, is this beginnin' to look good or is it?

So Fernandez was the chauffeur in the Aymes family under the name of Juan Termiglo, an' now he is Fernandez the big gambler out at the Hacienda. Now I am beginning to understand about the picture of me that was sent down there. Burdell sent it all right an' he sent it to Fernandez so's he would know who I was, an' it was Fernandez who let Burdell know where Henrietta's three letters was.

But wait just one little minute! Let's get this straight. How did Fernandez know where Henrietta had got them letters hidden?

I reckon that he knew where they was hidden because he was the guy who planted them there. Didn't I tell you that I found them letters a durn sight too easy? The way they was stuck in that cut out book of poetry looked to me as if they was just shriekin' to be found by anybody who had enough sense to look in the right sorta places.

An' if I am right about this—an' I believe I am—then Burdell is a double liar. All that stuff he told me about Henrietta findin' the letters in Granworth's desk an' takin' 'em away is just a lotta punk.

O.K. So we found something out ain't we? Something that is beginnin' to look good. I have already got a bunch of ideas stewin' around in my head about this new set-up.

I grab a piece of paper an' a pencil an' I write it down just to sorta analyse it in my mind. Here it is:

Point 1:—Burdell gets the servants to say at the inquest that Henrietta is outa town on the night of Aymes' death. He gives the Cotton's Wharf watchman one thousand bucks to keep his mouth shut about the woman in the car.

Point 2:—When the counterfeit dollar bond is passed by Henrietta and Caution is brought on in the job, Burdell tells him the same story as he told at the inquest. Right then he gets the three letters which he has found in Granworth's desk an' sends them to Fernandez who is out at the Hacienda and tells him to plant them somewhere where they will be found easy in Henrietta's room at the rancho. He then writes an anonymous letter to Caution an' tells him to get out to Palm Springs an' grab the letters which will tell him a lot.

Point 3:—Caution goes to Palm Springs, finds the letters, and also the picture and begins to think there is something screwy going on. He comes back to New York and sees Burdell. Burdell tells Caution a swell story which explains his change of front.

Caution makes out that he is falling for this an' checks up on the next 'phone conversation.

So what do we know? We know one thing certain an' that is that the Burdell Fernandez set-up are tryin' to pin a first-degree murder rap on Henrietta.

O.K. Well if this is so perhaps you can tell me something? If these two guys are tryin' to frame Henrietta for the murder of Granworth Aymes, then why in the name of everything that is sizzlin' is Burdell so keen that Henrietta should get herself married to Fernandez?

Ain't that a sweet question? Because that is the thing that is stickin' in my mind an' I have gotta find the answer somehow, otherwise this case is goin' to get me nuts in a minute.

But there's one thing you can rely on. The explanation is always durn simple. They always are when you finally find 'em out, but at the time they look tough.

Like once when I was in Oklahoma a dame who I was very stuck on hit me right on the top of the head with a tent mallet. When I come to an' I asked her how come she said she was gettin' so durn fond of me that she knew that unless she done something about it she would break up her home an' family because she was so fond of my ugly mug. She said that she had thought it all out an' the best way out was for her to sock me one with a tent mallet because it would create a situation that would clean things up.

She was right. After she had one sock I left Oklahoma.

The point is that I am goin' to use the same technique—as the professors call it. I am goin' back to Palm Springs an' I am goin' around with a tent mallet bustin' guys wide open until somebody stops two timin' me an' comes across with a spot of real honest-to-god truth.

An' here we go!

CHAPTER SIX
WOMAN STUFF

WHILE I am flying back to Palm Springs I think out how I am goin' to handle this bezusus. First of all it is a cinch that it is no good my jumpin' around pretendin' to be Mr. Selby T. Frayme of Magdalena, Mexico, any longer, because it looks to me like all the guys that I don't wanta know I am a "G" man have known about it for a helluva long time. Here is where we come right out into the open.

As far as Henrietta is concerned I reckon I have got enough on her to make her talk, because you have gotta realise that although I am certainly partial to this dame I have never allowed my personal feelin's to interfere with my business, well, not much, an' after all the fact that a jane is pretty don't mean a durn thing because it is always the hotcha numbers who get into jams.

I reckon if you was to stick an ugly jane on an island where there was a coupla hundred tough guys stickin' around nothin' much would happen; but you plant a little lady who has got this an' that in the middle of a jungle you can betcha sweet an' holy life that some guy will be busy startin' a big lion hunt just to show her what a swell guy he is.

I will go so far as to say that a travellin' salesman in Missouri once told me that if there wasn't any dames in the world there wouldn't be no crime. We talked this thing over an' after he had had half a bottle of rye he got all sentimental about it, an' said that anyway he reckoned he would sooner have crime *an'* dames.

He got his way all right, because eighteen months after some jane slugged him with a car spanner after which he handed in his order book an' took a one-way trip to the local cemetery.

Just how Henrietta is breakin' with these guys out at the Hacienda I do not know. This is another thing I have got to find out because it certainly looks a bit funny to me that she is stickin' around in a place actin' as hostess an' bein' kissed by some big guy who used to be the chauffeur. Maybe this Fernandez has got some pull over Henrietta, an' is makin' her toe the line which would account for her tellin' me that she might *have* to marry him.

It is eight o'clock when I pull in at the Miranda House in Palm Springs, an' I am good an' tired, but I reckon that I am goin' to getta move on with business an' not let any grass grow in my ears while I am doin' it.

After I have had a shower an' a meal I put a call through to the Hacienda an' ask if Mrs. Aymes is around. Some guy at the other end—an' I reckon by the way he talks it is Periera—say what do I want with her, an' I tell him that what I want with her is my business an' that if he don't get her to the 'phone pronto I will come out there an' slug him one with a blackjack. After this he decides to go an' fetch her.

Pretty soon I hear Henrietta cooin' into the telephone an' I ask her if she knows where Maloney is. She says yes he's around. I tell her that I am the guy who said he was Selby Frayme an' that I am not Selby Frayme but Lemmy Caution, a Federal Agent, an' I wanta see Maloney pronto, an' that he had better get around to the Miranda House good an' quick because I wanta talk to him.

She says O.K. an' about nine o'clock Maloney blows in.

I take him up to my room an'

I give him a drink.

"Now see here, Maloney," I tell him. "I reckon that you are stuck on this Henrietta, an' that maybe you wouldn't like to see her get into a jam, because it looks right now that that is the way things are goin'. I reckon that Henrietta has told you who I am, an' what I am doin' around here, so I don't have to explain any of that, but what I do wanna wise you up to is this little thing. When I come down here first of all I wasn't interested in how Granworth Aymes died or whether he committed suicide or was bit to death by wild spiders, I was just musclin' around tryin' to get a line on this counterfeitin' business. All right. Well, now I reckon that I am very interested in the Granworth business because it looks to me like the two things are tied up.

"Since I have been to New York I have found out a lotta things that make it look pretty bad for Henrietta. Maybe they're right an' maybe they ain't, but it's a cinch that she's gotta watch her step—or else . . .

"Now murder ain't a nice charge. Maybe it's my duty to advise New York about this suggestion that Henrietta bumped Granworth, but I ain't goin' to do that. I ain't goin' to do it just for one reason an' that is it won't help me any in the counterfeitin' business, an' that is the thing that I wanta clean up right now. If Henrietta did bump Granworth then she'll fry for it some time, but maybe she didn't an' if she didn't then I'm goin' to advise her to talk plenty an' quick, otherwise she may find herself elected for the hot squat an' they tell me that dames fry just as quick an' sweet as *hombres*.

"O.K. Well here's the first thing I'm askin' you to do. You get back to the Hacienda an' you have a talk with Henrietta, an' you tell her that I'm comin' out there to-night around midnight an' that I want a statement from her an' that she'd better make it the truth. If I think she's tryin' to pull anything on me or hidin' anything then I tell you I'm goin' to hold her right away as a material witness in this counterfeitin' business, hand her over to Metts, the Chief of Police here, an' produce what I know about her bein' tied up with Granworth's death. An' if I do that there's goin' to be plenty trouble for Henrietta. Got that?"

He nods. He is lookin' durn serious.

"I got it, Caution," he says, "an' I'm certainly goin' to advise her to come clean to you. It's the only thing she can do. But," he goes on, "I tell you she didn't murder Aymes. She couldn't do a thing like that. Why . . ."

"Can it, Maloney," I bust in. "You don't know a thing. Just because you are stuck on the jane you think she couldn't kill somebody. I have known dames who usta go to church twice Sundays who have killed guys so I don't wanta hear you tellin' me why Henrietta couldn'ta done it. She can do that for herself."

He shrugs his shoulders and lights himself a cigarette.

"All right," I go on. "Now here's something else you can do. Before I went to New York I had a talk with her, an' she said that she might *have* to marry Fernandez. Now I reckon that was a funny thing for her to say, because I have got the impression that she is stuck on you. Maybe you got some idea about that, huh?"

He shrugs his shoulders again.

"I can't get it," he says. "All I know is that Fernandez an' Periera are the big guys around the Hacienda, that they are sorta partners, an' it might be that Henrietta feels she would be better off if she married Fernandez. It was only when I saw that Fernandez was ridin' her an' givin' her a tough time that I sorta chipped in. I was kinda sorry for her an' I think she is a swell femme."

He sits quiet for a minute sorta thinkin' to himself. After a bit he goes on.

"Now you come to mention it," he says, "it certainly looks as if Fernandez has gotta nerve to think that Henrietta would fall for a punk like him. He speaks good English but he's a lousy breed."

"That's all the more reason why she shouldn't even listen to a guy like that," I say. "Tell me something, Maloney, have you asked this dame to marry you?"

"Sure I have," he says with a grin, "an' she said she'd think it over. I reckon I ain't ever been so sorry for any dame as I am for Henrietta, an' the more so because she's a swell kid an' she don't go grievin' all the time when she's in a jam like dames usually do."

"O.K. Maloney," I say. "Well, be on you way an' don't forget to tell her that I'm comin' out at twelve an' that I wanta hear some sense outa her."

He says all right an' he scrams.

I stick around until twelve o'clock an' then I get the car an' drive out to the Hacienda. There ain't many people there, because you gotta realise that at this time of the year there ain't a lotta people makin' holiday around this part of the world, an' I am wonderin' why Periera don't shut this place up for the bad season an' scram off somewhere else like most of the other guys around here do.

The band is playin' a hot number an' there are one or two couples pushin' each other around the dance floor an' some city guys from Los Angeles makin' hey-hey. I walk straight across an' up the stairs an' into the room at the top where the card playin' goes on.

There ain't anybody there except a waiter guy who is puttin' the place straight an' I ask him where Periera's office is. He shows me one of the rooms away along the balcony on the other side, over the entrance door to the main floor, an' I go along there. I open the door an' I go in.

Inside there is Periera sittin' behind a desk drinkin' a glass of whisky an' Fernandez is sittin' in the corner smokin'. They both give me a cold once-over as I go in.

"Well, bozos," I say, "here I am again, an' how's tricks?"

Periera looks up with a nasty sorta grin.

"Everytheeng is ver' good, Mr. Frayme," he says with a sorta sneer.

"Cut that out, Periera," I say. "You know durn well that my name ain't Frayme. My name's Caution, an' I gotta little badge in my pocket if you'd like to see it."

Fernandez cuts in.

"What the hell do we care about your badge," he says. "I reckon that we ain't got any call to be gettin' excited about Federal badges. You ain't got anything on us, an' we don't like dicks anyhow."

"You don't say," I tell him. "I bet you don't like dicks, an' I bet you certainly don't like one who gave you a bust in the kisser like I did last time I saw you. However," I tell him lightin' myself a cigarette, "my advice to you is to keep nice an' civil otherwise I'm probably goin' to smack you down some more. Where's Henrietta?"

He grins.

"She's just stickin' around," he says. "She's outside on the side porch with Maloney, an' the sooner you get done the better I'm goin' to like it because you make me feel sick."

"Just fancy that," I say. "Well while you're waitin' for me to come back I'll tell you something that'll help you pass the time away, Fernandez. Just you get yourself a good story about what you're doin' out here callin' yourself Fernandez an' puttin' on a big act when your name's Juan Termiglo an' you used to be chauffeur in New York to Granworth Aymes, an' see that it is a good one, otherwise I might get a bit tough with you about some phoney evidence you gave at the coroner's inquest."

"You got me wrong, copper," he says. "I never give any evidence at the coroner's inquest because I never knew anything about anybody bein' anywhere. I was at home that night an' I never saw a thing of Henrietta or anybody else, an' how do you like that?"

"O.K. sour puss," I say, "but I wouldn't be above framin' you for something or other, Fernandez, so watch your step otherwise you'll feel sick some more."

He grins an' lights himself a cigarette. He has got his nerve all right.

I go down the stairs an' across the floor an' out on to the side porch. Henrietta is sittin' there talkin' to Maloney. She is wearin' a blue frock made of some flimsy stuff an' she looks a peach. Maloney says so long an' scrams out of it.

I pull up a chair an' sit down.

"Well, Henrietta," I say, "I reckon that Maloney has told you about it, an' what are you goin' to do?"

She looks at me an' in the moonlight I can see that her eyes are sorta smilin', as if she was amused at something.

"All right, Mr. Caution," she says. "I'm going to tell you anything that you want to know. Jim Maloney says that if I tell the truth everything will be all right, an' that if I don't it may go hard with me. Shall I begin?"

"Justa minute, honey," I tell her, "an' you listen to me before we get down to cases. I don't know what's been goin' on around here but I guess it's something screwy an' I don't like it, an' I'm goin' to get to the bottom of it. Me—I like workin' along with people nice an' quiet an' no threats an' no nonsense—that is if they come clean. If they don't, well it's their own business if they get in a jam. Now I'm tellin' you this, Henrietta. You're a swell piece an' I'm for you. I think you got what it takes an' maybe you know it, but you're in a jam over this business of that phoney bond as well as the other stuff, an' the thing for you to do is to spill the works an' not forget anything. All right, now you tell me what happened the night you went to New York an' saw Granworth—the night he died."

"That's easy, Mr. Caution," she says. "It's all quite simple, only I'm afraid that I couldn't very well prove it. I wrote some letters to Granworth telling him I wanted to see him. I'd heard that he was making a fool of himself over a woman and although I'd believed for some time that he was unfaithful I'd never had any actual proof. I was never very happy with Granworth. He drank;

he was excitable and often silly, but when he made this money and said that he was going to turn over two hundred thousand dollars' worth of bonds to me I thought that maybe he'd turned over a new leaf. He talked about starting a new life together. He even went so far as to buy some more insurance—an annuity policy payable in ten years time or at his death—so that, as he said, we should be able to face the future without worry. I remember him joking about the fact that the Insurance Company insisted on having a clause in the policy under which they would not pay if he committed suicide, because, as you may know, he tried to kill himself after a drinking bout two years ago.

"I was actually beginning to feel that maybe he meant what he said for once. I was in Hartford, Connecticut, staying with friends, when I received a letter. It was unsigned and it said that I would be well advised to keep an eye on Granworth who was making a fool of himself with a woman whose husband was beginning to get nasty about things.

"I don't take notice of anonymous letters usually, but I telephoned through to Granworth and told him about this one. He did not even trouble to deny the fact. He was merely rude about it. Then I realised that the letter was true and I wrote him two other letters, asking him what he was going to do about it, and eventually telling him that I proposed to come and see him, and to get tough with him."

"Justa minute, Henrietta," I bust in. "What happened to those letters. What did Granworth do with them?"

"I don't know," she says. "After his death, when Burdell telephoned me an' I went to New York, I saw them lying around on his desk with a lot of other papers. I meant to pick them up and destroy them, but I was worried and unhappy at the time and I forgot."

"O.K." I say. "Go right ahead."

"I went to New York," she went on, "and arrived early in the evening of the 12th January. I did not go home to the apartment. I telephoned the butler and asked where my husband was. He said that he was in his office. I then called Granworth at his office and he spoke to me. He said that he just received my third letter and that he would talk to me that evening.

"He asked me to meet him at a down-town café. I went there and after a while he drove up. He was rather excited and seemed a little drunk. We discussed the situation and he told me that he was not going to give up this woman. I said that if he did not do so I would divorce him. Then he said that if I did so he would rather leave the country than pay me alimony. He was furious and his eyes were blazing, and when he tried to drink his coffee he could hardly hold the cup because his fingers were trembling so.

"I told him that I had no need to worry about alimony; that I had the two hundred thousand Dollar Bonds that he had made over to me. For a moment I thought he was going mad, he was so enraged. Then, after a little while he said that I'd better go back to Connecticut for a week or so and that he would think it over and write me and we could come to some decision. But he said definitely that if I divorced him his life would be ruined and he would finish everything.

"I went straight back to the depot and left for Hartford. Two days afterwards Langdon Burdell telephoned me that Granworth had committed suicide. I reproached myself terribly. I thought that perhaps I was responsible for his death; that possibly I should have handled the situation differently.

"I returned to New York immediately, but when I arrived the inquest was over. Langdon Burdell told me that he had instructed the servants to say nothing about my being in New York that day; that if this fact had been mentioned the police would probably be unpleasant and question me. Burdell had said at the inquest that I was in Connecticut at the time. I was grateful for this.

"I stayed in New York for a little while, and Granworth's affairs were settled up. In his will he had said that he wanted Burdell to carry on and to have the business and offices, and there was an instruction that certain debts including the mortgage on the Hacienda Altmira—which Granworth had built years ago—were to be paid out of his insurance.

"But the Insurance Company refused to pay because of the suicide clause, and so Periera who held the mortgage on the Hacienda couldn't get his money. If he hadn't been so unpleasant about the fact I would have paid him—or tried to do so—out of the bonds which had been handed to me and which were my own personal property, because Granworth had given them to me.

"You know the rest of the story. When my banking account ran down here I took one of the bonds down to the bank and tried to collect on it. They told me it was counterfeit, and that the rest of the bonds were too. Then I was in a spot. I had no money at all, and so Periera allowed me to stay on at the Hacienda in return for my services as hostess.

"That's the story, Mr. Caution. Some time ago Fernandez—whose real name is Juan Termiglo and who was our chauffeur—asked me to marry him. He seems to have acquired a sort of partnership with Periera. When I laughed at him he told me that it might not be so good for me if the police knew that I had concealed the fact that I had quarrelled with my husband an hour or so before his death, and when I discovered that the bonds were counterfeit he asked me again and practically suggested that the safest thing for me to do would be to marry him in order that the other servants should keep quiet about what they knew."

"O.K. Henrietta," I tell her. "If that's the truth it's a good story an' if you made it up it's still good. Tell me one little thing, who was this dame that Granworth was runnin' around with?"

"I don't know," she says, lookin' out across the desert, "but I believe that whoever she was she was the wife of the man who wrote the anonymous letter."

"How'd you get that idea?" I ask her.

"For this reason," she says. "The letter was handwritten, and it was in a manly hand. In one place before the writer used the words 'this woman' I could see that something had been scratched out. I looked at it through a magnifying glass and under the attempt at erasure I could see the words 'my wife.' I guessed he had been going to refer to his wife and thought better of it."

"Have you got the letter?" I ask her.

"I'm afraid I lost it," she says.

I get up.

"O.K. lady," I tell her. "I'm believin' your story because I always trust a good-lookin' dame—once! If it's true, well, that's O.K., an' if it's not I bet I'll catch you out somewhere. Stick around an' don't worry your head too much. Maybe something will break in a minute, but right now this bezusus looks to me like a mah-jong game played backwards."

She looks at me and sorta smiles. Her eyes are shinin' an' there is a sorta insolence about her that goes well with me. This Henrietta has got guts all right I guess.

"You've got it in for me, haven't you," she says. "Right from the beginning I've felt that everything you say and do is to one end, the pinning of this counterfeit business on to me. Maybe you'll accuse me of killing Granworth next. You're tough all right, Mr. Caution."

"You're dead right, honeybunch," I tell her. "What's the good of a guy if he ain't tough. Me—I think you're swell. I reckon that I ain't seen many dames around like you. You got class—if you know what I mean, an' I like the way you move around an' talk. In a way I'm sorry that you're so stuck on Maloney because maybe if things was different I'd like to run around with a dame like you. But you see they ain't different, an' I've got a job to do an' I'm goin' to do it even if you don't like it. So long, an' I'll be seein' you."

I scram down the steps of the porch an' go around the back an' get my car. I am so tired that I am almost seein' double an' I reckon that I am goin' to call it a day an' get back to the hotel an' have a piece of bed.

I have got about five miles away from the Hacienda an' am passing a place where the road narrows down an' there is a joshua tree standin' way back off the road in front of some scrub on a hillock when somebody has a shot at me. The bullet hits the steerin' wheel, glances off an' goes through the wind shield.

I pull a fast one. I tread on the brakes, slew the wheel round an' drive the car into a cactus bush just as if I was shot. Then I slump over the wheel, an' lie doggo with one eye open.

I wait there for a coupla minutes an' nothin' happens. Then, over at the back of the patch of scrub, in the moonlight, I see somebody movin'. As he gets out into the open I go after him. He starts to scram out of it an' this guy can certainly run. I let him go because I have got another idea. I go back to the car, turn her around an' step on it. I drive straight back to the Hacienda an' ask if Fernandez is there. They say he ain't, that maybe he won't be around to-night. I find Periera an' ask him where Fernandez is livin' an' he tells me that he has gotta cabin just off the Indio road. I find out where this place is an' I start to drive there pronto.

As I go speedin' down this road towards Indio I begin to think that this desert is a helluva place for things to happen. Some of these guys who are always talkin' about the wide open spaces might not think that deserts are so good if they got around on 'em a bit more.

Presently I see this dump. It is a white cabin fifty yards off the road, railed in with some white fencin' an' white stones. I pull up the car by the side of the road an' I ease over to the cabin. There is a window by the side of the door an' I look through an' there, sittin' at a table smokin' a cigarette an' drinkin' rye all by himself, is Fernandez.

I knock on the door an' after a minute he comes over an' opens it.

"What do you want, copper?" he says.

"Get inside an' shut your trap, Fernandez," I tell him. "Because to me you are just one big bad smell, an' if I have any trouble outa you I am goin' to hurt you plenty."

He goes inside an' I go after him. He hands over a chair an' I sit down an' take a look around.

The cabin is a nice sorta place. It is furnished comfortable an' there is plenty of liquor kickin' around. I light a cigarette an' look at Fernandez.

He is standin' in front of the hearth lookin' at me. He is a lousy-lookin' guy an' I think that I should like to give him a good smack in the puss with a steam shovel, just so that he wouldn't think he was so good.

I have got an idea as to how I am goin' to play this so-an'-so along. I reckon that there was never a crook who wouldn't do a trade if he thought that he could do himself some good that way.

"Listen, Fernandez," I tell him. "It looks to me I ain't popular around here, some guy has tried to iron me out to-night while I am goin' back to Palm Springs, but he wasn't quite good enough an' he just dented the steerin' wheel an' bust the wind-screen. I suppose you wouldn't know anything about that, Fernandez?"

He looks at me like he was surprised.

"You don't think I'm such a mug, do you?" he says.

"What good do I do by tryin' to bump you? You tell me that."

"I wouldn't know," I tell him, "but there's somebody around here has got one in for me—but maybe it's Periera."

"I don't get that," he says. "Why should he wanta bump you?"

"I wouldn't know that either," I say. "However, I ain't partial to guys shootin' at me, an' I just wanta know which side you're on, so you listen to me."

I help myself to some of his rye.

"Thanks for the drink," I say. "Now here's how it goes. It looks to me like I am goin' to make a pinch down here pretty soon, an' I'll give you two guesses as to who it is. Well, it's little Henrietta. That dame looks screwy to me an' I believe she knows a durn sight more about Granworth Aymes' death than a lotta people think. O.K. Well the thing is this. There is some dame who is playin' around with Granworth Aymes an' this dame's husband is supposed to write some letter to Henrietta tellin' her that he is bein' a naughty boy an' that she'd better do something about it. Well, either that story is true or it ain't true.

"Now I hear that you are stuck on marryin' Henrietta. Whether that is a true bill or not I don't know, but I know one thing an' that is this that you were Aymes' chauffeur, an' you usta drive him around, an' if he was stuck on some woman you would know who it was."

"I was for Henrietta," he says, "an' I offered to marry her when she was broke an' hadn't any friends, but maybe after that phoney bond business I sorta changed my mind. I don't say she ain't a very attractive number," he goes on, "but I don't know that a guy is justified in marryin' a dame who is gettin' herself all mixed up in counterfeitin' stuff an' who may have to face a murder rap."

I do some quick thinkin' because this is a very interesting situation. You will remember that Burdell told me that he was all for Henrietta until he suspected her of the counterfeitin' job, an' here is another guy who was supposed to be hot for marryin' her pullin' the same story. It looks like these guys have been takin' time out together, don't it.

"Looky, Fernandez," I say. "Here's the way it is. It's goin' to be pretty easy for me to find out whether Aymes was runnin' around with a woman if I get the boys in New York on the job, but I reckon you can save me the trouble. I'm goin' to make a bargain with you, although I don't often do a deal with a lousy two timer like you, an' the bargain is this. I want the truth outa you about this woman that Aymes was supposed to be gettin' around with, an' I wanta know what was goin' on. If you like to cash in well an' good. If not, I'm pinchin' you here an' now on a charge of attemptin' to murder a Federal Agent because I think that you are the guy who had a shot at me way back on the Palm Springs road."

His eyes start poppin'.

"Say listen, Caution," he says. "You can't say that. I can produce about six guys who will say I was around with them all the evenin'. Besides, anything you wanta know I'll be glad to tell you."

"O.K." I say, "listen to this."

I then tell the story that Henrietta has told me. He stands there smokin' an' listenin'. When I have finished he starts in.

"I reckon that she is stringin' you along," he says with a grin. "It stands to reason that since you know she was in New York on that night she has gotta have some sorta story to give a reason for bein' there. If she ain't got a reason then it looks as if she just came down from Connecticut for some other reason that she don't want you to know—such as bumpin' her husband off. I reckon that she made up that story about the other dame.

"I used to get around with Aymes a lot," he goes on. "I usta drive him around the place an' he had dames all over the place, the usual sorta dames, but there wasn't anything special about that. There wasn't any special one that he went for. Nope, there was just a whole lot of 'em an' I could make you outa list of 'em if you want it. But I reckon you'd be wastin' your time."

"O.K." I say. "Now you listen to me, Fernandez. An hour ago some palooka has a shot an' tries to iron me out. Now that mighta been you or it mighta been Henrietta or it mighta been Maloney or it mighta been Periera. Well, as the professors say, for the sake of this argument, I am goin' to say it was you."

I slip my hand under my coat an' I pull my Luger outa the shoulder holster an' cover him with it.

"Look, sweetheart," I say. "I have gotta reputation for bein' plenty tough, an' I am goin' to be tough with you. If I have any nonsense outa you I'm goin' to drill you. Then I'm goin' to say that it was you who tried to bump me earlier to-night; that I followed you out here to pinch you an' that you tried another shot an' then I shot an' killed you, an' how do you like that?"

He stands there an' I can see that he is beginnin' to sweat.

"An' if you don't want me to do that," I tell him, "you're goin' to tell me the name of that dame who was kickin' around with Aymes. *There was one, an' I wanta know who it was.* If you ain't made up your mind who she was an' where she is livin' right now, by the time that I can count up to ten, I am goin' to give it to you in the guts. See?"

He don't say anything. I start countin'.

When I have got to nine he puts his hand up. His forehead is covered with sweat an' I can see his hands tremblin'.

"O.K." he says. "You win. The dame's name is Paulette Benito, an' she's livin' at a dump called Sonoyta just off the Arizona line, in Mexico."

"Swell," I tell him, putting the gun away.

I get up.

"I'll be seein' you, Fernandez," I crack, "an' while I am away don't you do anything your mother wouldn't like to know about."

CHAPTER SEVEN
GOOFY STUFF

I DRIVE back to the Hacienda.

On my way I am thinkin' plenty. I am thinkin' that this guy Fernandez knows a durn sight more than he is lettin' on. I reckon that he only blew this stuff about the dame Paulette Benito just because he was afraid that I was goin' to blast a bunch of daylight into him, an' even then I don't think he woulda come clean if he hadn't thought that I'd known something about a dame anyway.

But I am very interested in the way this guy tries to bust down Henrietta's story about there bein' some other woman. It is a cinch that this Fernandez an' Burdell are workin' together on some set-up that they have thought out, but just what they are gettin' at—search me, I just don't know.

An' for all I know Fernandez an' Burdell an' Henrietta an' Maloney can be all playin' along together, I've known crooks put on good acts before an' when you come to think of it I know just as much about this bezusus as when I started in. All the way along the thing has got sorta confused with new people an' things bustin' in.

But one thing is stickin' outa foot. Both Langdon Burdell an' Fernandez want me to think that Henrietta bumped Granworth off. Everything they have done an' said is calculated to get my mind workin' that way. What are they gettin' at?

I reckon that I have gotta get next to this Paulette Benito. Because I reckon that she is goin' to be able to tell me more about Granworth Aymes than anybody else. If she was the woman he was chasin' around after, an' if he thought enough of her to give a swell dame like Henrietta the go-by for her, then she must have some little thing that the others haven't got. She must have plenty, an' I reckon that Granworth never had any secrets from her.

Because, an' I expect you have noticed this too, a bad guy always likes to kid himself that he is goin' for a good dame, but in the long run he always makes a play for some jane who thinks along the same lines as he does. He does this because she always talks the same sorta language an' believes in the same sorta things. Maybe Henrietta made Granworth feel like two cents just because she was so much better than he was an' so he takes a run out powder an' hitches up with this Paulette, who knows how to play him along. In nine cases outa ten like goes for like.

I remember some high-hat jane in Minnesota. Her pa wanted her to get hitched to some young Bible-student who was kickin' about the place, but she wouldn't have it at an' price. She goes off one night an' she runs away with a two-gun man who finally gets fried for murder, after which she comes back an' marries the church guy with a contented mind. I reckon that if she hadn't gone off with the other guy she wouldn'ta been able to appreciate the Bible-puncher.

There is one idea that I have got in my head an' that sorta sticks. It is that Burdell an' Fernandez an' anybody else who is playin' in with them woulda expected me to have pinched Henrietta before now. After all I have got evidence that she was in New York that night. I am entitled to suppose that she knew somethin' about the counterfeitin' an' most people woulda pulled her in before now—as a material witness at least.

An' the reason why I have not done this is just because I have got this idea that they expect me to do it, an' I am a guy who never does what other people expect. That is why I told Fernandez the story that Henrietta had told me. I wanted to see what his reaction to it was, an' sure as a gun the big palooka starts to throw it down, even though, if what he told me before was true, he didn't know anything about what had happened that night in New York because he was stickin' around at his own place.

I pull up around the back of the Hacienda, an' walk around to the front entrance. It is a lovely night, hot as hell, but there is a moonlight that is making the old adobe walls look like silver an' castin' shadows all around the place like it was some sorta fairyland.

I go in the entrance an' I see that some of the lights are out. When I get on to the main floor I see that the band is just packin' up an' that all the tables are deserted. I look up the stairs an' I see a guy an' a dame disappearin' into the room where the play is held so I think that maybe Periera has fixed a game for to-night.

Just then I see him. He comes outa the storeroom behind the bar, an' he opens the flap in the counter an' walks across to me.

"Meester Caution," he says. "There ees a little game to-night— not very beeg. I know that eet ees not legal, but I theenk that you don't mind, eh? Eet don' matter to you?"

"You bet it don't," I tell him. "I'm a Federal Agent not a Palm Springs dick, an' it ain't my business to worry about people breakin' the State gamblin' laws. Maybe I'll come up an' take a look."

He says thank you very much an' looks as pleased as if I had given him a thousand bucks. I have already told you that I do not like this guy Periera one bit. He is a nasty bit of business an' I personally would like to take a sock at him any time, but right now I am feelin' like playin anybody around here along. I want 'em all to think that they're gettin' away with everything, that I am just a big dumb cluck with no brains, because I reckon that this way, sooner or later, somebody is goin' to do something that is goin' to give me an idea to get goin' with.

So I ease up the stairs an' go into the gamin' room. There are a bunch of people there. Maloney is there an' Henrietta an' about six or seven other guys an' a few dames. One of the waiters is servin' liquor around an' there is a faro game goin' on at the top table an' they are just startin' to play poker at the centre table.

I stick around an' take a straight rye an' just look. Henrietta is playin' at the poker table—she is evidently playin' on the house, an' Maloney is sittin' behind a stack of chips an' lookin' pleased. Maybe he is winnin' for once. Periera is just hangin' around lookin' nice an' benevolent. In fact it is a nice quiet evenin' for all concerned. Fernandez ain't there an' I reckon that he is sittin' way back in that swell cabin of his doin' a spot of quiet thinkin'.

An' what will he be thinkin' about? I reckon that he will be thinkin' about this dame Paulette Benito that he has told me about.

First of all you gotta realise that he only told me about this jane because he was good an' scared an' because he thought that if he hadn't come across I was goin' to give him the heat. I reckon that when I pulled that gun on him he was scared plenty. An' the reason I pulled it was just this: I knew that there *was* some dame besides Henrietta in this business. I always had that sorta idea an' I had it just because Burdell, who had always talked plenty, had never even mentioned about there bein' another dame or not. Even when he was suggestin' to me that Henrietta took the letters she had wrote from Granworth Aymes' desk just so's nobody would know that she had written 'em, he never said whether she had been justified in writin' them.

If she hadn't been, that is if he'd known there wasn't another dame in the business, he coulda said so then. But he didn't say a word about the dame that brought Henrietta to New York an' that is one of the reason why I thought that Henrietta was tellin' the truth.

An' I reckoned to take Fernandez by surprise an' it came off. You gotta understand that the last thing that Fernandez heard from Burdell was on that phone call, that I had been along to the Burdell office an' heard all that stuff he pulled on me an' believed it. Neither of 'em guessed that I had their telephone conversation plugged in an' listened to.

Now here is another thing: Fernandez tells me that he thoughta marryin' Henrietta but that he has changed his mind. Yet when Burdell telephoned through he tells Fernandez to go ahead with this marryin' business. Fernandez makes out that he has changed his mind about it an' tells me so because it looks to him that I am goin' to pinch Henrietta, but just when he gets this idea into his head'n thinks that everything is hunky dory I pull a fast one an' a gun an' bust the story about this other dame outa him.

So I can certainly rely on one thing, an' that is that when I go an' see this Paulette Benito—an' I am certainly goin' to contact that dame—she is goin' to be all ready for me. It is a whisky sour to all the beer in Brooklyn that Fernandez or somebody is goin' to tip her off that her name has been mentioned to me an' that she can expect little Lemmy to come gumshoein' around. Well, they'll be right about that, only maybe I will do the gumshoein' in a way that they won't expect.

Me—I think that the guys who are playin' this business along are makin' one big mistake an' I'll tell you what it is. They are concentratin' too much on the Granworth Aymes death. They evidently think that if this death can be pinned onta somebody as a killin' that I am goin' to think that whoever did the killin' was also responsible for the counterfeitin'. They will think that this idea will be the easiest way outa the business. But they got me wrong. I never take easiest ways out an' the reason I have scored a bull in some tough cases before was because I just play along an' talk to people without gettin' excited about things. I have discovered that talkin' to people who may be crooks is a swell thing to do, especially if you tell 'em the truth. Sooner or later they are goin' to pull a very fast one, that don't check up, an' then you got somethin'.

An' as I have told you before, the main thing that I am workin' on is the counterfeit job. The death don't matter one jig to me. I'll tell you why. Guys are always dyin' an' gettin' themselves killed some way or other, an' it is a very good thing to grab the people who do it. At the same time a guy like Aymes more or less don't make very much difference, but a big counterfeitin' organisation does, an' I reckon that somebody who was organised enough to print off two hundred thousand bucks worth of phoney Registered Dollar Bonds is good enough to get a little attention from Uncle Sam. Even if Henrietta bought them phoney bonds off some counterfeitin' set-up, or ordered 'em to be made, the thing still stands. We gotta get 'em because their work is a durn sight too good. Why it nearly took in the bank manager an' Metts told me he'd never seen such a swell job.

I look over at Henrietta an' grin. She has just won a hand an' cleaned up about fifty dollars. She smiles back at me friendly like an' when I look at this dame sittin' there smilin' with her pretty little fingers pickin' up the chips I certainly get one swell kick out of it.

I'm tellin' you that she is a swell number. She is wearin' a little filmy sorta cloak over her shoulders. It is made of chiffon or somethin', an' every time she moves her arm it is worth lookin' at.

She gets up. Then she hands her chips to Periera who pays her out of some bills he pulls outa his pocket an' she looks over at Maloney. Maloney looks up at her sort of inquirin' as if he was askin' if she wanted somethin' an' she shakes her head a little bit an' sorta glances quickly at me, as if she was sayin' that she wanted him to lay off because she was goin' to pull one on me or somethin'. I pretend to be lookin' at the game an' that I have not noticed anything.

Then she walks around to me.

"I wonder if Mr. Lemuel H. Caution, the ace 'G' man, is going to do a forlorn woman a good turn and drive her home," she says. "Or maybe he's to busy?"

I get it. When Maloney looked up he had meant should he drive her home, an' she had signalled back no she was goin' to ask me. I reckon that she is goin' to try somethin'.

I give her a big grin.

"O.K. Henrietta," I say, "an' I won't even make you walk. Do you want me to drive you to that rancho where you live?"

She says yes, an' I say good-night to everybody an' follow her down the stairs. She waits on the front entrance while I drive the car around an' then gets in an' we go off.

There is a swell moon, an' when there is a current of air caused by the car startin' up I get a whiff of perfume that she is wearin'—carnation, an' I always did go for carnation. Only it is not that heavy sorta perfume, but nice an' mild, you know what I mean. It makes me remember the night when I went over her room an' sniffed that scent for the first time. I remember all her shoes an' ridin' boots standin' in a row, an' I suddenly get a big idea. I get the idea that I am becomin' much too interested in this dame, an' that I had better watch my step otherwise I may be fallin' for her just around the time when I am goin' to be makin' a pinch.

Which, I oughta tell you, is one of the loads of grief that a dick has to bear. Any sorta copper, no matter whether he is Federal, State or local, is always comin' up against swell dames. Why? Well, because it is always swell lookin' dames who get in jams. You never heard of a dame with a face like the elevated railway startin' anything, didya? Well, if a guy has gotta eye for a swell shape, a nice voice an' a well-cut pair of ankles, it stands to reason that if he don't watch out his mind is goin' to stray from the business in hand.

She starts talkin'.

"Jim Maloney was going to drive me home," she says, "but I thought that I'd like you to do it. I wanted to drive back with you."

I grin.

"I know," I tell her. "I saw you two signallin' to each other, an' I thought somethin' was boilin' up."

She laughs.

"There isn't much you don't see, is there, Mr. Caution?"

"Not very much, lady," I tell her. "There have been times when I have been caught off base. There was a dame in a garage flat near Baker Street, London, England, named Lottie Frisch, who once shot me through the bottom of her handbag when I thought she was lookin' for a letter. I never knew what she was at until I got a .22 bullet through the arm, which just shows you that you gotta keep your eyes skinned, don't it?"

She gives a little sigh.

"I expect you've seen some real life," she says.

I look at her sideways.

"Yeah," I tell her, "an' I've seen a spot of real death too. There ain't really a lotta difference between the two. Life comes slow an' death comes pronto sometimes. Take for instance Granworth," I go on, takin' a peek at her, "I bet that guy didn't have any idea on the mornin' of the 12th January that he was goin' to be fished outa the river on the mornin' of the 13th. That's the way it goes, ain't it?"

She don't say nothin'. She just looks straight ahead.

Pretty soon I pull up outside the little rancho where she lives. There is some fat Mexican dame sittin' on the front porch, an' she gets up an' goes in as the car stops. This is the hired girl who is lookin' after the place an' cleanin' up I guess.

Henrietta gets outa the car an' walks around, an' stands lookin' at me as I am sittin' in the drivin' seat. Her eyes are shinin' an' she looks as if she was happy.

"I enjoyed that ride," she said, "and if you'd like to come in and drink one glass of straight bourbon, you'd be welcome."

I jump out.

"You said it, Henrietta," I tell her. "That is just the thing I feel like, besides which I wanta ask you a question."

She laughs as we start walkin' up towards the porch.

"Don't you ever stop working?" she says. "Are you always trying to find out something about somebody?"

"Most of the time," I say. "But the thing I wanted to ask you is quite a simple little thing. I wanted to ask you what sort of a guy Granworth was."

We go inside. She shuts the wire door on the porch an' leads the way into the livin' room. Her face looks pretty serious.

I don't wonder, at it, because, if you are a woman you will realise that I have asked her a sweet question. I have really asked her to tell me what she thinks about her own life, because if you ask a woman about a man she is or was in love with you are really askin' her about herself, an' the way she thinks.

She slips off her little cape, an' she goes over to the sideboard an' brings a bottle of Kentucky straight whisky an' a glass, with another glass for a chaser. She musta been watchin' me at the Hacienda to know that I like it that way. Then she opens the shades on one side of the room so that the air an' the moon can come in, an' she sits down in a rocker chair an' looks at me.

"What did I think of Granworth," she says. "I think that's a question that would take some thinking over. I don't even know why I married him, except that I was bored and unhappy and thought that in any event marriage could not be more annoying than my life at home.

"But I liked Granworth. I suppose that I didn't believe in love very much and I thought that it was one of those things that arrived after marriage. It didn't take me long to find out about Granworth. He was the type of man who would find it impossible to be faithful to anything or anyone. He imagined that he was a good sportsman, but he would cheat rather than lose a game. He even thought that he was an idealist and yet I've never known any one with less ideals.

"He had two main troubles—money and women. He had to have both, and I don't think that he was awfully particular about either. He was spasmodic in his business—one week he would be very industrious and the next let everything go.

"He got tired quickly. He couldn't stick, and if anything needed concentration or real thinking he would quit.

"I believe he had a good business organisation. Burdell was the clever, efficient one as regards work. I believe that he was the one who made the money when it was made. Granworth was a gambler. He had to try for bigger and bigger money all the time, and the result was that very often we were broke and then, suddenly, he'd make some money and all would be well."

She gets up outa the chair, and walks over to the french windows. She stands there lookin' out. She looked as miserable as hell.

"He was weak, nervous and excitable," she went on, "and he was untrustworthy. I had ideas for a long while that he had been running around with women, but I thought that they were the usual sort of women that men like Granworth went for—chorines and such like. It didn't matter to me anyhow because during the last three years of our married life we were practically strangers to each other. I saw him occasionally and as often as not he was drunk.

"Then, quite suddenly, he made this quarter of a million. And he seemed to take a pull at himself. He told me that he was giving me the two hundred thousand Dollar Bonds so that I should know that there was something for our future. He said he was going to start over again; that he was going to think ahead and maybe we could string along together like we had in the old days when we were first married. He seemed so sincere that I almost believed him."

I light myself a cigarette.

"If you knew that he was runnin' around with dames," I say, "then why was you so burned up when you got this unsigned letter from this guy who said that Granworth was runnin' around with a dame, an' that he was goin' to get nasty about it. Didn't it look a bit funny to you that this guy should write *you* about it. Didn't you wonder why he didn't write an' tell Granworth to lay off?"

She turns around.

"The answer to both those questions is the same," she says. "Granworth knew that whilst his love affairs were confined to people who didn't matter, that I wasn't fearfully interested in either him or them, but I had told him that if he made any scandal or caused any more annoyance or bother to me that I would divorce him.

"He didn't like the idea of divorce and so he kept his so-called love affairs out of my existence. It seemed to me that the man who wrote me that unsigned letter might have told Granworth that if he didn't stop fooling around with his wife he would write to me.

"When I got the letter I was furious. I was even more furious when I telephoned Granworth about it from Connecticut and he seemed quite disinterested in what I had to say. I was amazed at the change in his attitude after all the protestations I had heard such a short while before. I made up my mind that either he would give up this woman or I would divorce him."

She smiles as if she was rememberin' somethin'.

"I suppose that I'm like most women," she says. "In the first place I thought I could make something of Granworth. I suppose every woman who marries a weak type of man thinks that she can improve him. We are all would-be reformers."

I grin.

"You're tellin' me," I crack at her. "That's why the bad guys get such a break. If a guy is a good sorta guy women ain't interested in him much. If he's a bad egg then they think that they oughta get out an' start reformin' him.

"I'm tellin' you dames are the funniest things," I tell her. "I once knew a dame in Illinois an' she was for reformin' some guy that she was stuck on. This guy usta drink a coupla bottles of rye every day an' she reckoned that she'd gotta stop this before she married him. She said she wasn't goin' to marry no rye vat.

"O.K. Well, I met this dame two years later. She had got so interested in reformin' this guy that she'd taken up drinkin' rye an' she could drink him under the table any day. He was sore because he said if she'd only left him alone in the first place he woulda been dead through drinkin' hooch by now an' out of trouble, but he'd got so fed up with watchin' his wife drink that he was considerin' turnin' prohibitionist. It just showed me that the reformin' gag don't always work out the way it seems to the reformers."

I give myself another cigarette.

"So you didn't like Granworth," I say. "That's what it boils down to, don't it? Say, Henrietta, what sorta guy do you like? Are you sure that you wasn't stuck on some other guy yourself? This eternal triangle bezusus can be played two ways you know!"

The smile goes off her face. She looks durn serious at me, an' she walks over an' stands lookin' down at me where I am sittin'.

"You listen to this, Mr. 'G' man," she says. "I've never been really interested in any man in my life until now—just when it's not likely to be of the slightest use to me."

I grin.

"I don't get you, lady," I tell her. "This Maloney is a good guy. He'd probably make you a swell husband."

She smiles at me.

"I wasn't thinking of Maloney," she says. "I was thinking of you."

I am hit for a home run. I get up an' stand there lookin' at her. She don't bat an eyelid. She just stands there lookin' at me smilin'.

"You're the only sort of person in the man line who's ever meant a thing to me," she says. "If I ever thought about Jim Maloney, it was because I know he's straight and a good friend."

She steps a little bit closer.

"I think that you're a swell man," she goes on, "and you're tough and very much cleverer than you allow people to believe. If you want to know exactly what I think about you, here it is!"

She takes a step forward an' she puts both her arms around my neck an' she kisses me, an' boy, can that dame kiss or can she? I stand there like I was poleaxed. I am wonderin' to myself whether this is a pipe dream or whether it is really happenin', an' all the while at the back of all this comes the idea that this Henrietta is puttin' on one big act because she thinks that I am workin' up to a pinch an' she imagines maybe that she can play me for a mug.

I don't say a word. She turns around an' goes to the table an' pours out another shot of the Kentucky. She brings it over an' she hands it to me. Her eyes are smilin', an' she can hardly keep herself from laughin' outright.

"That scared you, didn't it?" she says. "I guess I'm the first woman to ever scare the great Lemmy Caution. Well, here's your drink and after you've had it, you can be on your way."

I sink the whisky.

"I'm goin'." I tell her, "but before I get outa here I wanta tell you somethin', an' it's this. I think you're a swell baby. You got everything an' you know all the answers. I could go for a dame like you in a big way, an' maybe forget where I was while I was doin' it. But if you think that a big kissin' act is goin' to get you outa this jam you're in, you're wrong. I been kissed before— plenty, an' I like it. I am also very fond of dames in general, but lady, if I make up my mind to pinch you in this business then all the kissin' in the world ain't goin' to save you. So get that behind them sweet eyes of yours."

She laughs.

"You're telling me," she says, imitating the way I talk. "That's what I like about you. Well, good-night, Lemmy. Come around some more when you've got the handcuffs ready."

An' with this crack she walks outa the room an' leaves me there with a glass in my hand.

I scram. I go outside an' start up the car, an' ease off towards Palm Springs. I am doin' a lotta heavy thinkin', but believe it or not the way that dame kissed me has got me in a spin.

There is another thing that is stickin' out a coupla feet an' that is that this Henrietta is a clever number. She tells me that I am clever but believe me she knows her onions an' maybe she is tryin' to play me for a sucker.

I put my foot on the gas an' whiz. I have made up my mind about somethin'. I am goin' to see Metts an' fix a little thing with him. I am sorta sick of all these people takin' me for a ride. I am goin' to start somethin', an' I am goin' to start it pronto.

Work it out for yourself. I been kickin' around here talkin' to people till I'm sick. I been back to New York an' heard a lotta phoney stuff from Burdell. The only time I got anything worth while was when I pulled a gun on Fernandez an' he told me about Paulette.

Every time I get nice with people they give me the ha-ha, an' it looks to me that all there is left for me to do is to get myself some silk shirts an' go in for bein' a sissy.

Whoever is behind this bezusus has got one helluva nerve. They have only kept me kickin' around findin' out sweet nothin', but they have also ironed out Sagers an' are kiddin' themselves that they got away with that too.

O.K. Well, if they want it tough they can have it tough. So here we go.

CHAPTER EIGHT
A FAST ONE

I NEVER did like mornin's after. They get in my hair. You always think about the one you oughta have pulled the night before, the one you didn't think of.

When I wake up the sun is shinin' through the window curtains an' I feel that I am goin' to get movin' so fast that some of these guys are goin' to think they was bein' chased by lightnin'. Me—I'm a patient sorta cuss, but there is a time when you gotta do somethin' an' it looks to me like the time is right now.

I get up an' I take a shower an' drink some coffee. While I am drinkin' it I am thinkin' of all the things that I oughta have pulled on Henrietta last night that I never did. Work it out for yourself that this dame is doin' one of two things. She is either stuck on me so much that she will tell me anything I want, or else she is twicin' me an' has gotta put up a front that she will tell me anythin' I want. So either way I reckon that I missed a lotta opportunities.

Sittin' on the edge of the bed I start rememberin' when I was back at the Federal school learnin' my stuff. I remember some old guy who used to give us lectures on this an' that:

"Do somethin'," this old palooka usta say. "Don't stick around an' think too much. If you ain't gotta lead, make one. If you don't know what to do start measurin' up the room or talkin' to people, or creatin' situations in which guys who are tryin' to hide a fact you want, will get scared an' blow it."

Was he right or was he. O.K. This is where I start.

First of all you are goin' to agree with me that I am entitled to think that everybody connected with this set-up is playin' me like I was a mug who is so dumb that he has got moss growin' out of his ears through not thinkin'. Everybody in this bezusus is tryin' to two-time somebody else. Start with Burdell; this guy, after doin' a big kind-friend act with Henrietta an' gettin' the Aymes servants to say that she wasn't in New York on the night of the death, is now doin' everything he can to get the idea in my head that she bumped Granworth. Fernandez is helpin' him along. He pretends that he wanted to marry Henrietta until he got the idea that she was responsible for this counterfeitin' stuff an' then he changes his mind. Burdell helps along in this idea by sayin' that he only started to blow the works after *he* thought that Henrietta was in on the counterfeitin'.

An' what about Henrietta?

She just sticks around an' she don't say a durn thing that matters except to make a big play for me an' tell me that I am the cat's lingerie; that she could fall for me like a ton of old coke an' that generally I have only gotta go for her an' I am right in the front row with bells on.

Me—I could go for Henrietta all right. But I do not make a play for dames that are suspects in murder cases. I think that it would interfere with business. Anyway she knows what my job is an' therefore she must not blame me if I kinda think she is tryin' to pull something very fast.

Maybe some of these guys are goin' to get surprised an' that goes for Henrietta too, because I am goin' to start somethin' an' I am goin' to start it right now.

An' I am not bein' side-tracked. If Burdell or Henrietta or anybody else think that I am the sorta guy who can be locoed off the job then they have gotta think some more.

There is only two angles on this job that interest me right now, an' I reckon you will agree with me when I say what they are. First of all I am very interested in the state of mind of this guy Granworth Aymes just before he died. It's stickin' out a mile that this palooka ain't got any cause to commit suicide. He has got dough; he has got health—because the Insurance Company passed him as fit—an' I am certainly not goin' to believe that he was goin' to commit suicide just because Henrietta tells him that she is goin' to take a run-out powder on him an' get a divorce. Why should he? A guy who is chasin' around with a lotta other dames—like Fernandez said he was—ain't goin' to get burned up just because his wife gets wise an' jibs. The fact that he tried to commit suicide once before don't cut any ice. When he tried it before he was so drunk that he didn't know a thing.

When he said that he was goin' to start over again an' be a good guy maybe he meant it. It certainly looks like he did, because no guy is goin' to be mug enough to take out a big insurance policy an' pay a helluva down premium if he is goin' to bump himself off knowin' that the company have barred payment over suicide.

The fact that Granworth took out this policy stands out as bein' important to me.

The other thing is this Paulette Benito. The first idea that bumps into anybody's head is that maybe this dame has got somethin' to do with it. But I don't reckon that this is so because you gotta realise that if Burdell and Fernandez had wanted to get her in bad they coulda blown this woman stuff before and dragged her into it. No, I reckon that nobody thought that she was important in this thing an' that they didn't mention her because they wanted to concentrate attention on Henrietta.

But it is a cinch that this Paulette dame has got to know somethin'. If she was aces high with Granworth then I bet he woulda spoke to her about his wife; more so if he an' Henrietta was in bad with each other, an' maybe this Paulette can tell me somethin' about Henrietta that will shed a spotta light on the counterfeitin' job. I reckon I am goin' to see this Paulette just as soon as I have pulled a coupla other things around here, an' that dame is goin' to talk, an' talk plenty, even if she is in Mexico an' outa U.S. jurisdiction; because you gotta realise that this dump Sonoyta where she is stayin' is right on the Mexican side of the Arizona state line an' if I have to get her into U.S. territory to make her talk I am goin' to do it, an' I am not goin' to wait for any extradition either, even if I haveta take her over the line by her back hair.

An' all of this stuff will make it plain to you that I am gettin' good an' burned up about this business. Somebody is tryin' to take me for a ride an' I don't like it.

I put a call through to Metts, the Police Chief in Palm Springs, an' I have a little talk with him an' we fix things up.

Metts is a good guy an' has got intelligence. Also he is good at co-operatin', which is more than you can say about some coppers I have known.

We fix it this way. He is goin' to get two highway cops to run out to the Hacienda an' pick up Henrietta. They will bring her into Metts' office at eleven o'clock. At half-past twelve, just when Periera an' Fernandez are wonderin' what it is all about, the cops will go back an' pull in those two heroes an' bring them along. After which I reckon that we will get goin'.

I fix myself up nice an' pretty. I put on a swell grey suit I have got an' a light grey fedora an' a silver grey tie, just so's to kid myself that I am goin' places, an' then I ease over to Metts' office at the police headquarters an' say how-do.

Metts gives me his office an' a cigar I sit there an' wait.

Pretty soon the two cops bring in Henrietta. She is lookin' good an' surprised, an' she is also lookin' very swell. Boy, can that dame pick clothes *an'* wear 'em!

She is wearin' a lemon coloured suit that comes from some place where they know how to cut 'em. She is wearin' a brown silk shirt, a lemon panama with a brown silk band, brown an' white buckskin shoes an' tan silk stockin's.

She sits down in the chair that they have put for her on the other side of the big desk an' I see her lookin' at my hat which I have got well over one eye. The two highway cops go out an' leave us.

"Good-morning, Lemmy," she says, like we was very old friends. She smiles at me. "What's happening?" she goes on. "Am I under arrest? An' I do wish you'd take your hat off to a lady."

"Nuts, sister," I tell her. "An' getta load of this. Whether I'm goin' to pinch you this mornin', or hold you as a material witness, or just grill you, I ain't quite decided. But I don't have to take my hat off when I'm talkin' to suspected crooks if I don't wanta, an' you can can all that nice stuff because you are beginnin' to make me tired. Got that?"

She looks as if she had been hit with a black-jack. Is she surprised? An' I don't wonder at it. Last night she is doin' a big act with me an' maybe thinks that she has got me where she wants me an' this mornin' I come back with some tough stuff that shakes her plenty. Wouldn't *you* be surprised?

"I've got it," she says finally, sorta cold. "And where do we go from there?"

"Just this far, sweetheart," I tell her. "I've decided to have the investigation into your husband's death reopened. I've come to the conclusion that Granworth Aymes was murdered, an' I think that maybe you know a durn sight more about it than you'd like to tell. I am also inclined to believe that you are holdin' out on me over this counterfeitin' business. I may also bring charges against you for endeavouring to pass here, at this Bank in Palm Springs, a counterfeit United States Registered Dollar Bond, knowin' at the time that it was phoney, an' how do you like that?"

"It doesn't interest me very much," she says. "But I don't like it and I don't like you at all to-day. You're behaving like a pig. I suppose you think that after last night . . ."

"Can it, Henrietta," I tell her. "Why don't you turn that stuff off. Say, do you think that dames haven't tried to make me before. That's old hooey. You thought that I was gettin' after you; that maybe I was goin' to make a pinch, so you try that soft stuff last night an' think that I'm goin' to go all goofy. You remember that guys can play dames just as well as dames can play guys."

"I see," she says. "I suppose that's why you thrashed Fernandez. You wanted to get the idea into my head that you were a decent sort of man instead of a cheap, blustering Federal cop. All right, I'm wise now."

"Swell, sister," I say, "an' so am I. Now you get a load of this an' just answer my questions, otherwise I'm goin' to make things hot for you."

"Are you?" she says sorta insolent. "And supposing I don't want to answer them. Supposing I refuse to answer any questions unless I have a lawyer here?"

"O.K." I say. "If you wanta lawyer you get one, but I'm tellin' you this, if you getta lawyer around here I'm goin' to send you back to New York so that the police there can grill hell outa you, so if you wanta getta mouthpiece you get busy."

She smiles again—a sorta sneering smile. She looks at me like I was something that crawled out from under some rock.

"All right," she says. "I'll answer your questions. But I wish I were a man. I'd like to thrash you until all that cheap lousy conceit was knocked right out of you. Do you get that? Another thing," she goes on, sorta gettin' into her stride, "I've got a better name for you. They made a mistake when they called you Lemmy—they should have called you Lousy, it would have matched up better."

"You don't say," I tell her. "Just thinka that now. O.K. Well, now, if you've had your little say, I'll get busy an' then you can get outa here an' try come of that soft stuff on somebody else—Maloney or Periera or Fernandez or anybody else that's around. But in the meantime I just wanta know this an' I advise you to make it straight too. I wanta know just how you was dressed on the evenin' of the 12th January, the time you had your last talk with Granworth? Now get busy."

I take a sheet of paper an' a pencil an' I wait. When I look up I see that she has opened her bag an' is takin' a cigarette out.

"An' you can cut that out too," I tell her. "This is a police station an' you ain't smokin' here. Put it away."

She flushes red an' puts the case back inta her bag. As she does this I take out a packet of Camels an' give myself one. She watches me light it an' if she coulda murdered me at that moment she woulda done it an' liked it.

"Come on now, Henrietta," I say. "Quit stallin' an' cash in. What were you wearin' when you come up to New York from Connecticut on the 12th January? Start at the top with your hat."

She smiles. This dame can certainly be annoyin'.

"I may not be able to remember," she says, "but I'll try. I suppose you want to know *everything*—even to the colour of my step-ins."

She hands me out another sarcastic smile that was just poison.

"To tell you the truth I hadn't thought about your underwear," I crack, "but since you mention it you can tell me about that too!"

She gets up.

"You cheap gorilla," she says. She is white with rage. "I . . ."

"Sit down an' take it easy, sister," I say. "Cash in with the description *includin'* colour of underwear—remember you suggested it, not me—an' get busy. If you don't I'll seriously consider handin' you over to the woman warder here an' getting her to search, strip an' photograph you for birthmarks. So just play along before I get really tough."

Henrietta sits down. She is almost chokin' with rage.

"Now honeybunch," I say nice an' soothin'. "Here we go. Start at the top. What sorta hat was it?"

It is a coupla minutes before Henrietta can talk. She is near speechless an' I can see her hands tremblin'. Finally she gets going.

"I was wearing a hat made of Persian lamb," she says, an' her voice is shakin', "a toque—but you probably wouldn't know what that means. Also I had on a Persian lamb swagger coat and underneath I was wearing a black suit with a white silk shirt. I had on beige stockings, black patent shoes with french heels and silver Louis buckles, and black suède gauntlet gloves."

"An' very nice too," I tell her. "I woulda like to have seen you, I reckon you musta looked swell, an' what about the step-ins?"

I look at her dead serious an' she looks up an' our eyes meet. She goes red an' drops hers. Then she sticks her chin out an' says:

"They were eau-de-nil—but you wouldn't know how to spell it."

"Oh, yeah," I crack, "I know. I've known dames before who used to wear eau-de-nil step-ins, only they wasn't so secret about it."

I ring the bell an' after a minute a copper comes in. Henrietta thinks that I am through with her, an' she gets up an' picks up her bag an' is just turning for the door when I start talkin'.

"Take Mrs. Aymes to the record office an' finger print her, officer," I say. "Then when you've done that have her photographed, front and side faces, with an' without hat."

Henrietta spins around. Her eyes are blazin', an' for a moment I thought she was comin' for me with her bare hands, but the State policeman puts his fist out, grabs her an' starts to hustle her off.

She looks at me over her shoulder.

"You . . . you heel!" she hisses.

"Now, now, now, Henrietta," I tell her, shakin' my finger at her. "You mustn't talk like that to your little playmate, Lemmy! Bring her back when you're through," I tell the officer.

When they are gone I look at my watch. It is just after twelve. I ring the bell again an' another State copper comes in—it looks like Meets is keepin' 'em hangin' around for me—and says what do I want.

I tell him that a coupla his buddies are bringin' Periera and Fernandez in at twelve-thirty o'clock, an' that when they arrive at the station they are not to be brought into me until I ring for 'em. I tell him that two rings on the bell is the signal that they are to be brought in an' he says O.K.

I then look through the list of Henrietta's clothes, an' I fix it the way I want, an' I then take it in to the stenographer in the next office an' tell him to make three copies of it.

While he is doin' this I light another cigarette an' go an' look outa the window. Pretty soon I see a police car draw up outside an' I see the officers bring in Periera and Fernandez. These two birds are lookin' good an' surprised I can tell you. I then go an' park myself in the chair an' put up my feet on the desk.

A coupla minutes afterwards the door opens an' the first copper comes in with Henrietta.

"Everything O.K.?" I ask him.

He says yes, that they have finger printed the dame and photographed her like I said, an' the records clerk is makin' out a card now for the index.

I say all right an' that he can go. He goes an' leaves Henrietta standin' there in the middle of the floor lookin' at me.

She looks at me as if I was a large lump of mud. She looks from the tip of my fedora down to the soles of my shoes which are restin' on the top of the chief's cigar box. Then she gives her lip a curl an' looks just as if she was goin' to be sick.

Just at this minute I press the desk button which is fixed my side of the desk twice, an' in a coupla seconds the door opens an' the two State coppers come in with Periera and Fernandez.

I tell the coppers to scram. Then I wave my hand to the two guys.

"Sit down, boys," I tell 'em, very cheerful. "I wanna talk to you."

I motion them to go over an' sit on the long seat that is up against the wall. Henrietta is still standin' in the middle of the floor.

They go an' sit down.

"Periera," I say, "I want you to do something an' you gotta watch your step in doin' it, because if you slip up then I'm goin' to get funny with you."

I point to Henrietta.

"It's about this dame here," I go on. "I ain't got any particular charge that I want to bring against her at the moment, but it's on the cards that I'm goin' to want her as a material witness for the State of New York. Metts, the Chief of Police here, ain't got any spare room around to keep her in, an' I've got to get outa town for a few days. So Metts is goin' to swear you in as a deputy an' it's goin' to be your business to keep an' eye on this dame until we want her. Got that?"

He nods.

"I get eet," he says.

I turn around to Henrietta.

"You heard what I said, sweetheart, didn't you?" I tell her. "I'm lettin' you blow outa here an' you get back to the Hacienda Altmira until I want you, an' don't try an' get outside the Palm Springs limit otherwise I'm goin' to have you pinched pronto. O.K. Now you scram outa here an' once you're outside you can smoke as much as you like. So long, baby, I'll be seein' you."

I give my fedora a sorta cheeky flip so's it's right over one eye, an' I waggle my feet on the desk. It works. She blows up.

"Yes," she hisses like a snake, "and you'll be seeing me," she gulps. "If you think that you can get away with this sort of thing you're very much mistaken," she goes on, "you're just a conceited, insolent, rough-housing gorilla who's no more fitted to carry a Federal badge an' have the authority that goes with it than the dirtiest creep that ever crawled over into this country. You're cheap and nasty, and one day I'm going to make you squirm for this. In the meantime you can take this to go on with."

She takes a quick step forward an' before I can move she leans across the desk an' busts me in the face with her clenched fist. I tell you I was quite surprised.

Then she steps back, turns around on her heel an' walks out. I was watchin' her while she went, an' believe it or not she looked a picture. That Henrietta can certainly walk.

Fernandez grins.

"It looks like she ain't so pleased about something," he says. I laugh.

"You wouldn't be if you was her," I say.

I take my feet off the desk an' at this minute the stenographer comes in with the duplicate lists of Henrietta's clothes.

"Now listen, Fernandez," I tell him. "I gotta idea. I gotta idea that we can pin this Aymes bump off on Henrietta all right, an' I reckon that once we got a capital charge against her I can make her squeal the rest of the stuff about the counterfeitin'. But I got to prove that she was the woman who was in the car with Aymes, an' once I can do that I got her all set. Once I can pin that on her an' it looks as if there's a life sentence for her in the bag, I reckon she'll blow the works on anything if she thinks that talkin' is goin' to help her any.

"Now I gotta idea how we can work. I been grillin' this Henrietta good an' plenty this mornin', an' I gotta description of the clothes she was wearin' on the 12th January, the day that Granworth died."

I get up an' I hand one of the duplicate clothes descriptions to Fernandez. He looks at it a long time.

"Do you remember her wearin' any stuff like that?" I ask him.

"I sorta remember the coat an' the hat," he says, "but I wouldn't know about that day. You see, I never saw her that day. I was off duty."

"That's O.K., Fernandez," I say, "but here are two guys who could swear to those clothes. One of 'em is the maid at the Aymes apartment. I reckon that she packed Henrietta's bags an looked after her kit before she went away to Hartford, didn't she?"

"You bet," he says. "Marie Dubuinet—that's the maid—would know, an' I can tell you where you can contact her. She's still in New

York. She's personal maid to Mrs. John Vlaford, an' she'd know. She's a durn intelligent girl is Marie. She never forgets a thing."

"O.K.," I say, "an' there's somebody else too. There's the watchman on Cotton's Wharf. I reckon if this guy's sight was good enough to see that it was a woman who got outa Granworth's car, it was good enough for him to remember the fur coat an' hat she was wearin'. I'm takin' this description to New York, an' I'm goin' to get the police to check up with the maid an' the watchman. If they can identify those clothes then I'm comin' back here to pinch Henrietta, because I tell you now that I'm dead certain that she bumped Aymes.

"There's another thing, Fernandez," I go on. "I reckon that I mighta made a mistake about you bein' the guy who had a shot at me the other night. Maybe it wasn't a guy at all—maybe it was a dame."

I look at him sorta old-fashioned.

He grins.

"Well, you might be right at that," he says. "It certainly wasn't me. Periera here an' a coupla the boys know I was stickin' around there all the time. But," he goes on, "I reckon that maybe you're right. I like Henrietta, but I don't hold with murder an' it looks like you say that she bumped Granworth all right, but I'm sorry all the same," he says, "because she is a swell dame."

"You're tellin' me," I say. "An' it's always swell dames who start the trouble. They're always worse than the worst he-killer. They just don't care."

I get up.

"O.K. boys," I tell 'em. "Be on your way. Don't you forget, Periera, that you're responsible for Henrietta, an' thanks for the tip-off about the maid, Fernandez. I'll take care of that job right away."

When they have gone I sit down at the desk an' do a little quiet thinkin'. I reckon that maybe this thing is goin' to work out, an' if it don't well it's just too bad.

Metts blows in. He is grinnin' all over his face.

"You certainly handed it to the dame," he says. "I thought one time that she was goin' to crown you. I was listenin' in the next room," he goes on. "I just couldn't miss it. You see I don't get much excitement around here."

He hands me the developed photographs of Henrietta an' the finger print card, an' the record card. I put 'em on the desk.

"Where do we go from here, Lemmy?" he says. "I don't know what this set-up is, but whatever it is you gotta helluva technique I will say. Can I do anything else?"

"Yeah," I say, "there is just one or two little things that you can do around here. One is just get it around this burg that I have scrammed outa here for New York an' that I am not expected back for a week or so. The other thing is that you can keep a quiet eye on the Hacienda Altmira an' see that dame Henrietta don't start gettin' windy an' takin' a run-out powder on us, an' the third an' last thing you can do is to fix me an airplane. I wanna go places."

"You flyin' to New York?" he says.

"New York my eye," I tell him. "I'm flyin' to Yuma an' then I'm goin' to coast along the Arizona State line an' bust into Mexico. I got a date with a dame."

He grins.

"Is she a good dame, Lemmy?" he says.

"I wouldn't know," I tell him. "I ain't ever seen her, but I reckon that she is due to get acquainted with me. Now will you be a good guy an' fix that plane?"

He says O.K. an' he goes off. I grab the telephone an' I send a code telegram to the "G" Office in New York. I send the list of Henrietta's clothes an' I ask 'em to check on this list with the maid Marie Dubuinet, an' the watchman at Cotton's Wharf an' to telegraph me the result back to Palm Springs to wait for me when I come back.

Just when I have got this done Metts comes in. He has been on the 'phone in the next room an' fixed about the airplane. He is a pleasant sorta guy this Metts an' he is feelin' good an' talkative.

I am sittin' at the desk lookin' at the police pictures of Henrietta. I read the record card:

"Henrietta Marella Charlsworth Aymes. Widow. Wife of Granworth Aymes. Suicide 12-13 January, 1936. Height five

*feet seven and one half inches. Brunette. Eyes blue. Complexion
healthy. Features regular. Figure slim. Carriage erect. Speech
educated voice cultured. Weight 135 pounds.*

This is a pretty good picture of Henrietta I think. Then I look
at the finger prints. They have certainly made a neat job of these,
an' the photographs are very swell.

"Nice work, chief," I tell him. "You gotta good staff around
here."

I nod. He comes around behind me an' looks over my shoulder
at the pictures an' the finger print an' record cards.

"I put you to a lotta trouble, chief," I tell him, "so you won't
get burned up when I do this?"

"Do what?" he says, lookin' at me.

I tear up the pictures an' the finger print an' record cards, an'
I throw 'em in the waste basket.

He looks at me with his eyes poppin'.

"What the hell?" he says.

I grin.

"Just technique, chief," I tell him. "Just a spotta technique.
I'll be seein' you."

I scram. Mexico is callin'.

CHAPTER NINE
HEY PAULETTE!

IT IS seven o'clock an' a fine evenin' an' I am drivin' along the
state road that runs along the Mexican border between Mexicali
an' Sonoyta.

There is one swell moon. There is a lotta people who don't
like this desert scenery, but me, I go for it. I'm for the wide open
spaces where men are men an' women are durn glad of it.

An' I am plenty curious about this Paulette. Speakin' confidentially, I am keen to have a look at this dame. Why? Because I
like lookin' at dames and, speaking confidentially some more, I
am hot to get a look at the dame that Aymes turned down Henri-

etta for, because believe it or not this baby has gotta have what it takes in a big way to get a start of Henrietta. Get me?

Besides which I am not certain just where Henrietta is breakin'. I told you how I tore up the record card an' finger print cards an' pictures of her I had taken at Palm Springs, an' maybe you are wonderin' why I done this. If you got intelligence you will realise that the show I put up down at the Palm Springs police station was a big act an' if you stick around you'll see why I played it that way.

I start singin' Cactus Lizzie again because I have always found that I drive quicker when I am singin' this jingle.

I go on eatin' up the miles an' wonderin'. Sonoyta is about ten miles over the Mexican side of the Arizona-Mexico State line, an' it is about a hundred an' fifty miles from Mexicali, but what the roads are goin' to be like when I pull off the road I am on is another business.

It is eight o'clock when I get to the intersection. The left road runs inta Arizona an' the right inta Mexico. I pull the car round an' find myself on some helluva lousy road that shakes up my liver like a broncho. About five miles down this road I see a Mex sittin' on the side of the road, smokin' a cigarette an' thinkin'—which is what Mexicans is always doin' when they ain't tryin' to come the neat stuff with a dame or makin' a swell try to stick the other guy who is one jump ahead of 'em on the same game.

I pull up an' ask the guy if he knows a jane called Señora Paulette Benito who is livin' in some hacienda around here, an' after gettin' over a lotta surprise at findin' an Americano who speaks his own lingo he says yes, an' he tells me how to make this place which is about six miles from where we are.

After stickin' me for two cigarettes an' thereby provin' that there ain't even one Mex who will even give you some information for nothin' I ease off an' ten minutes later I see the hacienda.

It is a swell little dump. It is all white an' stuck on the side of a little hill with a lotta tropical stuff an' cactus around behind it. There are some white palisades around the front an' old-fashioned rancho gate, an' I drive in, get outa the car an' walk up to the door. There is a big knocker an' I bang plenty.

Pretty soon the door opens an' a Mexican jane stands lookin' at me. She is as ugly as a gorilla, an' by the looks of her pan I reckon that there is durn little Spanish about her. Maybe she had a Spanish mother about ten generations back who didn't know how to say no to Great Leapin' Moose or whatever the local chief's monniker was, an' since then her ancestors ain't met up with anybody except Indians.

I say good-night very polite an' I ask her if I can talk with the Señora Benito an' she gets very excited an' says that the Señora ain't around an' that she is at some dump called the Casa de Oro, after which we go inta a huddle an' eventually I find out that this Casa de Oro is the nearest thing they got to a road house around these parts. She tells me that I can know this dump by the lamp that is hangin' outside an' I say thanks a lot an' scram.

I go on down the road an' after a bit I see this Casa de Oro. It is an ordinary adobe house standin' off the road with an old Spanish lamp hangin' outside. I drive the car off the road an' park it around by the side of the house an' I go in.

There ain't anybody around, but I can hear the sound of some guy playin' a guitar. I go along a stone passage, an' at the other end I stop an' look with my eyes bustin' because the place is like a fairyland.

All around the patio at the back there is an adobe wall, an' fixed on this wall is a lotta trellis work. There is flowers an' things stuck all over this trellis an' swung across the top from side to side is a lotta candle lamps.

All around the patio are tables with people sittin' around. The guy playin' the guitar is standin' over in the far corner lookin' like he was nuts—he is so carried away with the song he is singin'. In the middle of the patio there is a sorta smooth stone floor about twenty feet square.

I sit down at a table. Mosta the guys turn around an' take a look at me like I come out of some museum, an' after a minute some Mexican waiter comes an' does a big bowin' act an' asks what is my pleasure.

I tell him that my pleasure is usually dames, but that at the moment I'll take a glass of *tequila*. Then I ask him if he knows the Señora Benito.

He nods an' makes a gesture towards the dancin' space, an' as I look over a couple get up an' start dancin'. I look over an' I see that the dame is American an' I know that this is Paulette.

Boy is she good or is she? Get this: I seen plenty janes an' I'm tellin' you that this Paulette has got the makin's. She is one swell bundle of woman an' I get thinkin' that maybe if I wasn't so busy on this case I would like to get around an' try out my personality on this baby.

She is a honey. She is as cute as Henrietta, but in a different way. She is as different like a pineapple is to a plum.

She has got curves that woulda made King Solomon sign off the roster an' turn into a one-woman man, an' she has got the sorta style that woulda made that Roman baby they called Juno look lika case of gallopin' consumption. If Henry the Eighth coulda taken one peek at her ankles he woulda figured to have got himself born about six centuries later just so's he coulda given Anne Boleyn a quick bum's rush an' made this Paulette top sergeant in the royal runaround squad.

An' can she dance? I have seen dames dance plenty an' I reckon that she can swing a mean hip. I tell you she is as supple as a snake, an' as she turns around in the tango she is dancin' I catch a look at her white teeth flashin' an' see her mouth smilin' up at the guy she is dancin' with, an' I start thinkin' that dames are very interestin' things an' that I would like to know very much just what a swell dame like this was doin' kickin' around with a cheap mug like Granworth Aymes.

An' the guy is good too. He is wearin' tight black Mexican pants with a silk shirt an' a bolero jacket. He has got a silver cord in his shirt an' all the trimmin's. He is a tall, wiry lookin' cuss, with a lotta black hair an' a little black moustache. He dances swell an' I reckon that if this guy went to Hollywood he would probably be such a success that maybe he could get married to some film star for a coupla months before she got sick of ante-ing up all the time to keep this palooka in hair-oil.

He also looks dangerous to me. He has got that sorta wicked look like a rattlesnake, only I reckon that this baby wouldn't even rattle before he started spittin'.

After a bit the music stops an' they sit down again. I sit at my table sippin' the *tequila* an' watchin' them. You gotta understand that it is not quite so easy for me this side of the border an' as I don't wanta get mixed up with the local cops I have gotta play my hand easy.

Lookin' at Paulette I try an' make up my mind as to how I am goin' to play this thing, but lookin' at her don't help me any. You never know how a dame is goin' to take anything. You never know with females; whatever you do they ain't satisfied.

I remember hearin' about some high-hat butler in some swell dame's house in England. One day this butler guy busts into the bathroom just when the dame is takin' a shower. Now this butler has gotta lotta tact so he just says "Excuse me, *Sir,*" an' scrams, an' thinks that he has got himself outa that one very good.

But he didn't feel so good next day when she made him go an' get his sight tested.

So I just sit there an' just as I am beginnin' to get tired of stickin' around, Paulette looks my way an' sorta gives me the once over, after which she gives me a sorta little smile.

I reckon that this is only because she reckons that I am an American in Mexico, but I act quick. I get up an' I ease over to her table an' I say how are you an' haven't we met some place before.

She says she don't remember me but maybe she has met me somewhere.

"Anyhow, lady, I've been waitin' years to meet you," I tell her. "My name's Caution—Lemmy Caution—an' I wanta have a little talk with you sometime."

"Sit down, Mr. Caution," she says, "an' have a drink. This is Señor Luis Daredo."

I sit down. The Mexican gives me a sorta look that might mean anything. I reckon he ain't so pleased with my bustin' in like this. He just nods.

I send the waiter to get the *tequila* that I have left on my table. While I am waitin' for it I see her watchin' me sorta interested, with a little smile playin' around her red mouth.

"And what was it you wanted to know, Mr. Caution?" she says. "I'll be glad to help you."

I look at her quick an' see a big laugh in her eyes.

I give myself a cigarette.

"It's this way, Mrs. Benito," I tell her. "I'm makin' a few inquires about a guy called Granworth Aymes who bumped himself off last January in New York. I thought that maybe you could help me. But I reckon that we can't talk here very well. Maybe I can take you back home some time an' have a little talk there."

She stops smilin'.

"Perhaps that wouldn't be convenient," she says. "You know, Mr. Caution, this is Mexico—*not* the United States, and possibly I don't want to talk about Granworth Aymes. Perhaps you're wasting your time here."

It is obvious to me that this dame is bein' fresh.

"I get you, lady," I tell her. "You mean that it ain't possible to hold anybody here as a material witness without a lotta funny business an' office stuff at Mexicali. Well, that's as may be, but if I was you I reckon I'd do what I want an' not make too much trouble over it, an' what will you have to drink?"

I order some drinks for all of us. The Mexican is watchin' me like I was a bad nightmare.

She starts smilin' again.

"I' like your direct methods, Mr. Caution," she says, "but I still don't see why I should make appointments to talk over somebody's death with people I don't know."

"O.K., lady," I say. "In that case I'll go back over the border an' get extradition for you as a material witness. Then I'll take you back an' hold you. It'll take me two days to get a Federal plea for your extradition through with the Mexican authorities, an' if they ain't quick enough for me maybe I'll try something else. I'm a Federal Agent an' I got a badge in my pocket that ain't very much use on this side of the' border but maybe it's enough for me to get hold of the local Rurales officer an' tell him you've got a pinched passport. Even if it ain't true it's goin' to make things plenty tough for you. Get me?"

She is just goin' to say something when Daredo puts his hand on her arm an' stops her.

"Señor," he says, "thees ees Mekkiko. I don't like that you talk to thees señora like you talk. I don't like you at all. You get out of thees place queek or else I order them to t'row you out. Sabe?"

"Nuts, gringo," I tell this guy. "I don't like you neither, an' I reckon that you'll have to get all your friends around you before you can throw me outa any place, an' just so's you'll know that I don't mean maybe, get a load of this."

I smack him across the puss an' he goes off the chair pronto. He gets up an' comes around the table an' I bust him another one. Some guy at the next table gets up an' starts emittin' a lotta Mexican noise an' easin' over to me so it looks as if I've gotta start something.

I stick my hand under my coat an' pull the gun. Around me I can see a lotta ugly mugs an' I reckon that I gotta fix this job.

"Listen, lady," I say to Paulette. "Get a load of this. If anybody starts anything around here, I'm goin' to give 'em the heat first an' talk afterwards. I'm takin' you back to your own place for a little talk an' if you don't like that I'll take you right over the border now an' smack you in the first sheriff's lock-up in Arizona I come to. You make up your mind what you're havin'—your own sittin'-room or the hoosegow—I don't give a continental."

She 'gets up.

"It's all right, Luis," she says. "You don't have to get excited. Maybe I'll go along with Mr. Caution here an' straighten this out."

"That's talkin'" I tell her, "an' I don't even mind if Luis does get excited. Any time he wants somebody to kick them tight pants off him I'll elect myself for the job. Maybe he's a big guy around here, but to me he's just a big sissy with whiskers. Come on, lady."

I put some money on the table an' we go out. I have still got the Luger in my hand an' over my shoulder I can see Luis lookin' at me like a tiger with a gumboil. This guy is certainly not so pleased.

We get in the car an' we go off. Outa the corner of my eye I can see Paulette lookin' at me. She is wearin' some swell perfume an' I can just sniff it. I get to comparin' it with Henrietta's "Carnation" an' I ain't quite certain which I like the best.

"That's a swell perfume you got, Paulette," I tell her. "I could go for that stuff. I always was keen on nice smells."

I can hear her gurglin' in the dark. I told you this Paulette is a helluva piece.

"You've got a sweet nerve," she says. "You burst into the Casa, smack Luis down, take me away just when I'm beginning to enjoy myself, and then tell me that you like my perfume. I reckon that you must go well with your lady friends, but you ought to remember this is Mexico."

"You don't say, Paulette," I tell her. "So what? I been in Mexico before, and it ain't ever frightened me any. Say, did you ever hear of a Mexican called Caldesa Martinguez—their ace stick-up guy?"

She nods.

"Well," I go on. "This guy got pretty big an' he reckoned to get over the border one day an' pull a fast one on the Arizona mail cart. He pulled a fast one—three times. First he stuck up the mail car; second time he stuck it up an' cut the driver's ear off, an' the third time he pumped so much lead into the driver an' the guard that they both looked like ammunition factories when we found 'em."

I get out my cigarette pack with my left hand an' give it to her. She lights a couple—one for herself an' one for me.

"O.K.," I say. "Well, the U.S. authorities got plenty mad at this guy. So they send some wise guy down to the border an' this guy pulls a coupla fake stick-ups, an' eventually Martinguez gets to hear of him an' cuts him in on the business. The wise guy plays along with Martinguez, an' one night gets him good an' high on doctored liquor. Then he ties him on a horse an' runs him over the border to a nice lock-up an' a six foot drop—they still hang 'em in Arizona.

"The joke was that when Martinguez arrives at the lockup he is nearly nuts because the wise guy has filled the seat of his pants with cactus spines an' stingin' nettles, an' every time the horse bumps Martinguez lets go a howl like he was demented. If you've ever sat on a cactus spine you'll get what I mean. I tell you this bad man was hard-hearted, but when they come to execute him his seat was so tender that hangin' was just a sweet relief."

"Very nice," she says, "an' who was the wise guy?"

"A palooka name of Caution," I tell her sorta modest. "Lemmy Caution was the name."

We go on drivin'. It is a lousy road an' I haveta concentrate. She don't say nothin'. Suddenly she puts her hand on my knee.

"You're a helluva man, Lemmy," she says. "After these guys . . ." She sorta sighs. "It's fine meeting you."

She looks at me sideways.

I keep my eye on the road. It looks to me like this dame is fallin' for me too fast even if she is a quick worker, but I play along.

"Gee, that's swell," I tell her. "I reckon you're the sorta dame I've been lookin' for. A swell dame an' a swell night," I say, noddin' my head at the moon, "an' what more could any guy ask?"

She don't say nothin'. She just lets go another big sigh. There is silence for a bit an' then she says:

"Listen, Lemmy, what's all this stuff about Granworth Aymes?"

"Oh, it ain't nothin' much," I tell her. "I ain't really interested in Aymes. I'm interested in a little counterfeit job that's sorta got mixed up with it. I'll tell you about it in a minute."

She don't answer an' I reckon she's doin' some heavy thinkin'. Pretty soon we pull up at the hacienda. The Mexican jane is waitin' in the doorway an' she takes my hat. The place is pretty swell inside—the furniture is good an' it looks like Paulette knows how to fix herself.

We go into some room on the right of the hallway. Paulette points to a big rocker chair that is standin' out on a veranda that runs along one side of the house. I go an' sit down an' give myself a cigarette an' she goes over an' starts mixin' high-balls. I can hear the ice clinkin'.

In a minute she comes over with a drink in each hand. She gives me mine an' sits herself down in a chair opposite me.

"Well, Lemmy," she says, "shoot."

I give her a cigarette an' light it. As I am holdin' the match she looks up into my eyes an' I'm tellin' you that I get an idea that she knows more about wireless telegraphy than Marconi. It was one helluva look. I go an' sit down again.

"Here's the way it is," I tell her. "This guy Granworth Aymes bumps himself off last January. Some time before he does this he has given his wife two hundred grand worth of Dollar Bonds. O.K. After his suicide she gets up to some dump near Palm Springs an' tries to cash one of these bonds at the bank. Well, it is phoney. I get stuck on this job an' I've been musclin' around plenty, but I ain't doin' myself any good. I know just as much about this thing as when I started on it."

While I am talkin' she is lookin' out across the Mesa. I can just see the outline of her face in the dark, but it don't tell me anythin'.

"Now I've got a hunch," I go on still watchin' her. "I've got a hunch that this dame Henrietta knows plenty about this counterfeitin' business, but I can't find any way to make this baby talk. While I am jumpin' around on this job Langdon Burdell who was secretary to Aymes give me an idea that Granworth didn't commit suicide at all; that he was bumped, and that Henrietta bumped him, an' between you an' me, honey, that's just the way it looks to me.

"But supposin' for the sake of argument I prove that she bumped Granworth an' pinch her for it, what good do I do. I still ain't goin' to find out where she got those phoney bonds an' who made 'em, because if she is stuck up on a first degree murder charge she knows durn well she ain't goin' to do herself no good or get any time off or save herself from the chair by squealin' about the counterfeitin'.

"O.K. Well, I find out that you used to get around with Granworth Aymes plenty, an' I reckon maybe you can help me on this job. If Aymes was stuck on you I reckon he told you plenty about Henrietta, because guys always tell the 'other woman' a lot, an' maybe you can slip me a little information rememberin' all the time that the thing I want to know is this:

"First, did Aymes give her the real bonds or did he slip her counterfeit ones? Second, did he slip her the real ones an' has she got 'em salted down some place an' got somebody to give her a duplicate set of phoney bonds so's she could have it both ways, takin' advantage of the fact that everybody would think she had the real ones an' therefore the phoney ones she was passin' was O.K.?"

I throw my cigarette stub over the veranda.

"So I want you to talk, Paulette," I tell her, "an' plenty, because they always say that the 'other woman' knows the works, an' it looks to me like you are the 'other woman'."

She turned round in her chair an' she looks at me.

"Nuts," she says. "It looks to me as if somebody's stringing you along, but I can certainly help you, Lemmy."

She gets up an' she stands leanin' against the veranda rail lookin' down at me.

"Listen, Mr. 'G' man," she says, "you can take it from me straight that Henrietta Aymes got those phoney bonds from some place and she knew they were phoney. I'll tell you why. Granworth Aymes didn't give her any 200,000 dollars worth of Registered Dollar Bonds. I know he didn't!"

"You don't say," I tell her. "But listen, honey," I go on. "We know he had got them bonds. We know he bought 'em. If he didn't give 'em to her, where are they? Who did he give 'em to?"

She starts laughin', a little soft gurglin' laugh that makes me think of all sorts of things.

"I'll tell you who he gave them to, Lemmy," she says. "He gave them to me."

Her face gets tense an' the smile goes off it.

"Now listen to me, big boy," she says. "I'm going to tell you plenty. If anybody says I was running around with Granworth Aymes then that person is a lousy liar. I knew Granworth Aymes and I'm not going to say that I disliked him in spite of the fact that he did my husband down for plenty. Now listen to this:

"Maybe they didn't tell you I've got a husband. He's away down at Zoni, living in a doctor's house. The poor guy's dying of consumption. They reckon he's got about three months to live.

"Granworth Aymes was his broker, an' two-three years ago my husband was worth nearly a quarter of a million dollars. He wasn't satisfied with that. He had to have some more, so he starts playin' the market with Aymes buying stocks and bonds. And what happens? He loses practically all the money he's got, but it wasn't till just before last Christmas that he found out that it hadn't been lost on the stock market. Aymes had taken him for it. He'd made a sucker outa the poor sap.

"Just at this time Rudy gets examined by a specialist. The specialist tells him that the only chance he's got if he wants to live even for another year is to come down and live in a place like this where the climate's right.

"Well, you can bet I didn't feel so good when I discovered that Granworth had practically grabbed off every bean that Rudy had in the world, so I reckoned I'd go along to New York and have a show-down with this Granworth Aymes. I reckoned this wasn't going to be too difficult because Granworth had always been trying to make play for me but I wasn't falling for it—I didn't like his style, at least not so's you'd notice it.

"I go along to New York, and I saw Granworth Aymes on the 10th January, two days before he committed suicide, and I told him straight that I had heard that he'd made a lot of money playing the market. I told him that unless he cashed in good and quick I wasn't going to waste any more time talking, I was going to the District Attorney and I was going to stick him behind the bars for defrauding Rudy over the last two years.

"Granworth had a look at me and he knew that I meant it. He told me to come back next morning. He said he'd give me the money. On the morning of the 11th January I went and saw him at his office and he gave me 200,000 dollars' worth of those Registered Bonds. He also told me to tell nobody about it because these were the bonds that he'd made over to his wife, that he'd got them out of the safe deposit where they were being kept for her, and that as they were bearer bonds anybody could cash them. I gave him a receipt for them and that's the money that Rudy and I came down here on. That's the money we're living on now.

"And if Granworth Aymes bumped himself off the day afterwards then I reckon it was because he had a show-down with his wife. I reckon she'd found that the bonds were gone and made it hot for him, or maybe—" she says sorta soft, "maybe Henrietta got annoyed. I reckon I'd get annoyed if he'd done me out of two hundred grand. Maybe she slugged him, you never know."

I whistle.

"Well, well, well," I say. "So that's the way it goes, hey? It looks like we've got this job cleaned up. So Henrietta, findin' that the bonds are gone, thinks that Granworth has got rid of 'em somewhere else an' promptly gets somebody to make her a new lot."

I give myself another cigarette.

"Listen, Paulette," I say. "Is there anybody who could confirm this story. I mean the part about Granworth Aymes makin' a sucker outa Rudy an' gettin' all that money off him?"

"Surely," she says, "Burdell can. He knows all about it. He knew what Aymes was doing, but he was only a secretary. It wasn't his business to butt in."

"O.K." I say. "I get it. It looks like this Henrietta Aymes is a pretty cute number," I say. "I don't reckon that there's any doubt that she bumped Granworth. All right. Now maybe I can get ahead. By the way, Paulette," I go on. "Did you say that this husband of yours, Rudy, is around here with some doctor? Where's this Zoni?"

"It's about forty miles away," she says, "and if you go and see Rudy and ask him any questions, go easy with him. The doctor, Madrales, says the poor guy's only got about another eight or nine weeks to go, and I don't want him worried too much."

I get up and put my arm around her shoulder.

"Don't you worry, Paulette," I say. "I'll go easy with him. I don't want to ask him anythin' much. I just wanta confirm that stuff you told me about Aymes takin' him for the dough."

She is standin' pretty close to me an' I can see some tears come into her eyes. I feel pretty sorry for Paulette, because after all even if she is kickin' around with this Luis Daredo, what's a dame to do? I reckon she has to do somethin' to keep her mind off the fact that her husband is slowly handin' in his checks.

She sighs.

"Life can be tough," she says. "Listen, Lemmy, go get yourself another drink. I'll be back in a minute. I got to ring Daredo, that guy's doing some business for me—I'm thinking of buying this place and he's fixing it—and I don't want to get in bad with him."

"O.K.," I say.

She goes outa the room an' I mix myself another high-ball an' go back to the veranda. Standin' there drinkin' it, it looks as if I am beginnin' to make some sense outa this case after all. One thing is stickin' out a foot an' that is that Henrietta found out that the original bonds—the real ones—was gone. She gets herself a phoney lot made an' she gets out to Palm Springs an' thinks she stands a chance of changin' 'em there. That's how it looks to me. I have just finished my drink when Paulette comes back. She comes straight up to me an' she puts her hands on my shoulders an' she looks straight into my eyes.

"You know, Lemmy," she says, "a woman has a tough time. I reckon I've had one. A girl has only got to make one mistake an' she pays plenty for it. Mine was in marrying Rudy. He was always a weakling and I guess I was sorry for him. If I'd have married a man like you," she says, "things might have been very different."

She comes a little closer to me.

"When you've got this job finished, Lemmy," she says, "if ever you're tired or you need a rest, you'll always find me down here an' I'll be glad to see you."

"That's swell, Paulette," I say. "That's a little matter I'll take up with you pretty soon. In the meantime I got this job finished, so I reckon I'll go over to Zoni an' have a few words with Rudy, an' I won't even be tough with him."

"All right, Lemmy," she says, an' I can see that her eyes are full of tears. "You get along and see Rudy and you can give him my love. Just don't say anything about you finding me with Luis Daredo to-night. I wouldn't want Rudy to get any ideas about my getting around with good-looking Mexicanos."

She tells me the way to get to this Zoni, an' she stands in the doorway watching me as I drive off.

Me—I am doing a little more thinkin'. I am wonderin' why she couldn'ta waited until we finished talkin' before she put that call through to Daredo.

I reckon that I am a sort of suspicious guy. An' I reckon that this Paulette fell for me too easy. She is certainly a swell number but she can still play me for a mug if she feels that way.

But I ain't such a sucker. Just when a dame thinks I'm fallin'—well, I usually ain't!

CHAPTER TEN
MEXICAN STUFF

I DRIVE along pretty slow for two reasons. First of all the night ain't so bright as it could be an' the road I am on is not so hot neither. Second I am turnin' over in my mind the stuff that this Paulette dame has handed out, an' it is sure one helluva story.

Maybe it's true because believe me no dame with as much sense as Paulette has got is goin' to spin a lotta hooey about takin' two hundred grand off a guy like Granworth Aymes unless she was surely entitled to it.

An' I feel pretty sorry for the husband—Rudy Benito. I get a picture of him all right. I can just imagine him stringin' along with Paulette, playin' second fiddle to her all the time an' knowin' that he had got T.B. an' that it was goin' to get him in the long run. I can sorta see this guy suddenly findin' out that Granworth has taken him for plenty an' gettin' good an' excited about it an' knowin' that maybe the amount of time that he'd got to stick around before he was due for a casket depended on whether he could get the dough out of Granworth.

But there is something that I cannot get an' it is this: What the hell was Paulette doin' all that time while Aymes was swindlin' Rudy out of his dough? What was a fly dame like that doin' stickin' around an' not gettin' wise to it?

An' then I get another big idea. Supposin' that Paulette was wise to it. Supposin' that she was stuck on Aymes an' knew that he was takin' Rudy for the dough an' didn't do anything about it. Then, all of a sudden she hears that Rudy is goin' to die unless he can get away some place where the climate is right an' have a doctor stickin' around all the time. An' she feels that she ain't been so hot. She feels that she has gotta do something to try an' put it right. Just at this time Aymes makes a killin' on the stock market an' Paulette weighs in an' tells him that unless he cashes in she is goin' to blow what he has been doin' to the cops.

Ain't that just the sorta thing that a dame would do? Wouldn't it be like a dame to make a sucker out of her husband because she fancies a bum guy like Aymes, but when she finds out that the sucker is goin' to die she goes all goofy an' tries at the last minute to put the job right, an' wouldn't this business be a first-class motive for Henrietta to knock off Granworth?

An' then something else hits me like a rock. What about that letter that Henrietta told me about. Didn't she say that she got an unsigned letter from some guy tellin' her that Granworth was playin' around with his wife. Didn't she say that this guy had crossed out the words "my wife" an' put in instead "this woman." Ain't you got it?

It was Rudy Benito who sent that letter to Henrietta.

Here's my new idea of the set-up: Benito gets a hunch that Aymes is playin' around with his wife, so he writes a letter to Henrietta and tells her so, but he don't sign it. O.K. Then Paulette discovers that Benito is as sick as a rat an' she gets all washed up an' hates herself for what she has been doin', so she goes along to Granworth an' tells him he has got to kick in with the dough.

Granworth, who thinks a durn sight more of Paulette than he does of Henrietta, hands over the dough. Maybe he thinks that he can get it back again off Paulette when she has got over this sorta sentimental stuff that has got into her about Rudy.

O.K. Then Henrietta comes along to New York an' tells Granworth that she hears he's kickin' around with a dame an' that if it don't stop she is goin' to divorce him. Granworth cracks back that if she does he will leave the country rather than pay her alimony. Henrietta says back that she don't give a durn if he pays her alimony or not because she has got the two hundred grand in Registered Bonds. Granworth gets inta one helluva rage an' tells her she ain't gotta dime because he has given the bonds to this other femme.

An' then the hey-hey starts. I reckon that this news just about finishes Henrietta. I reckon that when he tells her this Granworth is sittin' in his car just gettin' ready to drive off—maybe she is sittin' beside him. Well, she is so burned up that she just grabs something an' crowns Granworth. Then she finds she's killed him an' she works out that the best thing to do is to drive this guy down to the wharf an' put a good front up for the job bein' a suicide.

That's the way it looks.

By now the road I was on which was bad anyhow has got worse. It has got narrow an' is a sorta wide bridle path runnin' up between the foothills. It is plenty dark an' I cannot see very well, an' I am drivin' slow an' concentratin' on the road.

Then I hit something. I hit a coupla rocks that are stuck in the middle of the road an' at the same time somebody jumps on the runnin' board an' hits me a smack across the dome with something that feels to me just like the Mexican for a blackjack. I see more stars than ever told a movie director where he got off an' I just go right out as graceful an' as quiet as a baby.

When I come to I am as stiff as an iron girder. The guys who have brought me along to this place ain't been at all gentle with me. I am covered with dust an' there is a trickle of blood down my coat where I have been bleedin' from the crack in the dome.

My feet are tied up with cord an' my hands are tied across my chest with enough manilla rope to have started a marine store.

I am in some dump that looks like the basement cellar of a small house. There is a candle burnin' on a shelf on the other side of the room an' I can just see the watch on my wrist. It is nearly eleven-thirty o'clock, so I reckon I have been out for about an hour. I have been just chucked up against the wall an' left there.

I don't feel so good. My head is buzzin' plenty an' I reckon that who ever took a flop at me with that club was pullin' his weight all right. Altogether it looks like I am in a jam. Just who has taken a fancy to me like this so that they have to corral me an' chuck me in this dump I don't know, although I have gotta pretty good idea. I reckon I had better get some action pronto.

I work myself up against the wall an' get as easy as I can after which I start singin' Cactus Lizzie good an' loud. This sorta works because after five-ten minutes I hear somebody comin' down some steps an' then the door in the corner opens an' some Mexican dame busts in.

She is carryin' a lantern, an' she looks like a coupla tarantulas who don't like each other, an' she weighs about three hundred pounds. I reckon that this dame is about the biggest ever. She waddles over to me an' she lifts up her foot an' she kicks me in the face like I was a baseball. I'm tellin' you that this daughter of a hellion cops me right on the top of the nose with a boot that a New York flatfoot woulda been proud to wear an' I just see a lot more stars an' I go as sick as hell an' go out again.

I come round pretty soon. I am drenched with dirty water that she has thrown over me an' my face is bleedin' like smoke an' she stands there lookin' at me an' havin' one helluva time.

Then she starts in. She starts bawlin' me out in a sorta bastard Spanish that I can just understand by keepin' my ears flappin' wide open. She tells me all about me. She tells me what I am an' what she hopes is going to happen to me an' what my father an' mother was an' the amazin' an' extraordinary way that I was born. After which she spills some stuff an' I begin to get the idea.

She tells me that she is durn glad that I have come around here doin' my stuff all over the place. She tells me that directly I got my foot inside the Casa de Oro some guy recognised me as the dick who pulled in Caldesa Martinguez—the guy who I took back with stingin' nettles in his pants. She tells me that this Caldesa was her son an' that by the time they are through with me, bein' boiled in prohibition whisky would just be sweet dreamin' to what I am goin' to go through. She tells me to stick around an' that in a coupla minutes, after he has got through thinkin' up just what he is goin' to do to me, her other son is comin' down to start operations.

By this time I reckon I am feelin' pretty annoyed with this lousy old eagle an' I tell her the equivalent of nuts in Spanish. Just at this minute the candle lantern she is holdin' decides to go out. She says a nasty word an' just chucks it at me, an' sure as a gun it hits me on the side of the head an' knocks me back in the corner.

Me—I am beginnin' to get good an' tired of bein' treated this way. I am beginnin' to wonder just who my pan really does belong to, because the way it is feelin' I must look as ugly as a gargoyle, an' I am beginnin' to realise that this old dame don't like me at all, an' that if she is just playin' around with me I wonder what her big boy son is goin' to do to me when he gets around to it sorta serious.

She calls me a dirty so-an'-so an' she scrams.

I wait for a bit an' then I look around an' start workin'. The floor of this dump is earth except in the corner where I am where there is a sorta cement patch. There are plenty of cracks in this patch an' I reckon that if I get enough time maybe I can get rid of the rope.

I start workin' myself around until I have got the lantern between me and the wall an' then I start pushin' it against the wall with my legs an' when I have got it there I put my feet against it an' press hard. It busts an' the broken glass falls out.

I roll over on my stomach an' work towards the biggest bit of glass. You gotta realise that I am lyin' on my hands which are tied across my chest an' I am hurtin' myself plenty. After a bit I get to where the biggest bit of glass is an' I start lickin' this with my tongue, lickin' it along the floor to where there is a little crack, an' I'm tellin' you that the taste of that floor wasn't like no raspberry soda neither. Every time I get this bit of glass moved an inch or so I have to start rollin' again so as to get in position for another lick, but after about twenty minutes I do it. I lick it so's it falls into the crack an' the crack bein' shallow I have fixed that a spike of glass is stickin' up outa the floor.

I get my legs over this spike an' after a bit I push the rope down over it an' start workin' it about an' after workin' like hell I manage to saw through the rope that is tyin' my legs.

I stand up an' move around quietly, stretchin' my legs. I start workin' my hands about tryin' to move the rope that is tyin' me but I can't do it. I can just fix to wiggle two or three fingers of my right hand that is not tied by the rope, but I can't do anything else, so I reckon I have gotta think something else up.

I think about this an' then I go an' I stand just behind the door, so's I'm goin' to be ready for whoever opens it. I stand there leanin' up against the wall an' hopin' that I am goin' to get a break because, believe me, an' I know, there ain't anybody as cruel as Mexicans when it comes down to cases.

After about half an hour I hear somebody comin' down the steps outside, an' I reckon that by the sound if it is a guy this time.

I get ready. I think I am goin' to surprise this guy, I am countin' on the fact that the old palooka who threw the lantern at me has told him that I am all out for none in the corner.

As he opens the door I take a pace back, an' as he steps into the room I kick him straight in the guts an' I don't kick soft neither I'm tellin' you.

This guy who is a big bum with whiskers an' side burns, gives a funny sorta whine an' just flops down on the floor. He is hurt plenty for which I am very pleased.

I reckon that I have gotta work quick. I close the door quietly with my foot, an' then I get to work on this guy. I turn him over an' over with my feet, until I have got him away from the door. He is still makin' funny whinin' noises an' he is crazy with pain. I reckon I have given him something to think about.

When I get him on his face I see that he has gotta knife in the usual place—stuck in his pants waistband at the back. I get down on my knees an' work this knife out with the bits of fingers that I have got stickin' out of the rope that is tyin' me, an' when I have got it in between the tops of my fingers I get up an' turn this guy over on his back again.

I get up an' I go over to the door. I stick the point of the knife into the door an' I press my chest against the handle. This way I have got the knife fixed so that I can rub the edge of the blade against the ropes that are around my chest. In another few minutes I cut the rope. The guy on the floor is not so good. He has rolled over into the corner, I reckon I needn't worry about this guy. He is hurt plenty.

I go over to him an' search him because I wanta find the Luger that they have taken off me, but he ain't got it. I leave him, open the door an' start gumshoein' up the stone steps. These steps lead up to the ground floor an' at the top I find another door that opens out into what looks like a rough sorta kitchen. There ain't anybody there, but I am very glad to see that my Luger is lyin' on the table in the corner. I cannot see my shoulder holster which they have taken off me, so I don't worry about it. I just stick the gun in my right hand coat pocket, a business which I am goin' to be very pleased about a little later on.

I look around an' I listen, but I can't hear a thing. I think that maybe there was only one guy in this business—the guy down-stairs—an' that he was the palooka who knocked me out an' drove me here. I got a hunch that the old dame has gone off to tell their pals that they have got me spread-eagled, an' I think I had better get outa this quick before somebody else starts something.

I also think that I had better get my business done around here in Mexico just as pronto as I can, otherwise some of these guys are goin' to start makin' one big mess of Mrs. Caution's little boy an' I certainly am not partial to that.

I scram outa the house an' stuck around at the back behind a horse-shack I find the car, an' believe me I am plenty glad to find it. I get in an' start off back again an' get on the road to get to Zoni. I am feelin' pretty lousy, my nose is hurtin' considerable where the old Mexican dame kicked it, an' generally I could do with a shot of rye.

It is three o'clock when I get to Zoni. It is the usual sorta one-horse-near-village with a few ranchos an' shacks stuck around. I pull up an' sittin' in the car I clean myself up as well as I can. Then I start lookin' around. Away over on my left is a white painted house in front of some trees. It is a two story place shaped like an "L" an' it looks to me that this is goin' to be the doctor's house, the place where Rudy Benito is hangin' out.

I drive over an' leave the car in front of this place. Then I bang on the door. A guy opens it. He is a young Mexican an' he is wearin' a white coat. He also looks as if he washed sometimes which is a good sign. An' he also looks very surprised to see me. I reckon he is right because I must have looked a funny sight.

I tell him that I want to see Señor Madrales, an' that the matter is very urgent even if it is in the middle of the night. He says all right an' tells me to go in. I go in. I am in a big hallway with doors leading off left an' right. In front of me is some stairs runnin' up to the first floor. The guy in the white coat tells me to sit down an' goes off.

Pretty soon he comes back an' with him is another guy who says that he is Doctor Madrales an' what do I want. He speaks swell Spanish. He is a tall thin guy; he has got a little pointed beard an' he wears eyeglasses. He is a clever lookin' cuss with long thin taperin' fingers which he rubs together while he is talkin' to me.

I tell him what I want. I tell him I am an insurance investigator an' that I am makin' some inquiries into the suicide of Granworth Aymes. I tell him I have had a conversation with Mrs. Benito an' that she has said that I oughta have a few words with her husband Rudy. I say what about it an' I hope that this Rudy ain't to ill to be woke up as I have not got a lotta time to waste.

He shrugs his shoulders.

"I don't think it matters whether my patient is awake or not, Señor," he says. "As Mrs. Benito has probably told you he is a very sick man. I am afraid that he will not be long with us."

He shrugs his shoulders again.

"It is, I think, merely a matter of a month or so. However, he is very weak and I suggest that you talk to him as quietly as possible. If you will wait here for a moment I will go and prepare him. I think I had better give him an injection before you see him."

He goes off.

While I am waiting I am doing some quiet thinkin'. I am thinkin' about this bezusus about bein' smacked over the dome while I was comin' out here an' I am thinkin' that it is durn funny that somebody should have recognised me in the Casa de Oro as being the guy who pinched Caldesa Martinguez. I have got a coupla ideas about this as you will see later on.

After a bit this Madrales comes to the top of the stairs. He says I am to go up. At the top of the stairs is another passage an' we go into a room on the left. One side of the room is practically all windows which are open, an' in one corner there is a screen. On the other side of the room pushed up against the wall is a low bed.

I look at the guy in the bed. He is lyin' there lookin' straight up at the ceilin'. He has got a thin funny sorta face an' there is a funny strained sorta look about it.

There is very little furniture in the room. Beside the bed there is a low table with a polished top an' there are some bottles on it an' a lamp. Madrales goes over an' stands by the side of the bed.

"Benito," he says, "this is Mr. Caution. He wants to ask you some questions. Just keep very quiet and don't worry about anything."

The man in the bed don't say anythin'. Madrales walks over to the other side of the room an' brings a chair. He sticks it by the side of the bed for me. Then he says:

"Señor Caution, I will leave you now. I know that you will treat my patient with as much consideration as is possible."

He goes off still rubbin' his hands together.

I go an' stand over by the bed. The sick guy turns his eyes so that they are lookin' at me an' his lips break into a little sorta smile.

I am feelin' plenty sorry for this guy. It looks to me like he has had a pretty low deal all round. I talk to him nice an' quiet.

"Listen, Rudy," I tell him. "Take it easy. I am sorry I gotta come over here askin' you things, but that's just the way it goes. I'm goin to make it as short as possible. I just wanta check up on what that swell wife of yours Paulette has been tellin' me to-night, an' while I think of it I gotta tell you that she sent you her love. I reckon maybe she'll be along in the mornin' to see you. Well, here's the way it goes.

"It's about this Granworth Aymes business. Your wife tells me that Granworth was takin' you for plenty since you was doin' business with him as a stockbroker. She says that you found it out, that she went an' saw Aymes an' gave him the choice of cashin' in or else she was goin' to the cops.

"She says that Granworth turned over two hundred grand in Registered Dollar Bonds to her an' that's the money you got now, the money that paid for you to be brought down here. Is that O.K. Rudy?"

He speaks very quiet. His voice sounds as if it was comin' from a long way away.

"Sure," he says slowly, "that's how it was, an' I am durned glad Aymes bumped himself off. If I hadn't been sick I would have liked to have shot that lousy guy."

"O.K. Rudy," I tell him, "that's that. An' there's just one little thing I wanta ask you an' maybe I'm sorry I've got to ask you it because I don't wanta make things tough for you right now. It's this way. Henrietta Aymes, Granworth's wife, got an unsigned letter from some guy. This letter tells her that Granworth is playin' around with this guy's wife."

I speak to him nice an' soft.

"Listen, Rudy," I say, "did you send her that letter? It musta been you. What about it?"

There is a long pause. Then he turns his eyes over towards me again.

"That's right," he says. "I sent it. I just had to do something."

I nod my head.

"Look," I say, "I reckon we're cleanin' this job up pretty swell. I don't wanta make you talk too much. You tell me if I'm right in my ideas. The way I look at it is this. Maybe your wife Paulette thought she was a bit stuck on Aymes. Maybe because you was sick you couldn't give her the sorta attention that a dame like she likes to have, so she falls for Aymes. O.K. Aymes thinks he's on a durn good thing. He starts doin' you left an' right for your dough an' maybe the reason that you don't find it out is that your wife Paulette is lookin' after your business, an' because she an' Aymes are gettin' around together it's easy for him to pull the wool over her eyes. She don't see he's takin' you for your dough because she don't wanta see it. Got me?

"An' then the works bust. All of a sudden at the end of last year she finds you're not so well. She hears that you're a durn sick man an' that there's got to be dough to get you down here to get you looked after. Maybe she finds out that you've got an idea about what's goin' on. Maybe you even tell her that you've sent that unsigned letter to Henrietta Aymes.

"She sees she's been pullin' a lousy one an' she tells you that she is goin' back to get that dough out of Aymes if it's the last thing she does. Am I right?"

He turns his eyes my way again.

"You're dead right, Caution," he says. "We had a big scene. I told her what I thought about her. I said it was pretty tough for me being sick to think that she was running around with a guy who had swindled me. Well, that broke her up. I reckon she was sorry, and you know"—I see a little smile come around his lips—"I haven't very long to be around, and I don't want to feel that I'm making things tough for anybody. She told me she'd put the job right. She told me she'd get the money from Aymes and that she was through with him once and for all, and she made good. She got it."

He starts coughin'. I give him a drink of the water that is by the side of the bed. He smiles at me to say thank you.

"I'm a dying man, Caution," he says, "and I know you've got to do your job, but there's one thing you can do for me." His voice gets weaker. "Just you try and keep the fact that Paulette was getting around with Aymes out of this," he says. "I'd like you to do that for me. I wouldn't like people to know that she preferred a dirty double-crosser like Aymes to me."

He smiles at me again. He is a piteous sorta guy.

"O.K. Rudy," I say, "that's a bet. I'll play it that way. It won't hurt anybody. Well, I'll be gettin' along. So long an' good luck to you."

I turn an' I start walkin' towards the door. When I am half-way I see something, somethin' that is just stickin' out behind the edge of the screen that is on the other side of the room. It is a waste-paper basket and when I see it an' what is in it, I get a sorta funny idea, such a funny idea that I have to take a big pull at myself. When I get to the door I turn around and I look at Rudy. His eyes are still lookin' straight up at the ceilin' an' he looks half-dead right now.

"So long, Rudy," I say again. "Don't you worry about Paulette. I'll fix that O.K."

Downstairs in the hall I meet Madrales.

"Listen, Doctor," I say, "everythin' has been swell, but there is just one little thing I am goin' to ask you to do for me. I have got all the information I want from Benito. I got my case complete but I have got to have a signed statement from him, because he is the guy who was swindled. Can you lend me a typewriter and some paper an' if you'll just get him to sign it I needn't worry him no more."

"But surely, Señor Caution," he says, "come with me."

He takes me into some room off the hall which is like a doctor's office. In the corner on a table is a typewriter. I sit down at this machine an' I type out a statement incorporatin' everything that Benito has said. When I have finished I go out to Madrales an' we go upstairs. It is a tough job gettin' this guy Benito to sign it. The doctor has to hold his hand because it is shakin' so much that he can hardly hold the pen, but he does it. I stick the statement in my pocket and say so long to these guys an' I scram.

As I start up the car I look at my watch. It is twenty minutes past four.

I have got one helluva hunch. I have got an idea in my head that is considerably funny, an' I am goin' to play this idea. Even if I'm wrong I'm still goin' to play it.

When I have got well away from the Madrales dump I pull up the car an' do some very heavy thinkin'. I am checkin' up on the idea that is in my head. I have got a very funny hunch an' I am goin' to play it in a very funny sorta way.

I reckon that I am goin' to take a look around at Paulette's hacienda, an' I reckon I ain't goin' to tell her either. I am just goin' to do a little quiet house-bustin' just to see if I can get my claws on somethin' that I would like very much to find.

I pull the gun outa my pocket an' lay it right by me. I reckon that if anybody else tries anything on me to-night they are goin' to get it where they won't like it.

The moon has come out again. It is a swell night. Drivin' along back on the Sonoyta road I get thinkin' about dames an' what they do when they are in a jam.

Did I tell you that dames get ideas to do things that a guy would never even think of?

You're tellin' me!

Chapter Eleven
PINCH NO. 1

I DON'T drive up to the Hacienda. When I get to within a quarter of a mile of it I pull off the road an' start drivin' round over the scrub. I make a wide circle, drivin' the car slow an' keepin' in top gear so as I don't make too much noise, an' I come up two-three hundred yards behind the house.

I stick the car behind a cactus clump an' I start workin' towards the house keepin' well under cover. I work right round the house in a circle but I can't see anybody or hear anythin' at all.

Then I get a hunch. Keepin' well in the scrub, I start workin' along the side of the road that leads from the hacienda to the State road intersection, an' I keep my eyes well skinned. After about five minutes I hear a horse neigh. I work up towards this sound an' I find a black horse tied up to a joshua tree about fifty yards off the road.

It is a good horse an' on it there is a Mexican leather an' wood saddle with silver trimmin's. There is a little silver plate just behind the saddle horn an' on this plate are the initials L.D.

When I see these initials I know that my hunch is right an' that Señor Luis Daredo is stickin' around waitin' for me somewhere. Way down on the edge of the road about a hundred yards away there is a patch of scrub an' cactus, an' I reckon I'll find him down there. I start crawlin' that way, an' when I get there I see I am right.

Luis has picked himself a good place. He has picked a place where the road is very bad an' narrow an' full of cart ruts. He is sittin' way back twenty yards off the road behind a big cactus. He is smokin' an' he is nursin' a 30.30 rifle across his knees.

I come up behind him an' I bust him a good one in the ear. He goes over sideways. I pull the Luger on him an' pick up his rifle.

He sits up. He is smilin' a sorta sickly smile an' he is lookin' at the Luger. I reckon he thinks that I am goin' to give him the works.

I sit down on a rock an' look at him.

"You know, Luis," I tell him, "you ain't got no sense, an' I'm surprised at you because Mexicans are about the only people in the world who can keep themselves one jump ahead of a very clever dame like Paulette Benito. An' I'm surprised at you because you didn't tell that guy that smacked me over the head when I was drivin' to Zoni to finish me off pronto, because I reckon it woulda saved a lotta trouble for you guys. When that old battle-axe started tellin' me that somebody had spotted me down at the Casa de Oro as the guy who took in Caldesa Martinguez, an' that she was his mother, I knew that she was talkin' a lotta hooey because I happen to know that Martinguez's mother was dead years before. I knew that you was behind the job all right, an' it's goin' to annoy you plenty before I'm through."

He gets up an' he lights a cigarette.

"Señor Caution," he says, "believe me you got what they call theese wrong ideas. Sabe? I don't know nothin' about some peoples who do sometheeng to you. I am jus' sittin' here waitin' for a gringo who work for me, see? I don't know what the hell you theenk you are talkin'. Sabe?"

"You don't say," I tell him. "Just fancy that now. O.K. Well you just listen to my renderin' of this little piece. I reckon that you're stringin' along with Paulette Benito. I reckon that Granworth Aymes wasn't the only guy that she took Rudy Benito for a ride over. I reckon you're number two. I gotta hunch that you two are just waitin' around for Rudy to die off an' then you an' Paulette was goin' to get hitched up. Well, you ain't—savvy?"

I think I will try this guy out. I get up off the rock an' I put my gun in the pocket, an' I make out that I am goin' to get myself a cigarette outa my pocket, an' he tries it. He takes a flyin' kick at my guts an' I am waitin' for him. I do a quick side-step, smack up his foot as it shoots at me an' bust him as he goes down.

We mix it, an' I get goin' on this guy. I am rememberin' that old sour-puss of a Mexican dame kickin' me in the face an' throwin' the lantern at me, an' I am also rememberin' just what the guy who came down to the cellar to fix me woulda done if he'd got the chance.

I bust this Luis like hell. I close both his eyes an' crack some teeth out. I twist his nose till it looks like it is as tender as mine is, an' generally I give him more short arm stuff than I have ever issued any guy with for a helluva long time.

Then I chuck him in the cactus. He is all washed up an' he don't even care that a cactus spine is stickin' in his leg. He just ain't got any interest in life at all. I go over an' take a look at him an' it looks to me like I won't have any more trouble with him for quite a little while. So I go back to where his horse is, take off the bridle, the bellyband an' the stirrup leathers, an' I come back an' I make a nice job of Luis. I tie him up so neat that I think it will take him about a coupla years to get outa this tie-up.

I take a knife off him which he has got an' his rifle an' I chuck 'em in a hole an' bury 'em. I take his pants off him an' bury 'em too. I do this because I reckon that even if he managed to get outa this tie-up he wouldn't be much good without pants—it would sort of affect his morale.

Then I go back to the Hacienda. I work round the back an' I bust in through a window that is easy. I reckon that Paulette an' the Mexican jane will be sleepin' upstairs, but I am still careful not to make any noise. The light is good an' I can see plenty. I am in a sorta kitchen at the back an' I get outa this an' gumshoe along the passage openin' doors an' lookin' in as I pass rooms. One is a bedroom that ain't bein' used an' one is a sorta store-room.

After a bit I get into the room where I was talkin' with Paulette before I went to Zoni, an' I look around. I am lookin' for somethin' that looks like a safe or a place where papers would be kept.

After a bit I find it. It is a wall safe behind a picture on the wall. It is let into the wall an' it has got a combination lock. I don't worry about the lock because after all the wall is only wood. So I get back to the kitchen an' get myself a can-opener an' a strong carvin' knife that I find there an' I start diggin' around the hinges of this safe until I have burst them off. After about a quarter of an hour I fix it. I get the safe open.

Inside there are two-three boxes with some jewellery in them an' a lotta papers. I leave the boxes an' I take the papers over to the veranda an' I start lookin' through 'em. After a bit I find what I want. It is a share transfer authorising the transfer of some shares in a railway company from Rudy Benito to Granworth Aymes. It is witnessed by Paulette.

I look through this pretty carefully, then I stick it in my pocket. I take the rest of the papers back to the safe an' I put 'em back like they was before an' fix the safe as well as I can, an' I put the picture back in front of it.

I am pretty pleased with the night's work one way an' another. I reckon I'll get this job cleaned up pretty soon. I look out over the mesa. It is near time that dawn was breakin' an' there's that peculiar sorta half light that comes between night an' mornin'.

On the table there is a box of cigarettes. I take one out an' light it. Then I go over to the sideboard. I give myself a drink. I have just sunk half the liquor when a light is snapped on. I turn around an' standin' in the doorway I see Paulette.

She is wearin' a very swell blue silk dressin' robe. Her ash-blonde hair is down an' is tied up with a ribbon. She stands there smilin' a funny sorta little smile, in her hand she has got a .38 Colt.

I finish the drink.

"Well, well, well, Paulette," I say. "Just fancy seein' you again so soon."

She comes into the room. She is still holdin' the gun on me.

"So you're back, Mr. 'G' man," she says very quiet, still smilin'. "Why don't you knock on the door when you want to come into a place?"

I take a drag on the cigarette.

"I'll tell you why, baby," I tell her. "I came back here because I had a big idea I might take a look around an' find somethin' I wanted, but I am sorry you interrupted me first. But there is just one little thing I'd like to know, Paulette. Why don't you put that gun away?"

She laughs.

"Maybe you'd like me to, Lemmy," she says. "I expect you would. You know I think you've had enough luck for to-night. Maybe it's time you had a little bad luck."

"You're tellin' me," I tell her. "Listen, Paulette," I say, "ain't you the mug? The worst thing about you dames is that you always overplay your hand. You're the sorta woman who would come in on a poker game with a pair of two's just hopin' that the other guys would think you'd gotta full house, but you made a big mistake to-night. You shouldn't have 'phoned through to Daredo.

"When some guy bumps me over the head on the road to Zoni, an' takes me off to some place to give me the works, I was wise that that was the telephone call you put through to Daredo, an' why? Well, there can only be one reason an' that reason was that you thought it would be pretty dangerous for yourself if I got as far as Zoni an' saw Rudy. So you fixed with Luis Daredo to get me before I got there.

"By the time I have got to Zoni an' seen Rudy, Luis' pals have wised him up that I have got away, so knowin' that I'll take this road back to get on to the main State road, he sits behind a clump of cactus way down from the house an' waits for me with a rifle.

"Well, it just didn't work. I have bust Luis good an' plenty, an' he's pretty sick right now."

She is still smilin'.

"That doesn't really matter, does it, Lemmy?" she says. "I'm still on top of the game."

"You're tellin' me," I tell her. "But what's the good of you bein' on top of the game. Where do we go from here? Listen, Paulette," I say, "why don't you get yourself some sense? What do you think you're goin' to do with that gun? Do you think you're goin' to shoot me? How come? Be your age."

She laughs out loud this time, an' she looks as sweet as pie. I'll tell you this Paulette has got one helluva nerve.

"Aren't you being a sap, Lemmy?" she says. "And do you think you'll be the first dick who's been killed in Mexico and not missed. I'm goin' to kill you, Lemmy, not because I particularly want to, because in several ways I find you rather attractive, but I think you're a little bit too consistent for my way of thinking. You're obstinate you know. You're the sort of man who would go on working and working, following his nose so to speak, until he might do all sorts of things that might even be inconvenient for me. I'm choosing the lesser of the two evils."

I flop down in a chair. She is standin' in the middle of the room right under the electric light. I look at the gun in her hand.

It is as steady as a rock. I reckon this dame will kill me without even battin' an eyelid.

I don't feel so good. I am burned up that just when I am gettin' ideas about this job that I should be ironed out by some dame. Me—I never thought that I would be bumped by a dame.

"You know, Paulette," I tell her. "I think you're bein' silly. What you got to bump me for? What harm can I do you? I don't get this sorta business at all."

She just smiles.

"Well," she says, "here it comes, Lemmy. I'm going to give it to you. And I'll try and do it so that it won't hurt too much. How will you have it—sitting down or standing up?"

"Justa minute, Paulette," I say. "There is just a little thing I wanta say to you before you start the heat."

"All right, Lemmy," she says. "I'm listening. Go right ahead, but don't be too long."

I start thinkin'. I think as quick as hell. You gotta remember that earlier in the evenin' I told you that Paulette came an' put her hands on my shoulders when she was talkin' to me. When she took her hands away she sorta let 'em drop down the sides of my coat an' her right hand rested for a minute on my Luger which was in it's shoulder holster under my left arm. O.K. Well, maybe she will think that the gun is still there. She won't know that the Mexicans pinched the holster off me an' that I have got the gun in my right hand coat pocket.

I get up. I let my hands hang loose by my sides.

"Well, well, well, Paulette," I say. "If I've gotta have it I reckon I'll have it standin' up. Maybe you're not very keen on doin' anythin' for me, but there are two favours I would like to ask you. One is that I would like to have another shot of that bourbon of yours before I hand in my checks an' the other thing is that I would like you some time or other to send my Federal badge to a dame in Oklahoma. I'll give you the address. You don't have to send it now. Send it in a year's time if you like, but I sorta feel that I'd like her to have it."

She laughs again.

"Just fancy now," she says, "the tough 'G' man getting sentimental about a woman."

I shrug my shoulders.

"That's the way it is," I say.

I turn round an' I walk over to the sideboard. I pour myself out a shot of bourbon, an' I drink it. I put the glass back on the sideboard, an' I turn around.

"O.K. Paulette," I say, "here's the badge. I'll leave it on this table."

I put my hand sorta quite natural in my right hand coat pocket, an' I fire through my coat. I fire at the electric lamp an' I get it. Right at the same moment I drop on my knees an' I hear Paulette fire three times. I take a leap forward like I was a runner gettin' off the mark, an' hit her clean in the belly with my head. She goes over backwards, I grab her arm an' twist the gun out of it.

"O.K. baby," I say. "Now let's take it easy."

"Damn you, Lemmy," she says. "What a fool I was to even give you a chance."

"You're tellin' me," I say. "Why you didn't plug me while I was drinkin' that bourbon I don't know. Still I never did know a dame who was really swell with a gun."

She don't say nothin'. She is just breathin' hard. I throw her gun over the veranda an' still holdin' her by the arm I walk over to the electric standard lamp that is in the other corner of the room an' I switch it on. Then I take a look at her. She is still smilin' but it is a hard sorta smile.

"Well, here's where we go, lady," I say. "I reckon you played your hand as well as you could an' it didn't quite come off. You know," I tell her, "if you'd had any sense you'da shot me while I was drinkin' that bourbon. Then I'da been nice an' dead by now. Then you coulda got your friend Luis to chuck me in some hole around here an' nobody would have ever known that that big bad wolf Lemmy Caution had come bustin' around annoyin' poor little Paulette. Tough luck, baby!"

"That's as maybe," she says—her voice is sorta tense—"but I'll be glad to know what you're charging me with. You say you're a Federal Agent, but I've no proof of that. I've never even seen your badge. I find you here in my house in the middle of the night. I'm entitled to take a shot at you. This is Mexico."

"That's O.K.," I say. "An' maybe you could get away with a story like that. But I ain't worryin' about them shots you had at me. I woulda worried if they'd got me an' they didn't. I ain't pinchin' you for them shots. I'm pinchin' you for something else."

She flops down on a chair an' she starts cryin'. The way she is sittin' her robe has fallen back a bit an' I can see a piece of leg. I get to thinkin' that this Paulette sure has got legs that are easy to look at. I don't say nothin'. I just stick around waitin' for her to try an' pull somethin' else.

After a bit she stops cryin' an' looks up at me. She looks sweller than ever. She sorta smiles through the two big teardrops that are hangin' in her eyes. I'm tellin' you that this Paulette is one helluva actress, an' I would back her, under ordinary luck, to kid a Bowery tough that he was travellin' in ladies' powder puffs an' likin' it.

"Get me a drink, Lemmy," she says.

I go over an' get her one. I give her a strong one. I reckon she needs it, an' she will need it more before I am through with her. I take it back to her an' watch her while she is drinkin' it.

She puts the glass down.

"I know I've been a fool, Lemmy," she says, sorta soft, with her eyes lookin' at the floor, "but you must try and understand. I told you how I felt about Rudy, and I had an idea that you were going over there to put him through the mill. I knew that once there you would drag up all that old stuff and remind him of something that I wanted him not to remember just now—that I'd made a fool of myself over Granworth Aymes. I didn't want him to be bothered just at the time when he is dying and trying to think all the best things of me that he can. So I telephoned Daredo. I told him to get somebody to wait for you and hold you somewhere so that you couldn't get at Rudy. But I told him that I didn't want you hurt."

Some tears started runnin' down her face again.

"You bet I didn't want you hurt," she goes on. "I don't expect you to believe me, Lemmy, but I'm telling you that, even though I've only known you for a few hours, I felt that you are the sort of man who might really mean something in my life."

She looks up an' her eyes are swimmin'.

"Don't you see, Lemmy," she says. "Don't you see . . . I love you!"

I look at this dame with my mouth floppin' open. I reckon that when they was issuin' out nerve they issued this kiddo with enough to run the Marines on. Here is a dame who has just been on the point of blastin' me down with a .38 gun an' she is now tellin' me that she loves me!

An' the joke is that the dame has got somethin'. She has got that sorta thing that makes you wanta believe her even though you know all the time that she is a first-class four-flushin' double-dealin' twicin' sister of Satan who would take a sleepin' man for the gold stoppin' in his right hand eye tooth.

I look at her an' wonder. Maybe you heard about that classy dame Cleopatra who slipped a bundle into Marc Antony when the guy wasn't lookin'. Maybe you heard of Madame de Pompadour who had the King of France so heel-tied that he thought backwards just so's he wouldn't ever come up for air an' know he was nuts.

Well, I'm tellin' you that this Paulette was born outa her time. She oughta been born in the Middle Ages just so's she coulda pulled a fast one on Richard Cœur de Lion an' kidded him that he was a Roman gladiator with knock-knees. This dame is so good that she almost believes herself.

"Listen, honeybunch," I tell her. "So far as I am concerned I reckon it is a great pity that you didn't find all this stuff about lovin' me out before you started that act with the gun. An' I can catch on that you certainly didn't want me around at Zoni askin' Rudy questions an' findin' out one or two things about you—such as the fact that you was stringin' around with Granworth Aymes; that he was your sugar daddy an' that you was the guy who helped pull the wool over the eyes of that poor sap of a husband of yours while Granworth was doin' the big plunderin' act.

"An' do you think that I don't know why you are pullin' this lovin' wife act now. I reckon it is because you wanted to make certain that you was goin' to have the dough after Rudy's dead. It wouldn'ta been so hot for you if he'd left it to somebody else because he didn't like your bein' Granworth's lovin' baby, huh? It woulda been tough if after kiddin' Granworth into handin' back the dough he'd pinched from Rudy, an' then dyin' an' gettin' himself outa the way, Rudy told you to take a bite of air an' handed over the money to some home for Mangy Rattlesnakes. That woulda been too much for you, wouldn't it?

"So you start doin' a big act with Rudy. You make out that you are the naughty little wife who only wants her sick husband to forgive her so's she can start all over, an' the poor mutt does it, an' even while he is dyin' you are kickin' around with that lousy gringo Luis Daredo."

She don't say nothin'. I just watch her like a snake just to see how she is takin' all this hooey that I am handin' out to her. She sits there lookin' at me with the tears runnin' down her face.

"O.K. Paulette," I tell her. "You an' me is goin' upstairs an' you are goin' to get yourself dressed an' then we are goin' places, an' don't try anything on willya, because I would just hate to get really tough with you."

She sticks her chin up.

"Supposing I refuse to go," she says. "I'm an American citizen and I've rights. Where's your warrant? Where are you going to take me? I want a lawyer."

"Baby," I tell her. "Don't get me annoyed. I ain't got any warrant but I have got a very big hand an' if I have any more hooey outa you I am goin' to put you across my knees an' I am goin' to knock sparks outa that portion of your chassis that was made for slidin' on. As for wantin' a lawyer, as far as I care you can have six hundred lawyers all workin' overtime with wet towels round their domes, but even that mob couldn't get you outa the jam you're in. So take it easy an' be a good girl otherwise I'm goin' to smack you plenty."

I take her upstairs an' I stick around while she gets her things on. After this I look around for the Mexican jane but she ain't there, so it looks as if she has scrammed some place.

Paulette ain't sayin' a thing. She just looks like hell. When she is ready I take her outa the house an' back to where the car is. In the car I got a coupla pair of police bracelets an' I shackle up Paulette an' stick her in the back so's she can't move.

I get in the car an' start off. I reckon I have gotta move plenty quick otherwise some of Daredo's pals may get around an' find him an' he might decide to start something else. I would like to take this Luis Daredo along too, but you gotta realise that this guy is a Mexican an' I do not want to start any complications, so I reckon I will take a chance about him not startin' anything when I have gone.

I tread on it an' get ahead as fast as I can. I pull on to the main road leadin' to the State intersection an' pretty soon we pass the spot where Luis is lyin' in the cactus without any pants. I take a peek behind an' look at Paulette. She sees him too, an' in spite of everythin' she has to smile. That guy certainly did look a sight.

After a bit the road gets better an' we whiz, an' pretty soon we pull on to the State road to Yuma.

The day has started an' the sun is comin' up. I start singin' Cactus Lizzie which, as I have told you before, is a song that I am very partial to.

I reckon that I have got to do a hundred an' fifty miles to Yuma, an' I wanta do it quick.

There are two-three things that I have gotta fix down there pretty pronto, because if the ideas that I have got in my head are right there is plenty goin' to start happenin'.

I light myself a cigarette, an' I throw a look over my shoulder at Paulette. She is lyin' back in the seat with her hands, with the steel bracelets on 'em, in her lap.

"One for me, Lemmy," she says, smilin'.

I light a cigarette an' lean back an' put it in her mouth. She nods her head. I turn around again.

"You know, Lemmy," she says after a bit. "Aren't you taking a bit of a chance? I imagine you are holding me as a material witness, but I have yet to know the authority on which a Federal Agent can handcuff and take an American woman out of Mexican territory just because he thinks that she may have important evidence. Because that's all you've got on me. I'm just a material witness. You can't bring charges against me for attempting to shoot you, because I'm entitled to shoot any man I find in my house at night."

She takes a puff at her cigarette.

"I think that I'm going to make things very difficult for you, Lemmy," she says.

I look at her over my shoulder.

"Look, Paulette," I say. "You take a pull at yourself an' don't talk hooey. I don't give a durn about your takin' a shot at me. An' I ain't takin' you back as a material witness or anything else like that, so don't start tellin' yourself what you're goin' to do to me, because you're takin' yourself for a ride, honeybunch, an' I'd hate to see you disappointed."

"I see," she says. "Then if I'm not a material witness, an' you're forgetting about the shooting, may I be so curious as to ask just for what you are taking me somewhere for?"

"O.K. honey," I tell her. "Here it is. I'm takin' you back to Palm Springs just because I wanta take you there, an' when I get you there I'm chargin' you with first-degree murder."

I give her another cigarette over my shoulder.

"I'm chargin' you with the murder of Granworth Aymes on the night of the 12th January," I tell her, "an' how do you like that?"

Chapter Twelve
HOOEY FOR TWO

It is eleven o'clock at night when I pull the car up outside Metts' house in Palm Springs.

Paulette seemsta have settled down a bit. She has also got the idea that she is goin' to make a big sap outa me before she is through.

I stuck around at Yuma for a coupla hours because I wanted to telephone through to Metts an' tell him one or two things so that he wouldn't be too surprised when I showed up an' I also had a spot of business to do over the 'phone with the Mexican authorities at Mexicali an' another spot with the New York Office. I stuck around there for a bit so's Paulette could get her hair done, an' also so that we shouldn't arrive at Metts' place at Palm Springs before night because I have got an idea that I don't want anybody to see Paulette. I am goin' to keep her nice an' secret for a bit.

I hand her over to Metts in his sittin'-room.

"This is Paulette Benito," I tell him, "an' I am chargin' her with first-degree murder of Granworth Aymes. I'd be glad if you'd book her on that an' hold her pendin' extradition to the State of New York. I think that maybe two or three days in the lock-up here would do this dame quite a lotta good. It might sorta get her mind nice an' peaceful so's she feels like talkin'."

"That's O.K. by me," says Metts.

He rings the bell an' tells a cop to get through to the Police Office an' have a sergeant take Paulette along an' book her. He says that she is to be held *incommunicado* pending' further instructions.

Paulette just stands there. She is lookin' fine. She has got her hair done very nice like I told you at Yuma, an' she has got a swell suit on an' ruffles. She looks like she would have to take two bites to eat a lump of butter.

She smiles at me an' Metts.

"Very well," she says. "You have it your own way now, Lemmy, but believe me I'm going to make the Federal Service too hot to hold you before I'm through with you. And I insist on a lawyer. I'm entitled to one and I'm going to have one. Any objections, or are you going to twist the legal constitution of the United States to suit yourself?"

"That's O.K. by me, Paulette," I tell her. "Mr. Metts here will get a good lawyer sent around to you in the morning. An' then what? I reckon you an' him can have a great time together while you tell him how you didn't kill Granworth. But you ain't goin' to be sprung. You ain't goin' to get no bail or get outside the lock-up until I say go, so you can bite on that an' like it."

She smiles at me. She shows her little white teeth an' I don't reckon I have ever seen such pretty teeth—except maybe Henrietta's.

The copper comes in to take her.

"Au revoir, Lemmy," she says. "What a cheap flatfoot you are? You didn't really think that I'd fallen for you, did you?"

"Me—I never think at all where dames are concerned," I crack back at her. "I just let them do the thinkin'. Well, so long, Paulette. Don't do anything that you wouldn't like your mother to know about."

The copper takes her away.

I tell Metts just as much of the works as I want him to know, an' I tell him just how I am goin' to play this thing from now on. Metts is a good guy, an' he has got brains, an' he sees that what I am doin' is the only way to play this job. So he cuts in an' says I can rely on him the whole durn way.

After which he gives me a wire that has come through from the "G" Office in New York.

An' when I read it do I get a kick or do I?

I told you that I sent a wire to the New York "G" Office before I went inta Mexico. In this wire I sent 'em a list of the clothes that Henrietta was wearin' on the night of the 12th January when she went inta New York to see Granworth, an' I asked the New York Office to check up with the maid Marie Dubuinet and the night watchman an' ask 'em if they could identify these clothes as bein' Henrietta's. Well, here is the reply:

"Reference your wire. The maid Marie Dubuinet now employed by Mrs. John Vlaford, New York, definitely identified clothes as being part of outfit packed by her for Mrs. Henrietta Aymes when proceeding to Hartford, Connecticut stop. James Fargal night watchman at Cotton's Wharf identified hat and fur coat as being those worn by the woman who got out of the car which afterwards drove over wharf edge with Granworth Aymes in driving seat stop. Both these identifications absolutely positive."

So there you are, an' I reckon that I have now got Henrietta placed in this job all right, an' I guess that when I have told this sweet dame just what I am goin' to tell her within the next few hours then maybe she is goin' to get such a surprise that she will not be quite certain as to whether she is standin' on her arm or her elbow.

It is now twelve o'clock an' Metts an' I go into a huddle an' we work out just what we're goin' to do now. Metts asks me if I was serious when I said that he could get a lawyer for Paulette next mornin', an' I say I do not mind if she has twenty-five lawyers because I reckon that when I'm through with her she won't even need one of 'em.

I then have a drink with him after which I go down an' get into the car an' start off for the Hacienda Altmira. It is a swell night an' while I am drivin' along I get to thinkin' what a lot has happened since the first time I was on this road. Life's a funny thing whichever way you look at it or even if you don't look at it.

Pretty soon at the end of the main street I come to the Hot Dog dump. I get out, go inside an' get myself a cup of coffee. The two swell wise-crackin' dames in their white coats are still issuin' out the eats an' the old dame they call "Hot Dog Annie," just as high as she was on the first night I saw her, is sittin' down at a table eatin' a hot dog with the tears runnin' down her face.

The red-headed dame looks at me with glowin' eyes.

"Gee, Mr. Caution," she says, "we was tickled silly when we heard you was a 'G' man. We remembered the first night you came in her an' started pullin' a lotta stuff on us that you came from Magdalena in Mexico. Gee, it must be a swell job bein' a 'G' man."

I drink my coffee.

"It ain't so bad, honey," I say, "an' then again it ain't so good. But you be careful or else I might get after you."

I give her a naughty look.

"Yeah?" she says, "I reckon I wouldn't mind. I guess it wouldn't be so bad bein' pinched by a guy like you."

"That's as may be, honey," I say, "but the sorta pinch I got in mind for you is one that you do with your fingers! I'll be seein' you."

I finish my coffee an' I go on my way. Drivin' along the desert road I get to thinkin' about Henrietta. I wonder how she has liked stickin' around the Hacienda under the supervision of Periera. I remember how she went for me the last time I saw her down at the police station when I got the description of her clothes from her an' when I wouldn't let her smoke. I reckon I ain't goin' so good with Henrietta, which makes me grin a bit more. Another thing is I think that before I'm through with her to-night she's goin' to hate me worse than I was poison. Still I have had dames dislike me before now.

Pretty soon the Hacienda comes in sight. The neon lights outside are twinklin', but there is only a few cars around. It looks like they are havin' an off night. I park the car an' walk in the front entrance an' standin' by a hat room on the right talkin' to the dame who checks in the hats is Periera. He grins when he sees me.

"*Buenos noches,* Señor Caution," he says. "I am ver' glad to see you some more. Everything has been very quiet around here, and the Señora Aymes—eef you want to see her you find her up een the card room."

"That's swell," I tell him. "You're a good guy, Periera, an' I reckon you've been useful to me. Maybe I'll find some way of makin' it up to you."

"They are all up there, Señor," he says, "Fernandez, and Maloney—the whole lot of them. But don't you pay for any drinks. Anytheeng you have here is, what you call, on the house."

I go into the dance room. There are not many people there an' the band is sittin' around lookin' like bands always do when there ain't nobody to listen to 'em. I walk across the floor an' I start goin' up the steps that lead to the balcony.

When I have walked up a few steps I remember that this is the place where I found Sager's silver shirt tassel. I stop for a minute and look around.

You remember I told you this balcony runs right round the wall of the Hacienda Altmira. It is about eighteen to twenty feet off the ground. At the top of the stone steps where I'm standin' is the card room. Next to it way down the balcony is the room where Henrietta took Maloney after Fernandez had socked him one. Farther down in the corner is another room an' there are two more rooms leadin' off the balcony on my right-hand side.

I go up the stairs an' inta the card room. There are about twelve people in there. Fernandez an' Maloney an' four other guys are playin' poker at the centre table, an' the rest of 'em includin' Henrietta are standin' around watchin'.

When I go in Henrietta looks up. She sees me an' I give her a grin. Her face freezes an' she turns her back on me.

"Well, well, well, Henrietta," I say to her, "you don't meanta say you ain't goin' to say good-evenin' to your friend Lemmy?"

"I've told you what I think of you," she says, "and I'll thank you not to talk to me. I hate the sight of cheap policemen."

"That's O.K. by me, baby," I tell her. "Maybe before I'm through with you you're goin' to hate the sight of 'em some more, an' if I was you, Henrietta," I go on, "I wouldn't get too fresh because I can make things plenty tough for you."

There is a sorta silence. The guys playin' poker have stopped. Everybody is lookin' at Henrietta an' me.

Maloney gets up.

"Say listen, Caution," he says. "I reckon you've got your job to do, but there's two ways of doin' it, an' even if you are a Federal Agent you don't have to get tough with Mrs. Aymes."

"You don't say," I tell him. "O.K. Well, if you want it that way, you have it. Fernandez," I say, turnin' to him where he is sittin' shufflin' the cards through his hands an' grinnin', "I guess you can do somethin' for me. Downstairs outside you will find a coupla State policemen. Bring 'em up here, will you?"

"O.K.," says Fernandez.

He gets up an' he goes outa the room. Maloney looks serious.

"What's the matter, Caution?" he says. "You goin' to make a pinch?"

"Well, what do you think, Maloney?" I tell him. "That's my business, makin' pinches. What do you think I've been kickin' around here for goin' into this an' that if I wasn't goin' to pinch somebody sometime?"

He don't say nothin', but he looks very serious. I give myself a cigarette an' while I am lightin' it the door opens. Fernandez an' Periera come in, an' behind 'em are the two State cops, the guys who have been waitin' downstairs for me like I fixed with Metts. There is a helluva lotta atmosphere in this room. Everybody is waitin' for somethin' to break. There is a little sorta smile about Fernandez' face as he sits down at the table again an' starts runnin' the cards through his fingers. I turn around to Henrietta.

"Mrs. Henrietta Aymes," I tell her, "I am a Federal Agent an' I'm arrestin' you on a charge of murderin' your husband—Granworth Aymes—on the night of January 12th last at Cotton's Wharf, New York City. I'm also arrestin' you on a charge of causin' to be made an' attemptin' to circulate two hundred thousand dollars' worth of counterfeit Registered United States Dollar Bonds, an' I am handin' you over to the Chief of Police here at Palm Springs to be booked on those charges an' held pendin' extradition for trial in the State of New York."

I turn around to the cops.

"O.K. boys," I say. "Take her away."

Henrietta don't say a thing. She is as white as death an' I can see her lips tremblin'. Maloney steps forward an' takes her by the arm. Then he turns to me.

"Say, this is tough, Caution," he says. "This ain't so good. I thought . . ."

"Impossible," I tell him, "you ain't got anythin' to think with. But if you want to be the little hero you can go back to Palm Springs with Henrietta."

"Thanks," he says, "I'd like to do that."

He goes out with Henrietta an' the cops go after 'em. I turn around to Periera.

"I wanta talk to you an' Fernandez," I say, "so I reckon you'd better close this dump down an' get these people outa here, an' you two go back to your office where we can sorta discuss things over."

Periera an' Fernandez an' the other guys go outa the room. After a minute downstairs I can hear people packin' up an' clearin' out. I go over to the sideboard an' I give myself a shot of bourbon. I stick around for about ten minutes, an' then Periera comes back an' says everything is O.K. He says would I like to go along to his office, we can talk easier there. I follow after him along the balcony, an' we go into his room. Fernandez is sittin' at the table drinkin' a high-ball an' smokin' a cigarette. He looks up as we go in.

"Well, Mr. Caution," he says, "it's turned out the way I thought it was going to turn out. I always knew she done it. Have a drink?"

I tell him yes. Periera hands me a cigarette an' lights it for me.

"I reckon I have played it the only way I could play it," I tell 'em. "It's stickin' outa foot to me that this dame Henrietta was the woman who got outa that car, started it up again an' sent it over the edge of the wharf, but I wasn't certain of that till to-night. I got a wire from New York to-night that tells me that the maid

Marie Dubuinet an' the night watchman on Cotton's Wharf identified them clothes she was wearin'. That's good enough for me an' it ties the job up."

"An' you reckon she done the counterfeitin'?" asked Fernandez.

"No," I say, "she didn't do it, but she got somebody else to do it for her. Who that is I don't know, but maybe when I talk to her to-morrow mornin' down at the jail, she'll feel inclined to do a little real talkin'. Maybe she can make it a bit easier for herself."

Fernandez gets up an' pours himself out another high-ball. This guy is lookin' pretty well pleased with himself.

"I'm surely sorry for that dame," he says. "I reckon that she has got herself inta a bad jam, an' one that'll take a lotta brains to get her out of."

"You're tellin' me," I say, "but you never know where you are with dames. Say listen, Fernandez," I go on, "what was the big idea in you callin' yourself Fernandez an' comin' out here after Aymes died?"

He looks up an' grins.

"I hadta do something," he says, "an' I'd met Periera here, before, when I was out here a year ago drivin' Aymes. An' I call myself Fernandez because it don't sorta hurt so much as my real name—Termiglo."

He gives me a fresh sorta look.

"Anything else you'd like to know?" he says.

"Yeah," I tell him. "The night Aymes died you wasn't on duty, was you?"

He stubs out his cigarette.

"No, I wasn't," he said. "I was just stickin' around. So what?"

"Oh, nothin'," I tell him, "but I thought that maybe you could let me know where you was. I suppose you musta spent the evenin' somewhere an' I suppose that somebody musta seen you."

He laughs.

"Sure," he says. "If you gotta know I took Henrietta's maid, Marie, to the movies. I didn't know I hadta have an alibi."

"You don't have to have any alibi, Fernandez," I tell him. "I just sorta wanta know where everybody was on that evenin', that's all."

He looks at Periera sorta quick. I walk over to the side table an' give myself a drink. I am just imbibin' this liquor when the telephone bell rings. Fernandez picks up the receiver an' then looks at me.

"It's for you," he says. "Metts, the Palm Springs Chief of Police, wants you."

"Say listen, Lemmy," says Metts. "There's a marriage threatenin' around here an' I wanta know what I oughta do about it. I suppose it's O.K.?"

"What are you talkin' about, Metts," I ask him. "Who's goin' to marry who an' why, an' what's it got to do with me? I thought that maybe somebody else had got committin' some crime or something. Who is it that's goin' screwy an' wantin' to get hitched up?"

"It's Henrietta an' Maloney," he says. "When they got back here Maloney says that you have pinched Henrietta for killin' Aymes an' on a counterfeitin' charge as well, an' that you're a heel. He says that she's broke—she ain't got any dough at all, an' that you're framin' her. He says that he reckons the best thing he can do is to get married to her so's there'll be somebody to look after her an' get her a lawyer an' generally hang around. He says that he's talked it over with her an' she's so het up that she's prepared to agree to anything.

"Well, what could I say? They both been resident here an' they're entitled to marry, so I rang up the Justice an' he's comin' around here in about half an hour to tie 'em up. After a bit I sorta got the idea that maybe you oughta know something about this an' so I called through."

"Thanks a lot, Metts," I say. "Don't you worry about it. I'm comin' back right now, an' I reckon I'm goin' to stop this marriage pronto. Say, what the hell does Maloney think he's doin' usin' your police office as a marriage bureau?

"Don't you say anything until I get around. Just stall 'em an' play 'em along, but don't you let any marriages take place around there. Got me?"

He says he gets me, an' scrams.

I put the telephone down.

"Fernandez," I say, "I often been wonderin' why you was so keen to get yourself hitched up to Henrietta an' then suddenly shied off. I suppose it was because you thought that she'd had a hand in this counterfeitin'?"

He nods.

"That's the way it was," he says. "An' when you come gumshoein' around here it began to look to me like she knew a durn sight more about Aymes' death than a lot of us thought, so I sorta laid off."

"I got it," I tell him. "Well, I gotta scram now, but there's just one little thing I gotta say to you guys an' that is that I'll probably have to ask both of you to take a trip back to New York with me to-morrow. I reckon that you're both goin' to be material witnesses in this case against Henrietta. Anyhow, I reckon the D.A. ought to hear what you gotta say."

Periera starts a lot of stuff about not being able to leave the Hacienda, but Fernandez shuts him up.

"If we gotta go we gotta go," he says. "An' personally speakin' a few days in New York at the government's expense wouldn't be so bad neither."

"O.K.," I say. "Well, the pair of you had better be ready to go back there with me to-morrow. If you got any business to clean up here you better get it fixed. We oughta be leavin' pretty early in the mornin'. Well, so long, I'll be seein' you."

I scram. I get outside an' start the car up. I drive pretty fast for half a mile an' then look out for the cop that I fixed with Metts to have waitin' for me. In a minute I see him, sittin' behind a joshua tree off the road.

"Get along to the Hacienda Altmira as quick as you can," I tell him. "Come in by the back way, an' keep your mount under cover. Don't let 'em see you. Watch the place. There's only Periera an' Fernandez inside. If they come out an' go any place tail 'em, but I don't reckon they will. I reckon they'll be stickin' around. I'll be back in pretty near an hour or so."

He says O.K. an' he scrams.

I drive on. I go whizzin' along the road to Palm Springs like somebody has put hot lead in my pants, an' I am hurryin' because

I reckon I gotta stop this marryin' nonsense on the part of Henrietta an' Maloney.

But when I come to think this thing out, I sorta realise that I don't really give a continental durn if Henrietta does marry Maloney. It won't make any difference anyhow, except that it might sorta be inconvenient havin' regard to one or two things that I got in my mind about that dame.

My old mother always usta tell me that there was only one thing worse than one dame an' that is two dames. I reckon King Solomon musta been nuts. Just fancy stickin' around with four hundred dames an' tryin' to play ball with the whole outfit. Still you gotta admit that these old time guys had got something an' if you read your history books why I reckon you gotta say that as the centuries go rollin' by guys just get more and more indifferent all the time. Maybe you reckon that this English guy, Henry the Eighth, was a real he-man, just because he had six wives, but if you compare him with King Solomon he is nothin' but a big sissy. What's six against four hundred?

When I get to Metts' house, I bust right in to his room and he is sittin' behind the desk waitin' for me an' smokin' a pipe that smells like it was loaded with onions.

"What's all this hooey about Henrietta marryin' Maloney?" I ask him.

He grins.

"Maloney brings her back here," he says, "an' she is all burned up about bein' pinched for killin' Granworth an' she hasn't got any dough an' reckons that she won't be able to get a lawyer. So Maloney says he reckons that if they sorta get married he can see her through. So he speaks to me about it, an' I says it's O.K. by me. So I dig out the local Justice an' he's in there now gettin' ready to marry 'em."

"Well, he ain't goin' to," I say. "Look here, Metts. That pinch of Henrietta's was a fake. She never killed anybody, but I just hadta play it that way. Take me along to this weddin'."

He gets up an' puts his pipe away, for which I am very glad, an' we go into the next room.

Somebody has putta lotta flowers on the table an' standin' in front of it, with a Justice gettin' ready to shoot the works, an' a coupla State coppers for witnesses, are Henrietta an' Maloney.

"Justa minute," I say. "I think that I'm stoppin' this weddin' because it don't look so good to me."

I turn around to the Justice an' tell him that I am sorry that he has been troubled about this an' got outa bed but that there ain't goin' to be any weddin'. He scrams an' the two coppers go with him.

Then Henrietta starts in. She asks me what I think I am doin' an' who I am to get around stoppin' people from gettin' married. She says that she has got Metts' permission an' that she's goin' through with it. She says that I have been houndin' her around, bringin' false charges against her an' generally ridin' her around the place an' that if Maloney is man enough to try an' protect her against any more stuff on my part then he is entitled to go through with it.

I'm tellin' you that Henrietta was burned up. Her eyes are flashin' an' she looked swell.

"I don't think I've ever hated anybody like I hate and detest you," she says. "I told you that you were a heel and that is what I think you are."

She shuts up because she ain't got any more breath.

Maloney weighs in.

"Look here, Caution," he says, "have a heart. You've got no authority to stop a marriage. Somebody's got to look after Henrietta. She's in a bad jam, an' you're ridin' her an' makin' it a durn sight worse. An' let me tell you this . . ."

I put my hand over his mouth.

"Now shut up you two, an' listen to me," I tell 'em both, "an' you can be in on this too, Metts. Henrietta, I want you to get a load of what I am sayin' an' remember it because it's important.

"Just how much you don't like me don't matter a cuss. I'm doin' a job an' I'm doin' it in my own particular way. Maybe, Henrietta, when this job's over you'll be inclined to take a kick at yourself for bein' so durn fresh, but in the meantime get this:

"My arrestin' you to-night out at the Hacienda Altmira was just a fake. I done it for a purpose an' with a bitta luck what I want to happen will happen, an' then everything will be hunky dory. I hadta make Periera an' Fernandez believe that I was pinchin' you for this counterfeitin' job an' I've warned 'em both that I'm takin' 'em back to New York with me to-morrow.

"O.K. Well, right now I'm scrammin' back to the Hacienda, but before I go I wanta wise you up to something, Henrietta, an' don't you forget it. Sometime to-night you're goin' to meet Mrs. Paulette Benito—the dame that your husband was playin' around with; the dame that got the two hundred grand in *real* Registered Dollar Bonds.

"All right, now get this. I'm goin' to pin the murder of Granworth Aymes on this Paulette. I'm goin' to prove she did it. Now Granworth Aymes was bumped by one of two women, because there was only two women saw him on the evenin' of the 12th January. One was Henrietta here an' the other was Paulette.

"Right, now I'm goin' to eliminate Henrietta from this business by producin' a bit of fake evidence. I'm goin' to say that we've checked up at New York an' that we know that Henrietta here couudn'ta killed Aymes because she left New York on a train that left the depot five minutes before the night watchman saw the Aymes car go over the edge of Cotton's Wharf. I'm goin' to say that a ticket clerk an' a train attendant both identify Henrietta's picture as bein' that of a woman who was on the train goin' back to Hartford.

"Now have you got that Henrietta? You was on that train goin' back to Hartford, Connecticut, an' it left the depot at eight-forty. An' don't forget it."

She looks at me sorta curious. She is lookin' tired an' it looks like she might start weepin' at any minute.

"All right, Lemmy," she says. "I don't understand, but I'll remember."

"O.K.," I tell her. "Now I'm goin' to scram." I turn around to Metts. "Let these two stick around," I tell him. "Henrietta ain't under arrest for anything. But I don't want 'em to leave here. I want 'em here when I get back."

When I get to the door I turn round an' look at Henrietta. She is almost smilin'.

"An' when I get back, honeybunch," I say, "I'll tell you why I stopped you marryin' Maloney!"

CHAPTER THIRTEEN
DUET FOR STIFFS

I RECKON that I am glad I stopped Henrietta marryin' Maloney.

As I go whizzin' along the road towards the Hacienda I start doin' a little philosophising in regard to dames. I have told you that they got rhythm an' technique; but they also gotta helluva lot of other things as well some of which are not so hot.

Dames fly off the handle any time. They just go off anyhow; they are like skyrockets. You can take an ordinary honest-to-goodness dame an' mix her with a little bitta excitement an' maybe a spot of love an' she just goes nuts, an' when she goes nuts she always has to put some guy in bad just so's she'll be in company. It ain't the things that dames do that worries me it's the things that they get guys to do for 'em.

I've heard folks say that the difference between a man an' a woman is so little that it don't matter. Well, you don't want to believe these guys. They're wrong. A man is controlled by his head an' a woman by her instinct, an' in nine cases outa ten a woman's instinct is just the way she's feelin' that mornin'.

An' the way Henrietta feels now is that she would like to marry Maloney just because she's in a jam an' because she thinks that she ain't got any friends, an' that I am ridin' her like hell an' that in Maloney she will have a good guy who will look after her an' act as a buttress between her an' the wicked world.

Hooey!

Maloney wouldn't be any good at all for Henrietta. Why? Well, didn't I see all them little shoes of hers set out in rows, the night that I bust into the rancho where she is stayin'. Them shoes told me she had class an' although Maloney is a good guy he ain't in the same boulevard as Henrietta, not by a mile, an' another thing is that he only thinks he is fond of Henrietta. He ain't really in love with her at all. If he'd been really stuck on this dame he wouldn'ta let me play her around on this job the way I have had to do. He woulda done something about it.

I reckon I'll be pretty glad when I have got this case sewed up an' in the bag. You gotta realise that except for a coupla hours' sleep I had at Yuma I have been kickin' around for practically three days an' three nights without sleepin', an' I am a guy who is very fond of bed.

By this time I am half a mile from the Hacienda. I pull the car off the road an' leave it behind some sage brush. Then I start easin' over towards the house. Presently I come across the State policeman's motor-cycle where he has left it, an' a few yards farther on I find him.

He tells me that nobody has left the Hacienda except when Fernandez has come out an' driven a car from the garage around to the front. He says Periera an' Fernandez have been droppin' things into this car from the veranda over the front entrance so it looks as if my idea is workin' out.

I do not see that it is any good havin' this cop hangin' around, so I tell him to scram back to Palm Springs. When I have done this an' he is outa the way, I walk over to the back of the Hacienda. I go up past the wall that runs along from the garage an' up to the back door that leads into the store room, the place where I found Sager's body. This door is locked, but I work on it an' after a few minutes I get it open.

I go inside, lock it behind me, walk along the passage an' get down into the store room. I go across the store room an' very quietly I start movin' up the steps that lead to the door behind the bar. This door is not locked. I open it justa little bit so that I can put my eye to the crack an' look out.

In front of me I can see the dance floor of the Hacienda. All the lights are out, but from where I am I can see the door of Periera's office on the balcony along the opposite wall. The door is a little bit open an' there is a light inside. From where I am I can just hear Fernandez an' Periera talkin'.

I light myself a cigarette, hold it behind the door so that they cannot see the light, an' I wait there about ten minutes. I can still hear their voices dronin'. Then I hear Fernandez laugh. After a bit the door opens an' he comes out an' stands in the doorway. As the light falls on his face I can see that he is smokin' a cigarette an' lookin' pretty pleased with himself.

Then he goes back into the office an' comes out again in a minute carryin' a suitcase. He starts walkin' along the balcony towards the place where it ends which is just over the main entrance to the Hacienda. I think for a minute that he is goin' into the end room on the balcony, but he don't. He passes it. He keeps on walkin' an' he goes to where there is a big picture on the wall.

He waits there for a minute an' then Periera comes out. They both get hold of this picture an' start takin' it down. When they have done this, they lean it up against the wall, an' I can see that behind the picture is a sorta hatchway in the wall.

Periera goes back to the office an' closes the door behind him. Fernandez climbs through the hatch in the wall an' disappears. I push open the door an' step into the bar. I jump over it an' start gumshoein' up the stairs. I pull the Luger whilst I am goin' up.

I am very quick an' very quiet, an' the first thing that Periera knows is that I am standin' in the open doorway of his office with the gun on him. From this place I can keep an eye on the hatch down the balcony just in case Fernandez decides to come out.

Periera looks surprised. His mouth sags open an' some little beads of sweat come across his forehead. I reckon this Periera is a yellow cuss anyhow.

"Well, Periera," I tell him. "It don't look so good for you does it? It looks as if you two guys are not goin' to have such a good time from now on. Now you take a tip from me an' do what I tell you, otherwise things is goin' to look pretty bad for you. Have you gotta key to this door?"

He says yes an' pulls it outa his pocket. I take it off him.

"O.K.," I say. "Now I'm lockin' you in here an' leavin' you in here. Just take a word of advice an' stick around until I come for you again, otherwise I am goin' to get very tough with you. I'll be seein' you."

I step out on to the balcony, pull the door shut an' lock it. I reckon I am pretty safe in leavin' Periera there. I don't think he will try anythin' because he is not the sorta guy who would. He is frightened sick. Then I gumshoe along the balcony, keepin' my gun ready in case Fernandez comes through the hatch.

When I get to it I climb through. I find myself in a little room that would be right above the passage that leads from the front entrance to the dance floor. There is a lantern burnin' on the floor an' by the light from it I can see in the corner of the room a flight of iron steps curvin' down towards some place underneath on the left.

I slip along down these steps an' at the bottom I find myself in a long stone passage. I do a bit of thinkin' an' I come to the conclusion that this passage runs underground from the main room of the Hacienda along underneath the adobe wall that is at the rear end of the garage. I reckon this passage was originally a sorta cellar in the house. Anyhow it makes a pretty swell hide-out.

I go along the passage until I come to a wooden door at the end. There is a light comin' from underneath it. I kick this door open, step into the room on the other side quick. I am in a stone cellar. There is a couple of electric lights fixed up, and in the opposite corner I can see Fernandez packin' up some papers in the suitcase stuck against the wall. On the left hand side of the cellar are two big printin' presses an' packed against the wall on the other side are a lotta boxes an' on shelves above 'em are bottles, brushes an' stencil plates.

So I am dead right.

"Well, Fernandez," I say.

He spins around. I show him the gun.

"Take it easy, big boy," I tell him, "because gettin' excited certainly ain't goin' to get you nowhere now, an' you know so far as you are concerned it woulda been a lot easier for you an' Periera if you'd aimed a little bit better that night when you took a shot at me when I was drivin' back to Palm Springs. I knew it was you all along, but I thought at the time that you might like to think that I thought maybe it was Henrietta who was doin' the shootin'."

I walk over to him.

"Go an' get yourself against the wall on the other side an' reach for the ceilin'," I tell him, "an' I wouldn't move if I was you. If I see one twitch outa you I'm goin' to give it to you the same as you gave it to Sagers, you lousy heel."

He starts walkin' over but keeps his hands up.

"Say what the hell do you mean, Caution?" he says. "You can't get away with this stuff. You can't . . ."

"You shut your head an' do what I tellya, Fernandez," I say, "otherwise I'm goin' to execute you here an' now, which is a thing which I would not like to do because I would hate to do the electric chair outa a good customer, an' the day they fry you I'm goin' to give myself a big high-ball just to celebrate. Turn your face to the wall, keep your hands up an' stay quiet, otherwise I'll blast your spine in."

He does what I tell him. I look inta the case he has been packin' up. You never saw such a lotta stuff in your life. It is fulla stock an' share certificates, Unites States dollar bonds, United States gold certificates, 1,000 dollar bills, an' what will you. I take some of this stuff out, walk over to where the electric light is an' look at it carefully.

The whole durn lot is counterfeit.

"So that's the way it is, Fernandez," I tell him. "I thought I was guessin' right. I reckon that you an' Periera are bigger mugs than I thought you were. I knew when I told you that phoney stuff to-night about my takin' you to New York in the mornin' as material witnesses that you'd have to clean this stuff up so that nobody would find it while you was away. I reckoned if I came back here I'd find you at it. Well, I was right.

"I suppose now you're goin' to tell me that this ain't a counterfeitin' joint, an' even if it was, you wouldn't know anythin' about it. Well, it was a swell idea too. I reckon it was durn easy to work off some of this phoney stuff on clients up in the card room when they'd had too much liquor to tell the difference between a bad bill an' a good one. It was a swell idea, but it ain't goin' to be so swell for you. Come on, let's get goin'."

I take him up the stairs, push him through the hatch an' along the balcony. I unlock Periera's room an' I shove him inside. I go in after him an' close the door behind me.

Periera is sittin' at the desk lookin' as scared as hell. I frisk Fernandez an' take a gun off him that he has got on his hip. Then I tell him to go an' sit down alongside Periera. He calls me a nasty name.

"I oughta had more sense," he says. "I oughta have known that all that stuff you said about us goin' to New York as witnesses was a lotta baloney."

"You're dead right, Fernandez," I tell him. "You oughta have had a lot more sense. You guys are the fall guys all right. I put on a nice little act up here to-night in front of you arrestin' Henrietta for killin' Granworth Aymes an' counterfeitin', an' you fell for it. You thought that the big idea of framin' this poor dame for the jobs you've been doin' had come off. You musta thought I was a mug.

"You guys thought you'd get away with the whole works. Well you didn't. You made your mistake an' you're goin' to pay plenty for it."

I stand there lookin' at 'em.µ Periera is holdin' his head between his hands. He looks as if he is finished, but Fernandez has got his hands in his pocket. He is tiltin' his chair back, grinnin'.

"If you ain't the finest pair of lousy heels in the world, I'm a Dutchman," I say. "But you know you guys can still learn some-thin'. I never yet knew a crook who didn't get too clever an' catch himself out, an' that don't only go for you neither. Your pal Lang-don Burdell, Marie Dubuinet—the maid at the apartment—an' that wharf watchman guy—James Fargal, are all as big saps as you are. They've blown the works good an' plenty. Maybe you'll like to know how. Well, I'll tell you.

"You remember when I had you two guys down at the police station at Palm Springs just before I went away, the day I pulled that big act about gruellin' Henrietta about the clothes she was wearin? You remember, Fernandez, I showed you a list of the clothes an' I told you that I was goin' to send it through to New York an' that if Marie Dubuinet an' the watchman identified them clothes then that would show me that it was Henrietta who was in the car with Granworth? You remember that?

"Well I just didn't tell you guys one thing. I just didn't tell you that I altered that list. It wasn't the list of clothes I got from Henrietta. She was wearin' a black Persian coat an' hat on that night, but in the list I showed you—the one I sent through to New York—I altered it. I made out she was wearin' a brown leather hat an' a fawn musquash coat.

"An' the sap maid Marie Dubuinet an' the sap night watchman, both of 'em fell for the little trap I set for 'em. They both say they identify the list as being the clothes that Henrietta was wearin' that night. Well that told me all I wanted to know. It told me that she wasn't the dame in the car with Aymes, it showed me that the dame in the car was your little playmate Paulette Benito, an' it also showed me that the whole darn lot of you was in on this job, an' how do you like that?"

They don't say nothin'.

"I reckon I have met some lousy heels since I've been kickin' around in the Federal Service," I tell 'em, "an' I reckon I've met some thugs who wouldn't stop at anythin' at all, but I just think that you bunch of guys, with the big idea you've been tryin' to pull, are just about the top of the list. You make me sick."

Periera gives a moan. He starts cryin'. He is also sweatin' considerable. I reckon he is just ripe for me to fix him. I go over to the side table an' I pour out a shot of bourbon. I take it back an' I give it to him.

"Drink that up, big boy," I say, "while you've got the chance. I reckon they won't give you a drink on the day they fry you."

He looks up.

"Señor," he says, "they can't fry me. I done nothin'. I keel nobody."

"Yeah," I tell him.

I take a chair an' sit down, an' look at him.

"Listen," I say, "I reckon you've got enough sense to know what sorta jam you're in. If you're wise you're goin' to make things as easy as you can for yourself. Now, right now I'm not interested in the counterfeitin'. I know that was done here, an' I reckon I know the whole story of it. The thing that's takin' my notice at the present moment is this:

"Somebody here—one of you two guys—shot Jeremy Sagers. Now I reckon I know who bumped him. I've got it all figured out, but I made up my mind about one thing. The guy who shot him is goin' to fry for it, an' maybe the other guy will be lucky. Maybe he'll get away with from five to twenty years for being accessory to counterfeitin'."

I stop an' light myself a cigarette. I'm givin' these two guys plenty of time to stew. After a bit I go on.

"Now all you two guys have got to consider is which one is goin' to be tried for what. If one of you likes to squeal on the other, O.K. Otherwise I'm goin' to hold you both on the murder charge, an' if the Court don't feel so good about you I reckon they'll fry the pair of you. But with luck one of you can get away with it. So my advice to you is to get busy an' start thinkin', otherwise maybe two bums are goin' to get fried for one killin'."

I sit there waitin'. Fernandez is still grinnin'. He has still got his chair tilted back. He just looks at me an' sneers.

But Periera ain't feelin' so good, not by a long way he ain't. He is sweatin' more than ever, an' his hands are tremblin'. I reckon in a minute he will start to squeal just because he is that sorta guy. An' I am right. We stick around there for about half a minute an' then he starts talkin'.

"I don't shoot nobody, Señor," he says. "Me—I nevaire keel any guy, nevaire in my life do I keel a guy. I nevaire had no gun. I tell the trut'. I nevaire keel Sagers."

"So you didn't," I tell him. "All right, Periera," I say. "Now you listen to me. I will do the talkin', all you gotta say is yes if I'm right, an' all you've got to do is to sign a statement to that effect when I get you back to Palm Springs Police Station."

I throw my cigarette stub away, an' I go over to the side table an' give myself a drink. I'm pretty pleased with the way things are goin', an' I reckon that maybe in a coupla hours I'm goin' to get this job all over bar the shoutin'. I go back an' sit down. I light myself a fresh cigarette.

"Now here's the way it goes, Periera," I say. "When I got put on this counterfeitin' case first of all an' went along an' saw Langdon Burdell in New York, I reckon that he wised you guys up that the Federal authorities was gettin' busy on this job. But he didn't only wise you up, he found a picture of me, he cut it out of some newspaper—this is the picture I found down in a garbage can in the store room behind the bar, the place where Sager's body was parked in the ice safe—an' when he's got this picture out of the newspaper he writes on the side of it 'This is the guy' an' sends it along to Fernandez here so that when I get down here you'll know who I am.

"O.K. Well I get here. I blow in this dump thinkin' that nobody don't know me. I put on a big act with Sagers, so's to give him the chance to slip me any information he's got, an' you guys know all about it. You know who I am an' you see through the act I put on, so you guess that Sagers is workin' with me.

"All right. That night after the place is closed down—an' you get it closed down good an' early—Sagers comes up here an' tells you the stuff that I've told him to tell you. He says that some guy in Mexico has left him some dough an' he's goin' to fire himself an' scram for Arispe. He says good-bye to you fellers. He goes outa this room. He walks along the balcony an' starts goin' down the steps on the other side, an' I reckon that Fernandez here thinks that there is just a chance that this guy knows a bit too much—for all I know Sagers may have found somethin' out between the time that I left this dump an' the time that I found his body. Maybe he saw that hatch or somethin'.

"Anyhow, Fernandez goes to the door an' pulls a gun on Sagers. He fires over the dance floor. He hits Sagers in the leg. Sagers falls down the stairs an' Fernandez has another coupla shots, but he still ain't killed Sagers—the guy's too tough. So Fernandez goes along the balcony, down the steps an' puts another coupla shots into that poor guy at close range, so durn close that there was powder marks on his clothes an' his skin was burned.

"O.K. Well by this time the guy decides to die, an' then Fernandez leans over him an' starts to pull him up. He pulls him up by his silver shirt cord an' the tassel falls off on the stairs where I found it afterwards. Then this big guy Fernandez yanks him over his shoulder, takes him along an' parks him in the ice safe in a sack."

I stop. I look at Periera. He is cryin' like hell, the tears are runnin' down his face.

"Well," I say, "is that right or is it right?"

He can't talk, he just nods his head. Fernandez looks at him.

"Aw shut up," he says. "You don't know what you're talkin' about. I suppose you're goin' to let this lousy dick frame you into sayin' anything he wants you to say."

"Look, Fernandez," I tell him. "I'd hate to get tough with you. I bust you up once before, but I promise you one thing, If I get my hooks on you again, I'll hurt you plenty. Just keep that trap of yours shut. You stay dead in this act.

"O.K. Periera," I say, "so Fernandez shot Sagers. All right, that's that. Now you tell me somethin', Fernandez, since you're so keen on talkin', where did you bury the guy, huh?"

"Aw nuts," says Fernandez, "I ain't sayin' a word. I don't know what you're talkin' about. I ain't sayin' anythin' until I got a lawyer."

I laugh. "The way you guys get stuck on lawyers drives me crazy," I say.

By this time Periera can talk. He cuts in:

"I tell you, Señor, I tell you the trut'. What you say ees right. Fernandez here he keel Sagers. 'E theenk 'e know too much. 'E bury him at the end of the wall behind the garage. I see eet myself."

I look at Fernandez. He is still grinnin'. He is tiltin' his chair back an' forwards. He is tiltin' it so far back that I think that maybe in a minute he will fall over, an' then so quick that he has me guessin' he pulls a fast one. As he tilts the chair back he grabs at the desk drawer in front of him. It opens. He pulls out an automatic that is inside an' he puts four shots into Periera. Periera lets go a howl an' then starts whimperin'. He is shot in the body at close range an' he don't feel so good.

He slumps over the desk. At the same minute I come into action with the Luger. I let Fernandez have it. I give him two right through the pump.

He falls off the chair sideways. I go an' stand over him. Behind me I can hear Periera still whimperin'. Fernandez looks up at me an' starts talkin'. There is a little stream of blood runnin' outa the side of his mouth. He is still grinnin'. He looks like hell.

"Nuts, copper," he says. "You ain't goin' to fry me. You ain't ..." He fades out.

Periera is lyin' quiet. I reckon he's got his too. When I look at him I see that I am right. His eyes are glazin' over.

I look around at Fernandez. He is lyin' sorta twisted up on the floor with his eyes starin' up at the ceilin'.

An' there they are—just two big guys who thought they could beat the rap. Two mugs who thought they could kick around an' do what they wanted. Fernandez, a big, cheap walloper with nothin' but some muscles an' a gun, an' Periera, a dirty little creep, trailin' along behind him. An' they always finish the same way. Either they get it like these two have got it or they finish up in the chair, scared stiff, talkin' about their mothers.

These guys make me feel sick.

I step over Periera an' grab the telephone. I call Metts. Pretty soon he comes on the line.

"Hey-hey, Metts," I tell him. "I'm speakin' to you from the local morgue—because that's what it looks like. I have gotta coupla stiffs out here an' I reckon that you might collect 'em before mornin'."

I tell him what has happened. He ain't surprised much. He says that he reckons that Fernandez saved me a lotta trouble by gunnin' Periera an' gettin' himself bumped.

I ask him how things are at his end. He says that everything is swell. Henrietta is stickin' around talkin' things over with Maloney an' tryin' to figure out just what the hell I am playin' at. Maloney is so sleepy that he can't keep his eyes open an' Metts is playin' solitaire by himself.

"Swell," I tell him. "Now there's just one little thing that you can do for me. Get one of your boys to get around an' dig up a casket for Sagers. They got him buried around here an' I would like to collect what's left of him an' put him some place that is proper. If you got a mortician handy just get him goin'."

"O.K. Lemmy," he says. "I'll say you're a fast worker. Listen, just how long have we gotta stick up around here. Don't you ever want any sleep?"

"Keep goin'," I say. "This little game is just about endin'. I gotta get over to Henrietta's place an' do a little bitta gumshoein' around there, an' then I reckon that I am through out here. I reckon that I'll be back at your place inside forty minutes. Say, Metts, just how is my little friend Paulette?"

"She's all right," he says. "She is just about as happy as a cat with the toothache. I went an' saw her down at the jail half an hour ago. She is givin' my woman warden a helluva lotta trouble. She says she wants a lawyer an' I've fixed one for her first thing in the mornin'. Last thing I heard about her was that she had turned in the walkin' up an' down game an' was lyin' down. Maybe she's asleep."

"Right," I tell him. "Now listen, Metts, an' I gotta hunch that this is goin' to be the last thing that I'm goin' to ask you to do for me. In half an hour's time you wake Paulette up. Get her up outa that jail an' bring her up to the sittin' room in your house. If she gets funny stick some steel bracelets on her. But don't let her meet Henrietta or Maloney or anybody until I get around. Then when I get back I reckon we'll sew this business up."

"Okey doke," he says. "I'll have it all set for you. So long, Lemmy."

I hang up the receiver. I go over to the side table an' give myself a drink. Then I light a cigarette an' take a deep drag on it. It tastes good to me.

Then I straighten things up a bit. I get hold of Fernandez an' stick him back in the chair, an' I lay out Periera as best as I can. I pick up a piece of adhesive tape that I find on the desk an' I go over to the door an' take a last look at these two near-mobsters.

Then I switch off the light and scram out. I lock the door behind me and seal it in two or three places with the tape to keep guys out before Metts gets his coroner to work.

Then I stand on the balcony an' look down at the dance floor. The moonlight is comin' through makin' the place fulla shadows.

The Hacienda looks bum. It looks as bum as any place like that looks when the floor ain't filled with dancin' guys an' the band ain't playin'—when there ain't any swell dames doin' their stuff.

The moon makes this dump look sorta tawdry.

I go downstairs an' out by the back way, an' I ease along to the place where I have left the car.

It is a swell night, but I am feelin' good. As I start up the car I realise that I am plenty tired. I step on it an' make for the little rancho where Henrietta lives.

When I get there I bang on the door. Nobody answers so I reckon that the hired girl who looks after Henrietta has gone off some place. Maybe she's scared at bein' alone in the dark.

I get the door open an' I go up to Henrietta's room. Where I get inside I can sniff the perfume she uses—Carnation—I always did like Carnation. Right there in front of me is the row of shoes with here an' there a silver buckle or some ornament shinin' in the moonlight. Slung across a chair—just like it was before is Henrietta's wrap.

I tellya I am sorta pleased at bein' in this room. I am one of them guys who believes that rooms can tell you plenty about the people who live in 'em. I take a pull at myself because I reckon that I am beginnin' to get sentimental an' bein' that way ain't a long suit of mine—you're tellin' me!

I get to work. I start casin' this room good an' proper. I go over every inch of it but I can't find what I'm lookin' for until, just when I am givin' up hope, I find it.

I open a clothes cupboard that is in the corner. I find a leather letter-case. I open it an' inside I find a bunch of letters. I go through 'em until I find one written by Granworth Aymes. It is a year old letter an' it looks as if Henrietta has kept it because it has got a library list in it—a list of books that Aymes wanted her to get for him.

I take this over to the light an' I read it. Then I put it in my pocket an' I sit down in the chair that has got the wrap on it an' I do a little thinkin'.

After a bit I get up an' I scram. I lock the rancho door an' get in the car an' start back for Palm Springs.

I have got this job in the bag. Findin' that letter from Aymes has just about sewed it up. I am a tough sorta guy but I have a feelin' that I wanta be ill.

Why? Well, I have handled some lousy cases in my time, an' I have seen some sweet set-ups. I been bustin' around playin' against the mobs ever since there have been mobsters an' there ain't for me to learn.

But believe it or not this job is the lousiest, dirtiest bit of mayhem that's ever happened my way. It's so tough that it would make a hard-boiled murderer hand in his shootin' irons an' look around for the local prayer meetin'.

I woulda liked to have seen Fernandez fried. That guy oughta got the chair, an' I'm sorry I hadta shoot him. But before I'm through with this job, three-four other people are goin' to take that little walk that runs from the death house to the chair an' when they take it I'm goin' to have a big drink an' celebrate. I start singin' Cactus Lizzie. It sorta takes the taste outa my mouth.

CHAPTER FOURTEEN
SHOW-DOWN

I LOOK at 'em.

I am in the chair behind Metts' desk in his sittin' room. It is twenty minutes to four. Metts is in a big arm-chair in the corner smokin' his pipe an' lookin' as if this sorta meetin' was just nothin'. Henrietta is sittin' with Maloney on a big sofa on the right of the room, an' Paulette is in a chair on the other side smilin' a sorta wise little smile just as if we was all nuts except her.

Everything is very quiet. An' the room is kinda restful because Metts has turned the main light off an' there is only an electric standard lit in the corner behind Paulette. The light is fallin' on her face an' makin' her look sweller than ever.

I tell you dames are funny things. Take a look at this Paulette. Here she is, a swell dame with a swell figure, good looks, poise an' personality, but she can't play around along like an ordinary dame. She has to go around raisin' hells' bells.

I often wonder what it is that starts a dame off like this. I wonder what bug gets into 'em an' turns 'em into trouble-starters, because I never yet knew a crook or a bitta dirty work that some dame wasn't at the bottom of, an' I reckon that the French guy who said "cherchez la femme" knew his onions. An' I reckon every case I have ever handled has boiled down in the long run to "cherchez la femme." But maybe that's what makes life so interestin'.

I look at 'em all an' I grin.

"Well, people," I say, "here is what they call the end of the story. I reckon that I am bein' a bit irregular in havin' this meetin' right now, an' without havin' Paulette's lawyer around. But you don't have to worry, Paulette, I ain't goin' to ask you any questions an' I ain't goin' to ask you for any statement. What you are goin' to do or what you ain't to do it just up to you."

I look over at Henrietta.

"Honey," I tell her. "You have had the worst sorta deal. I reckon that I have had to make things tough for you, but the way I played it was the only way that it woulda worked. The day I had you down here at the Police Station an' grilled you about the clothes you was wearin' that night when you went to New York from Connecticut, was an act. It was an act that I put on for the benefit of Fernandez an' Periera. I was goin' to Mexico an' I had to do somethin' that was goin' to make 'em think that the case was all closed up, that you was the woman I was goin' to pinch for killin' Aymes.

"The same sorta thing had to happen earlier to-night when I pinched you for Aymes' murder. I hadta make them two guys believe that I had the case complete against you, an' that I was goin' to take them to New York as witnesses. I did this because I knew that if they knew they hadta leave the Hacienda in the mornin' the first thing they would do would be to clean up the counterfeitin' plant. I knew that plant was around there somewhere but I just hadta make 'em show me where it was an' that was the way I picked to do it. I'm sorry lady, but by the time I'm through I reckon you'll understand."

Henrietta gives me a little smile.

"It's all right, Lemmy," she says. "I'm sorry I was rude. I might have guessed that you were much too clever to suspect me of murder."

"Swell," I tell her. "Well, people, I reckon I'm goin' to do a lotta talkin', an' I reckon I want you to listen durn carefully to what I'm sayin'. Especially you, Paulette, because you gotta realise that this an' that are goin' to make one helluva difference to you. I told you just now that this meetin' is pretty well out of order from a legal angle; but I'm havin' it for your benefit. When you hear what I gotta say you can go back to the can an' think it over, an' you can also think over just what you're gonna tell that lawyer of yours in the mornin'.

"O.K. Here we go: Fernandez an' Periera are dead. Periera squealed on Fernandez an' Fernandez shot him. I croaked Fernandez an' that's that. Both these guys was tied up with the Granworth Aymes counterfeitin' an' the guy who was behind the counterfeitin' an' responsible for it was Granworth Aymes.

"Granworth Aymes had gotta great idea. He was supposed to be a gambler playin' the stock market. Well he did—sometimes. When things was good O.K., an' when they wasn't, well he reckoned that he could keep goin' by counterfeitin'. This Hacienda Altmira—the place that he built an' mortgaged over to Periera—was the place where the phoney stuff was made an' was it a good scheme? He started off by gettin' Periera to make phoney money because it was easy to get it inta circulation up in the card room. People who have drunk plenty ain't liable to examine the bills they won or got in change, an' most of the guys who used to play at the Hacienda Altmira was birds of passage. If somebody come along who was livin' in Palm Springs I reckon they'd lay off handin' him any phoney dough. It was when they got a mug that they issued him out with this fake money.

"You remember, Metts, you told me the first night I was here that you found some guy who'd been banged over the head out on the desert not far from the Hacienda? Remember you told me that you thought that this guy had got his up in the card room. Well, I reckon you was right. I reckon this was one of the few guys who'd been given some phoney dough an' made a song an' dance about it. So they croaked him. Altogether this idea of usin' the Hacienda as a place for workin' off this counterfeit on people was swell. They got away with it easy.

"It wasn't until afterwards that they started to make phoney stock an' bond certificates an' I'll tell you why they done this later on.

"This mob was well organised. Aymes was the head of it an' Langdon Burdell, the butler at the apartment, Fernandez the chauffeur and Marie Dubuinet the maid, was all in it. Periera was responsible for runnin' the Hacienda an' makin' the phoney stuff. I reckon they been gettin' away with this game for a helluva time.

"O.K. Well now I'm goin' to tell you why they started makin' phoney stock an' bond certificates an' transfers, an' I'm goin' to tell you why they made that two hundred thousand dollars worth of Registered U.S. Dollar Bonds, the stuff that was planted on Henrietta here. It's a swell story an' the dame responsible for it is sittin' right here with us now."

I grin over at Paulette. She looks back at me an' gives me a horse laugh. She is still fightin' fit an' don't give a durn for anything.

"I gotta apologise to you too, Paulette," I tell her. "I gotta apologise to you for bringin' you back here on a charge of killin' Granworth Aymes. You didn't kill him, but just at the time it looked like the easiest thing for me to do. Right now you are just bein' held on a charge of accessory to counterfeitin', but I don't want you to get too pleased with yourself. Just wait nice an' patient till I get finished, an' then you can laugh as much as you like.

"All right, well about a year ago Granworth meets Paulette an' he falls for her an' she falls for him. I reckon that he was a weak, silly sorta cuss an' the kinda guy who would fall for a swell dame with a strong personality like this Paulette. These two play around together an' Paulette gets to know about the money counterfeitin' business an' she thinks the idea is swell.

"An' then she gets a helluva idea. You gotta realise that she has gotta husband an' this husband is in a pretty bad way. He has got consumption bad an' he can't get around much. He don't get inta New York an' he don't suspect what is goin' on between his wife an' Granworth.

"But it looks as if he hasn't got very long to live, an' Paulette don't wanta wait until he's dead to get her hooks on the money he has got. So she has a helluva idea. She gets the very swell idea of gettin' Rudy Benito to do his investin' through Granworth Aymes, an' she suggests to Granworth that it would be one swell idea if all the stocks an' bonds that he is supposed to buy for Rudy could be made out here at the Hacienda. In other words she an' Granworth stick to the money an' issue Rudy with counterfeit stocks an' bonds.

"Rudy ain't goin' to get wise because Paulette is bein' the lovin' wife who is lookin' after his business affairs—got me? She will be the person who handles the certificates an' share documents an' Rudy is too sick to examine the stuff through a magnifyin' glass an' anyhow he trusts his wife.

"All of which goes to show you just how lousy a dame can be if she wants to be. I reckon most women whose husbands were sick an' dyin' woulda been glad to have stuck around an' given him a hand. But Paulette ain't like this. This lady is the real tough guy—an' is she tough?

"So the game works well an' they get away with it. In a few months they have cleaned Rudy out, an' all he has got is a bunch of phoney certificates.

"Okey doke. Everything is goin' hunky dory when something happens. One day—a day when I reckon that Paulette is away at New York Rudy gets in a specialist an' gets himself examined again. The specialist tells Rudy that he's pretty bad, but that he will last longer if he gets down to a good dry climate like Arizona or Mexico. Rudy figures to do this an' thinks that he'll take a look at his finances an' things, an' see how he is goin'. So he probably goes an' gets some of the stocks an' bonds that are in Paulette's safe an' maybe he gets around to some local broker just to see what the stuff is worth an' to see how quickly he can realise on it. Can you imagine what a helluva shock this Rudy Benito gets when he finds out that the whole durn lot is phoney, that it is not worth the paper that it's printed on?

"Can you imagine how that poor guy felt? When Paulette gets back he lets her have it. He asks her what the hell has been goin' on.

"So what does she say? She can't tell him that she has been in on this job from the first. She has to make out that Granworth has done 'em both in the eye. She tells Rudy that he needn't worry because Granworth has just made a bundle of dough on the stock market—which is a fact—an' that they will make him cough it up or else they will go to the police.

"But is she annoyed with Rudy? You bet in her heart she hates him like hell. She didn't like him in the first place because he was dyin'. She didn't like him in the second place because she had been twicin' him, an' sometimes if she ever thought about herself she must have reckoned that she was pretty lousy. But when this poor sick guy gets enough intelligence to know that he is bein' done left, right an' centre, then I reckon she does get burned up. After this she hates this guy like hell.

"Directly she gets the chance she gets on the telephone to Granworth an' tells him that Rudy is wise to the swindle an' that they will have to keep this guy quiet by payin' him back the dough.

"Granworth says O.K. but believe me he ain't so pleased an' I'll tell you why. He has just made two hundred grand legitim- ately on the stock market. He reckons that he is goin' to give up this counterfeitin' business an' go straight. Also he is beginnin' to get tired of Paulette. He has gone so far as to make over the two hundred grand to his wife Henrietta an' he has also taken out a big insurance. He don't feel so pleased at the idea of partin' with the dough back to Rudy, but he tells Paulette O.K. he will pay up an' that the great thing to do is to keep this Rudy Benito quiet.

"But Rudy is beginnin' to get suspicious. He reckons that Paulette musta known something about what was goin' on. He makes some inquiries an' he finds out that Paulette has been gettin' around with Granworth Aymes—that their names have been coupled together.

"The poor guy don't know what to do. He knows that Gran- worth is a crook an' he is beginnin' to suspect his own wife, so he gets down an' he writes an unsigned letter to Henrietta. He tells her that her husband is playin' around with some woman, but he don't say who. He writes this letter so that Henrietta will get after Granworth an' bust up the business between him an' Paulette.

"Now we are comin' close to the time when the works start shootin' properly. Henrietta writes some letters to Granworth from Hartford, Connecticut, where she is stayin', accusin' him of gettin' around with a woman, an' this puts Granworth in a jam. He has got to get his hooks on the two hundred thousand Registered Dollar Bonds that are in the safe deposit in Henrietta's name so as to give 'em to Rudy to keep him quiet, an' he has gotta do this without Henrietta knowin' anythin' about it. So what does he do? He gets goin' directly he gets the first letter from Henrietta. He gets Periera to manufacture counterfeit dollar bonds an' he sticks 'em in the safe deposit in the place of the real ones. This way he reckons he is safe. The phoney bonds will keep Henrietta quiet an' he can hand the real ones over to Rudy an' keep him quiet. Paulette has told him that Rudy ain't goin' to last long an' he reckons that when he dies he can get the real bonds back again.

"He tells Paulette about all this an' she thinks that it is a swell idea an' that if they play it carefully they can get away with it. But they don't reckon on one thing. They forget Rudy Benito. This guy is suspicious an' not only is he suspectin' Granworth but now he is also suspectin' Paulette.

"So now we come to the big day. We come to the 12th January—the day that Granworth Aymes goes over the edge of Cotton's Wharf. Now I reckon that this day is a pretty interestin' sorta day. In fact I will go as far as to say that durin' a long experience of crooks an' murderers an' what will you. I ain't ever heard of a day that was just like this 12th January.

"It is a day that all you guys are goin' to remember all your lives, an' personally speakin' I reckon I am goin' to remember it too.

"Now get the set-up. This 12th January is the day that Paulette has told Rudy that she is goin' inta New York to make the wicked Granworth pay up the two hundred thousand grand that he has swindled Rudy an' her out of. Rudy listens to all this stuff with his tongue in his cheek. He is gettin' pretty wise to Paulette an' reckons that when she goes to see Granworth he is goin' to string along too, but he don't tell her.

"O.K. Well Granworth ain't feelin' so pleased with the 12th January either. He knows that he has gotta hand over the two hundred thousand in bonds to Paulette an' he has also received the third note from Henrietta who has come back to New York an' in this note she tells him that she is goin' to see him an' have a show-down about this woman he is gettin' around with."

I look around at 'em. Metts is sittin' holdin' his pipe in his hand, lookin' at me as if he was hypnotised. Henrietta is starin' straight in front of her. Poor kid I reckon she ain't feelin' so good at hearin' all this stuff about Granworth. Across on the other side of the room Paulette is lyin' back on her chair keepin' her eyes on me. There is a sorta half-smile playin' around her mouth. She sits there, quite still, not movin' a muscle, just like she was petrified.

"O.K.," I go on. "So here we are on the afternoon of the 12th January. Paulette comes to New York for the express purpose of seein' Granworth Aymes an' gettin' the two hundred grand in dollar bonds from him, an' after her, keepin' well under cover, comes the poor sick guy, Rudy Benito, coughin' his way along, with his guts fulla hatred for his wife who has sold him out for the man who has helped her to do it.

"Rudy has got his own scheme. I reckon that in the afternoon he takes himself a room at some little quiet hotel and rests himself. He is preparin' for the big act he is goin' to put on with Granworth. Just for the minute I'm goin' to leave him there.

"In the afternoon Paulette goes along an' sees Granworth in his office. Maybe Langdon Burdell is there an' maybe he ain't, but anyhow Paulette spills the beans to Granworth. She tells him that the only way of keepin' Rudy quiet is to pay back the dough. She don't know that Rudy suspects her an' she tells Granworth that the guy is goin' to die soon anyway an' that then they can join up again.

"Granworth says O.K. He gives her the two hundred grand in dollar bonds an' he tells her about the fast one he has pulled on his wife, Henrietta. He tells her how he has got Periera out here at the Hacienda to fake up counterfeit dollar bonds to replace the real ones that he has just handed over to Paulette. I reckon that they think that this is one helluva joke. Maybe they sit there an' laugh their heads off.

"Well, after they have enjoyed this big joke, Granworth tells Paulette his big news. He tells her that his wife Henrietta is in New York an' that he has just received a note from her to the effect that she is goin' to see him that evenin' an' have a show-down about this woman he is supposed to be runnin' around with. Paulette is interested like hell. You bet she is. She is rather enjoyin' the joke. She asks Granworth what he thinks Henrietta will do. He tells her that he reckons that Henrietta will say that unless he gives up this dame he is gettin' around with she will divorce him. He says that she will be all the more inclined to take one helluva strong line because she thinks that she has got the two hundred grand in dollar bonds that was in the safe deposit. She don't know that they have been switched an' that they are fake.

"Then Granworth an' Paulette have another helluva big laugh.

"Paulette says O.K. but she is mighty curious to know about this interview that is comin' along with Henrietta an' she would like to stick around an' hear what happens an' Granworth says O.K., that when he is through with Henrietta he will come back to his office an' if she will be waitin' there for him about eight-thirty he will tell her the works an' they can have another big laugh.

"Paulette says O.K. an' she goes back to her hotel an' probably gives herself a facial an' a big drink. She thinks that she is doin' swell.

"All this time the poor sap Rudy is restin' up at his hotel, tryin' to get himself up enough strength to have the big show-down with Granworth. But maybe he can't make it. Maybe don't feel so good, so he just sticks around waitin' an' waitin' until he feels good enough to make it, an' if you people have ever known a guy who's got consumption real bad you'll know what I mean an' you'll feel for Rudy.

"An' Granworth just sits around in his office waitin' for Henrietta to telephone through.

"In the late afternoon she comes through. She tells Granworth that she has just gotta see him an' she asks him where. He says at some little down-town cafe an' when the time comes Henrietta goes along, an' he drives up in his car an' they have a big talk.

"Granworth has had a coupla drinks an' is fairly high an' fulla courage. He tells Henrietta he don't give a durn for her an' that she can do what she likes. When she says that she will divorce him if he don't give up this other dame, he says O.K. an' if she does he won't pay her any alimony, that he will leave the country first. Then she says she don't give a hoot about the alimony because she has got the dollar bonds an' then he just laughs like hell, because be is thinkin' what a funny story he will have to tell Paulette when he goes back to the office an' meets up with her again."

I stop talkin' because, there is a knock at the door. Metts gets up an' goes across. He talks to the copper at the door an' then he comes back across the room to me. He has got two telegrams in his hands an' he gives 'em to me. I bust 'em open an read 'em. One is from the "G" Office in New York an' the other is from a Captain of Mexican Police Rurales in the Zoni district to Mexican Police headquarters at Mexicali, who have forwarded it on to me from there.

They both look pretty good to me.

I put 'em down on the desk in front of me an' I go on.

"Henrietta can't say anything else," I tell 'em. "He is drunk an' she knows it. She gets up an' she leaves, an' she goes back to the depot an' takes the first train back to Hartford, Connecticut. We know she does this because two guys in the railway service, a ticket clerk an' a train attendant, have identified her picture as bein' on the train that left at ten minutes to nine.

"O.K. Well, returnin' to Granworth. He goes back to his car an' he starts it up an' he drives back to his office. By now it is about eight-thirty an' he is lookin' forward to havin' a big laugh with Paulette about his talk with Henrietta an' maybe he is reckonin' in takin' her some place to dinner.

"Right. Granworth goes up to his office an' there he finds two people waitin' for him. He finds Langdon Burdell an' Paulette. When he goes in the door of the outer office he is so high that he forgets to close it behind him. If he had I mighta not been tellin' this story.

"Anyhow he goes inta the inner office an' he gives himself another drink an' he starts laughin' his head off. Then he starts tellin' Paulette and Burdell about his interview with Henrietta. He tells these two that the poor sap Henrietta thinks that she has got two hundred grand in dollar bonds an' that the poor mutt is threatenin' him with divorce thinkin' that she has got plenty money an' that all the time all she has got is a bunch of counterfeit paper.

"They all start laughin' like hell. They all think that it is one helluva joke an' just when they are screamin' their heads off the door opens an' in walks Rudy Benito, and I reckon this guy has been standin' in the outer office an' has heard them tellin' the whole bag of tricks.

"Rudy starts in. He tells 'em all about it. He tells Granworth what a cheap four-flushin' devil he is an' then he turns around to Paulette an' tells her what he thinks about her. He tells her just what he thinks about a lousy daughter of hell who would help to swindle her dyin' husband an' who could sit down an' laugh about it.

"He stands there pointin' his finger at' em. An' then he tells 'em something else.

"He says that the fact that Granworth is prepared to return the money don't matter a durn to him. He says that he is goin' to the police. He says that he is goin' to bust the whole works an' hold 'em both up for all the world to see what lousy scum they are. He says that if it's the last thing he ever does he's goin' to put 'em behind the bars.

"An' then what! Well, I'll tell you. Paulette here is pretty burned up. She is furious at bein' caught out like this. Right by where she is sittin' on the edge of Granworth Aymes' desk is a big paper weight—the figure of a boxer, the same one that's there now. She gets up an' she grabs it. She smashes it down on Rudy's skull an' she kills him. He lies there dyin', a poor sick guy that never had a chance, an' there, sittin' in that chair lookin' at us, is the lousy dame who did it!"

Paulette cracks. She jumps up. She rushes across to the desk an' she leans across it. Her eyes are blazin' an' she is so worked up she can hardly talk.

"I never did it," she yells. "I tell you I never did it. It's all true but the killing. I didn't do that. Granworth did it. *He* killed Rudy. I tell you he killed him with the paper weight."

She falls on the floor in front of the desk. She lies there writhin'. I go around an' take a look at her.

"Thanks a lot, Paulette," I tell her. "Thank you for the tip. That's just what I wanted to know."

CHAPTER FIFTEEN
FADE OUT FOR CROOKS

I WALK around the desk an' I stand there lookin' at her as she is lyin' on the floor. I reckon she is goin' to give herself a double dose of hysteria in a minute.

I bend down an' pick her up. I carry her over to the chair an' while I am doin' it she tries—even fixed the way she is—to pull something. While she is in my arms she sorta turns her head an' looks at me an' she puts everything inta that look that she's got. I reckon that if that dame coulda cut off ten years of her life if she was able to kill me with a look she woulda done it. It was poison I'm tellin' you.

I throw her down in the chair.

"Take it nice an' calm, Cleopatra," I tell her, "because gettin' excited or raisin' hell around here is goin' to be as much use to you as red pepper on a gumboil. Sweet dame, you are all shot to hell, you are washed up like a dead fish in a waterspout. From now on you are the sample that got lost in the mail, you are the copy the news-editor spiked, you are the lady who got stood-up by a gumshoein' Federal dick that you thought was a pushover. You make me sick. Even if you was good I wouldn't like you."

She goes as red as hell. I reckon talkin' to her this way has stopped her hysterics anyhow. She takes a pull at herself.

"You cheap heel," she says. "I wish I'd shot you when I had the chance. I wish I'd hurt you so that it took you a year to die. But get this. Somebody will get you. Somebody will get you for this!"

"Nope, little buttercup," I tell her. "Somebody won't, an' if you keep them shell-like ears of yours flappin' an' stop thinkin' of new things to call me you'll hear just why 'somebody' won't. Another thing I ain't frightened of friends of yours, little dewdrop, an' though they may be all the world to you to me they are just bad smells. An' another thing, if every crook who has tried to iron me out had done what he wanted I would be so full of holes that they could use me for a nutmeg grater.

"Stay quiet an' take what's comin' to you like a lady."

I turn around to Henrietta. She is sittin' up starin'. She is tryin' to understand just where she is breakin'. You ain't never seen a dame as surprised as Henrietta.

"But, Lemmy," she says. "You say that Granworth killed Rudy Benito. Then what happened? I don't understand. Did Granworth commit suicide afterwards?"

"Take it easy, honeybunch," I tell her. "You ain't heard the half of it yet. By the time I'm through you'll begin to understand just what a lousy heel that husband of yours was, an' just how much trouble a cheap dame like this Paulette here can start if she feels like it.

"O.K. Well let's go on from there. There is poor Rudy Benito lyin' on the floor as dead as last month's prime cuts. Langdon Burdell, Granworth an' Paulette standin' lookin' at each other an' wonderin' what the hell they are goin' to do next, an' then Paulette gets another swell idea—an' is it a good one? I'm tellin' you that it was such a good one that they nearly got away with it.

"She remembers that Granworth has tried to commit suicide two years before—the time when he drove his car over the wharf. O.K. Well, nobody much knows about Rudy. He ain't known in New York an' anyhow he was just plannin' to scram down to Mexico. So nobody is goin' to miss him. So she suggests to Granworth an' Burdell that they take the clothes off Rudy, put Granworth's clothes on him, stick him in the car an' drive him over the edge of the wharf. Everybody will think that Granworth has committed suicide, an' Granworth can scram off with Paulette an' clear down to Mexico an' pretend that he's her husband Rudy.

"The only thing they have gotta be careful about is the police identification. But they know that Henrietta has gone back to Hartford. If they can keep her outa New York till Rudy's body is buried an' if Langdon Burdell fixes so that *he* is the guy who identifies Rudy's corpse as bein' that of Granworth then everything is hunky dory. Do you get it?

"Granworth thinks the idea is a jewel. It lets him out. All he has gotta do is to scram with Paulette an' get outa New York to some place where nobody won't know him an' he is as safe as the bank. Also be gets rid of Henrietta which is another idea he likes, an' anyhow he is a lousy dog who will do anything that Paulette tells him to. So he takes his clothes off an' they put them on Benito who is about the same size. Then they smash Benito's face in some more; then Granworth writes a suicide note an' they put it, with Granworth's letter-case, in Benito's pocket.

"Then they have a meetin' as to how they are goin' to get the body down to the wharf, an' Paulette has another big idea. She says that she will get in the car an' drive Benito's body down, because as Granworth was meetin' his wife Henrietta that night, if anybody sees her they will think it is Henrietta.

"So Granworth an' Burdell pick up the body an' they take it down by the service lift at the back of the block. Paulette is waitin' there in the car. They stick Benito in the passenger seat an' Paulette, drivin' round the back streets, gets down to Cotton's Wharf. Once there she gets out, leans in the car, puts her hand down on the clutch an' pushes the gear lever in, an' steps back an' slams the door. The car starts off an' after hittin' a wood-pile goes over the edge.

"But just as Paulette is scrammin' off she sees the night watchman Fargal. She goes back an' tells Granworth an' Burdell, an' Burdell says that don't matter a cuss because he can square the night watchman if he has seen anything.

"O.K. Paulette an' Granworth scram off. They have got the two hundred grand in dollar bonds an' before they go they pay off Burdell an' leave a cut for Fernandez, the maid an' the butler.

"When they get down to Mexico they begin to feel better, but Paulette still thinks that there is a chance of Granworth bein' recognised sometime. So she gets another swell idea. They get hold of the doctor—Madrales—an' they pay him plenty to take Granworth into his house at Zoni an' do a face operation on him that is goin' to change his face so that nobody will ever know he was Granworth.

"O.K. Well now lets go back to Burdell. Granworth an' Paulette have scrammed outa it. Early next mornin' he gets down to Cotton's Wharf an' sees the watchman. He gives this guy a thousand bucks to keep his trap shut about havin' see a woman gettin' outa the car the night before. The watchman says O.K.

"Then the police get the car up an' the suicide is reported. Burdell scrams along to the morgue an' identifies Benito's body as bein' that of Granworth Aymes. In the pocket is the suicide note in Granworth's handwritin'. The police accept the identification an' when the coroner has an inquest he brings in suicide. Ain't it natural? Granworth tried to commit suicide two years before, didn't he?"

I move over an' stand with my back to Metts' desk an' look around. Paulette is huddled up. Her face has gone grey. Maloney is lookin' at me with his eyes poppin' an' Henrietta is claspin' an' unclaspin' her hands. Metts is gettin' so worked up that he is tryin' to light his pipe with a match that's gone out. I go on talkin':

"Swell. Everythin' is goin' accordin' to plan. Burdell is wise. He waits two days before he phones through to Henrietta in Connecticut to tell her that Granworth has committed suicide. He does this so as to give time for the body to be buried before she can see it.

"Then he tells the maid, the butler an' Fernandez not to say anythin' about Henrietta bein' in New York that night, not because he wants to keep Henrietta outa trouble but just because he don't want anybody knowin' anything about *any* woman bein' around. He is thinkin' of Paulette.

"Well, the whole scheme works out swell, an' if they had been prepared to have left it alone there everything woulda been all right, an' we none of us woulda known anything about it now.

"But Burdell ain't satisfied. He ain't satisfied even although he is runnin' Granworth's old business an' makin' money. One day he is kickin' around in his office an' he finds two things. He finds first the insurance policy that Granworth took out that says that two hundred thousand dollars will be paid on his death *providin' he ain't committed suicide,* an' he finds the three letters from Henrietta that Granworth has left in his desk, the letters accusin' him of gettin' around with some other woman, the third one sayin' that she is comin' to New York to have a show-down with him.

"Then this Burdell gets an idea. He gets the rottenest, lousiest idea that a guy ever got. *He gets the idea that if it can be proved that Granworth Aymes was murdered by his wife Henrietta then the Insurance Company are goin' to pay. The money will go to the Aymes estate an' the Aymes estate is mortgaged to Periera— so the Insurance money will go to Periera because the Insurance Company have contracted to pay on anythin' except suicide!*

"Have you got it? Was it a swell idea or was it?

"So Burdell gets busy. He sends Fernandez out to the Hacienda Altmira to wise up Periera about the new scheme. An' after this he waits around an' persuades Henrietta to go out to the Hacienda to have a nice quiet time. She is glad to do this because she is upset about Granworth's supposed suicide. She even thinks that maybe she was responsible for it an' that if she hadn't been so tough with him he mighta not done it.

"O.K. Then Burdell sticks around an' waits. I'll tell you why he waits. He knows that Henrietta ain't got very much money. He knows that when that is spent she is goin' to start usin' the two hundred thousand in fake dollar bonds that she has got—the ones they switched on her, an' he knows that directly she tries to change this phoney stuff the Federal Government will step in an' start investigatin'. He knows that they will send an agent to him to ask questions about Granworth an' they will investigate the circumstances surroundin' the Aymes suicide.

"So he grabs the three letters from Henrietta outa the desk an' he sends 'em down to Fernandez an' he tells him to be ready to plant 'em where this Federal agent will find 'em.

"Sure as a gun it comes off. I get assigned to the job an' I go to New York an' see Burdell.

"While I am stayin' there he sends me an unsigned letter sayin' that if I will go down here to Palm Springs I will find some letters that may tell me a lot.

"I fall for it an' I come down here an' find the letters an' I begin to think that Henrietta here bumped Aymes, that he didn't commit suicide at all.

"Burdell knows that I will probably think that he has written this letter, an' that I will talk to him about it so he has a story all ready—a story that makes things look even worse for Henrietta. He tells me that he told the others to say that she wasn't in New York on that night just so's her name would be kept outa the business.

"But like all the other crooks these guys haveta make mistakes. An' that is a thing I am always waitin' for. I checked up on Fernandez an' found that he had been the Aymes chauffeur an' that got me thinkin'. The worst thing they did was to kill Sagers because that got me annoyed, but the durndest silliest thing they did was to be so keen on hangin' this thing on Henrietta. They was all so hot to prove that she had done it after they had tried to keep her outa it in the first place that I reckoned that there was something screwy goin' on.

"The second mistake was when Fernandez told me about Paulette. He told me about this because by this time Granworth had got his face changed O.K. an' nobody woulda recognised him as bein' Granworth Aymes. Fernandez thought that he was safe in tellin' me because he didn't think that I would take the trouble to go down inta Mexico an' take a look around for myself.

"Fernandez has been a mug too. He has been pullin' an act on Henrietta that if he don't marry her he can make things plenty hot for her. When I come on the scene he alters this tale first because I smacked him down for gettin' fresh with her an' secondly because it plays their story along for him to say that he don't want to marry Henrietta now, because he suspects her over the counterfeitin'.

"I get wise to this guy. I get wise to the fact that Fernandez an' Periera an' Burdell are all playin' along together. So I decide to go to Mexico an' see this Paulette, but before I go I have Henrietta down at the Police Station an' I grill her so that Fernandez an' Periera will think that I am fallin' for their stuff an' that I am goin' to New York to seal up the evidence against her.

"Instead of which I scram down to Mexico an' when I get there Paulette starts makin' mistakes as well. She rings through to her pal Luis Daredo to bump me off when I am goin' down to Zoni to see her supposed husband Rudy who is dyin' there. She thinks that it will be a wise thing to get me outa the way.

"Anyhow the job don't come off. I was lucky enough to get outa that, but I am still not suspectin' the truth. When I was on my way to see Rudy Benito at Zoni I hadn't got one idea about this business that you coulda called an idea.

"An' I got at the truth just because crooks are always careless an' because they always make one big mistake.

"When I get to Madrales' place at Zoni, an' I go upstairs an' see this poor dyin' mug, I feel sorry for him, I don't suspect a thing, an' he tells me a good story that matches up with what Paulette has told me. You bet he does because she has been on the telephone an' wised him up about me.

"But just when I am walkin' outa the sick room I see somethin' durn funny. Stuck behind a screen is a wastepaper basket an' in the bottom of this wastepaper basket is a big cigarette ash tray, an' in the bottom of the basket where they have fallen out are about sixty cigarette stubs.

"I get it. Somebody has cleaned up the cigarette ends an' made out to hide 'em before I was allowed up to see Rudy. They have done this because they know that I will be wise to the fact that a guy dyin' of consumption can't smoke about sixty cigarettes in one day.

"At last I was wise. Now I got it why Paulette tried to stop me goin' to Zoni. I get a big idea. I go downstairs an' tell Madrales that I have gotta have a statement from Benito. I type it out an' make him sign it, an' then I go back to Paulette's place an' I compare the signature on the statement with one of the real Rudy Benito's signatures on a duplicate stock transfer of about a year before.

"The signature was different an' that told me all I wanted to know.

"To-night just before I come down here I went inta Henrietta's room at her rancho. I found an old letter from Granworth Aymes an' I compared the handwritin'. The signature on the statement signed by Rudy Benito an' the Granworth Aymes handwritin' are one an' the same. The guy I saw at Zoni—the guy supposed to be dyin', who was laughin' his head off all the time thinkin' what a mutt I was, wasn't Rudy Benito—it was Granworth Aymes!"

I look over at Paulette. She is lyin' back starin' at the ceilin'. She don't look so good to me. She looks like she is due for a fit.

I pick up one of the wires that Metts handed to me.

"Just so's it'll help you when you see your lawyer in the mornin', Paulette," I tell her, "you might like to hear about this wire. It is from New York this mornin'. Followin' an instruction that I sent through from Yuma while you was gettin' you hair done, Langdon Burdell an' Marie Dubuinet was arrested early this mornin'. They grilled Burdell an' he squealed the whole works. They gotta full confession from him, an' he has said enough about you to fix you plenty."

Paulette pulls herself together. She sits up an' she flashes a little smile across at me.

"You win," she croaks. "I was the mug—I thought you was just another copper. How could I know you had brains?"

I look over at Henrietta. She is sittin' lookin' scared. Her lips are tremblin'.

"Lemmy," she says. "Then Granworth isn't dead. He's alive—in Mexico. I . . ."

"Justa minute, honey," I tell her. "I'm afraid I gotta bit of a shock for you."

I picked up the second wire an' I read it to 'em.

It is from the Mexican Police at Mexicali, an' it says:

"Following request from Special Agent L. H. Caution of the U.S. Federal Bureau of Investigation, confirmed by the Federal Consular Officer at Yuma yesterday, for the arrest of U.S. Citizen Granworth Aymes, otherwise known as Rudy Benito, and the Spanish Citizen Doctor Eugenio Madrales, both of Zoni, Police Lieutenant Juan Marsiesta sent with a Rurales

Patrol to affect the arrest reports that both men were shot dead whilst resisting arrest."

Henrietta starts cryin'. She puts her head in her hands an' she sobs like her heart would break.

"Take it easy, lady," I tell her. "I reckon that the way this job has finished is the best for everybody. Maloney, I reckon you'd better put Henrietta in your car an' take her along back home."

Henrietta gets up. I'm tellin' you that with her eyes fulla tears she looks a real honey. There is a sorta light in her eyes when she looks at me that is aces. I reckon that if I was a guy who was given to gettin' sentimental about anything I shoulda been sorta pleased with the way she was lookin'.

"I think you're swell, Lemmy," she says.

She goes out with Maloney.

I go over to Metts' desk an' I open the drawer an' I take out a pair of steel bracelets. Then I go over to Paulette an' I slip 'em on her. She don't like it very much.

"You better get used to the feel of 'em, Paulette," I tell her. "An' if you get away with twenty years I reckon you'll be lucky, an' that ain't even takin' inta consideration them shots you had at me."

She gets up outa the chair.

"I wish I'd got you," she says. "I reckon I woulda saved myself a lotta trouble if I had. Still that's the way life goes. . . ."

She takes a sudden step back an' then she takes a big swipe at my face with her wrists. I reckon if them handcuffs had hit me my face woulda been more like the Rock of Gibraltar than it is.

I do a quick side-step. She misses me. I get hold of her an' I am goin' to give her a good smackin' on the place intended for it, when I stop myself.

"No," I tell her. "I ain't goin' to smack you any, it would be like smackin' a tarantula. Paulette Benito," I go on "I'm arrestin' you on a charge of bein' accessory to first-degree murder of your husband Rudy Benito. I'm arrestin' you on a charge of being accessory to the makin' an' issuin' of counterfeit bills, bonds and stock certificates. I'm holdin' you here at Palm Springs pending extradition an' trial by a Federal Court.

"An' also," I go on, "speakin' personally I'd like to tellya that I'm durn glad that I ain't your husband. It would be like sleepin' with a rattlesnake."

She looks at me an' her eyes are glitterin'.

"I wish you were my husband," she says, "just for one week. If you were my husband, I'd give you rat poison!"

"Swell," I tell her, "an' if I was your husband I'd take it an' be glad. Take her away boys. Lock her up, an' if she wants to she can start a civil war in the can."

The cops who are waitin' outside grab her an' take her off. Metts brings out a bottle of bourbon an' we have a stiff one each. I am feelin' like I could go to bed an' sleep for twenty-four years without even turnin' over.

Metts tells me that he has sent a wagon out to the Hacienda Altmira with a casket an' a coupla cops with spades to dig up what is left of Sagers an' fix him properly. I reckon that these boys will be waitin' for me to go out an' show 'em where Fernandez buried the kid, so I scram downstairs an' get in the car an' drive out to the Hacienda.

The dawn is breakin'. I reckon the desert country looks pretty swell at this time.

I reckon that I would like to stick around here at this place just doin' nothin' an' doin' it all the time, instead of rushin' about the country pullin' in cheap crooks an' counterfeiters an' jumpin' around duckin' shots from dames like Paulette.

I leave the car at the front of the Hacienda, an' walk around the back. Two State coppers with a police wagon an' shovels are hangin' around. They have got a casket in the wagon. I show 'em where Sagers is buried an' they start diggin'.

Then I remember somethin'. I light a cigarette an' go back to the car an' drive over towards Henrietta's little rancho. When I get there I see Maloney just gettin' inta his car.

"Say, am I the big mug, or am I?" I tell him. "With all this depression that's been flyin' around, I forgot the only bitta good news I got for Henrietta. An' anyway where was you goin'?"

"I'm scrammin'," he says. "You see, now that Henrietta's in the clear I reckon I don't haveta stick around any more. I sorta wanted to give her a hand that's all, an' I reckon I sorta used the situation inta rushin' her inta a marriage with me. But she ain't that way about it. She says she'd like to think of me as a brother— you know the stuff."

He grins.

"Anyhow," he says, "I got a girl in Florida. I reckon I'll go along an' say how are you to her."

"Atta boy," I tell him.

I watch his dust as he goes down the road. Then I walk up to the door an' I bang on it. After a bit Henrietta comes along. She has changed her kit an' she is wearin' a white crepe-de-chine frock an' white shoes. That dame sure can look a honey.

"Say, Henrietta," I tell her. "I gotta bit of news for you an' I was a mug not to have thoughta it before.

"Granworth was insured for two hundred thousand, wasn't he? Well the policy covered everything except suicide, an' he never committed suicide. He was shot resistin' arrest yesterday by Rurales.

"O.K. Well the Company will pay. That means that you get plenty dough so I reckon you needn't worry your head about anything. I'll have a word with Metts on my way back so's if you want any dough quick the bank'll let you have some. I'll wire the New York Police to send the policy along, so's the bank can hold it against any dough you want."

She looks at me an' her eyes are sorta starry.

"That's fine, Lemmy," she says. "But won't you come in. There's one or two things I want to say to you. Besides there's breakfast coming."

I look at her.

"Listen lady," I tell her. "Maybe you ain't heard about me. I am one tough guy. I am not the sorta guy who you can trust around the place havin' breakfast with a swell dame like you. Especially if you are good at makin' waffles. I reckon that when I eat waffles I just get goin' an' they tell me that then I get to be the sorta guy that dames oughta be warned against."

She leans up against the door post.

"I was goin' to give you fried chicken," she says, "but after that I think I won't. I've got a better idea."

"Such as?" I ask her.

"Such as waffles," she says.

I look at her again an' I start thinkin' of my old mother. Ma Caution usta tell me when I was a kid that I always put food before everything.

An' for once Ma Caution was wrong.

THE END

Lightning Source UK Ltd.
Milton Keynes UK
UKHW012001030322
399530UK00001B/151